Christopher James Riethmüller

The Life and Times of Alexander Hamilton

Aide-de-Camp, Secretary, and Minister of General Washington

Christopher James Riethmüller

The Life and Times of Alexander Hamilton
Aide-de-Camp, Secretary, and Minister of General Washington

ISBN/EAN: 9783337058173

Printed in Europe, USA, Canada, Australia, Japan

Cover: Foto ©Raphael Reischuk / pixelio.de

More available books at **www.hansebooks.com**

THE LIFE AND TIMES OF ALEXANDER HAMILTON.

THE LIFE AND TIMES

OF

ALEXANDER HAMILTON,

AIDE-DE-CAMP, SECRETARY, AND

MINISTER OF

GENERAL WASHINGTON.

ILLUSTRATING THE HISTORY OF THE UNITED STATES, DURING THE

FIRST YEARS OF AMERICAN INDEPENDENCE;

AND CONTAINING SKETCHES OF THOMAS JEFFERSON, AARON BURR,

JOHN ADAMS, BENJAMIN FRANKLIN, THE MARQUIS

DE LAFAYETTE, GENERAL LEE, BENEDICT

ARNOLD, MAJOR ANDRÉ,

ETC. ETC.

BY

CHRISTOPHER JAMES RIETHMÜLLER,

AUTHOR OF " TEUTON, A POEM," " FREDERICK

LUCAS, A BIOGRAPHY," ETC.

LONDON:

BELL AND DALDY, YORK STREET, COVENT GARDEN,

AND 186, FLEET STREET.

RICHARD BAXTER, Esq.

MY DEAR BAXTER,

In our young days, when Reform was in the ascendant, it was the fashion for the liberal party to point to the United States of America, as the great example of the success of democratic institutions. Since then, events have occurred, which have shaken the faith of many, and led the majority of Englishmen to reconsider the subject. With our attention strongly drawn to what is passing in the bosom of the republic, we have naturally sought for an explanation of so dire a convulsion, and have not been able to rest satisfied with the narrow theory, that all this has arisen from a difference on a single question.

We have rather inclined to the belief, that the causes must be various and complicated, and only to be discovered by a diligent study of the past history of the Union.

Any contribution to that history should, therefore, be of some value; and it has struck me, that a brief account of the Rise of the American Constitution — in connexion with the life and opinions of the remarkable man, who did the most to call it into existence and to bring it into working order, while he foresaw its dangers from the beginning, and laboured incessantly to guard against them—might not be without interest at the present moment. In the career of Hamilton we trace the progress of the Constitution, from its first germ in the mind of the young soldier, through all the difficulties of its establishment, and the trials of its early years, until its administration passes from the control of its authors, to fall into the hands of the champions of an absolute democracy. But, apart from all political speculations, the story of Hamilton himself, his character, his services, and his fate, are well worthy of record and ought to be better known than they have hitherto been—especially in that England which he understood with the instinct of genius, and loved with the enthusiasm of a high and generous nature. Such knowledge can only tend to the honour of his name, and to the growth of kindly feelings between his country and our own.

In treating of this theme, I have written as a foreigner at a distance from the scene of action, and have had to collect my materials from such sources as were open to me. I have done my best, however, to arrive at the truth, and have little doubt as to the general accuracy of the following sketch. Though much indebted to the elaborate, and yet unfinished work, which Mr. John Church Hamilton has devoted to the memory of his father, I have distrusted the inevitable bias of filial reverence, and have tried, wherever I could, to test his statements by a comparison with independent authorities. With regard to Hamilton's contemporaries, I have for the most part endeavoured to estimate them by their own acts and words, rather than by the comments of friends or enemies;

and, if I have erred in my appreciation of any amongst them, I am conscious of no other motive than the wish to render justice to all.

To you, whose calm and sober judgment is so well fitted to form an impartial opinion of its contents, I dedicate this book. You will read it without passion or prejudice, and give due weight to the facts it has brought together; and, even should you not agree in some of its political conclusions, you will respect the sincerity of the convictions on which it is founded, and welcome it if only as a token of the esteem and affection of

THE AUTHOR.

London, *January*, 1864.

CONTENTS

ALEXANDER HAMILTON

AND HIS CONTEMPORARIES.

CHAPTER I.

WASHINGTON.

THE British Colonies in North America had risen in arms against the mother-country. No acts of gross cruelty and oppression, such as roused the Swiss to throw off the yoke of Austria, or nerved the people of the Netherlands to resist the power of Spain, could be urged in justification of this revolt. Yet a long course of unwise and vexatious measures, of just claims neglected and services ill-requited, had been sufficient to provoke the deep and bitter resentment of men of English blood, who, proud of their descent, and jealous of their rights and privileges, were already conscious of the strength derived from increasing wealth and numbers and from the

B

possession of a vast territory that seemed to promise an almost boundless future. In the memorable war which wrested Canada from the grasp of France, the colonists had taken their full share in the sacrifices and exertions necessary to bring it to a successful issue. They had cherished a strong feeling of loyalty and attachment to the parent-state; and there can be little doubt, that a generous and conciliatory policy on the part of England might have retained their allegiance for years to come. But narrow and petty restrictions on trade, prohibition of manufactures, interference with the freedom of navigation, and that general mode of dealing with the colonies which Burke described as " the system of a monopoly," excited and kept alive a growing spirit of discontent; and when to all this was added the attempt to tax the Americans by a parliament in which they were not represented, the discontent became disaffection, and took the shape, first of passive resistance, and then of open rebellion.

It is well to remember from the very commencement of this narrative, that the thirteen colonies, which were now united in opposition to the authority of the British Crown, could in no sense be considered as a single nation or people, but rather as an assemblage of small, distinct societies, founded at different times, under various circumstances, each with a character and history of its own, and with little to bind them together, save a common determination to uphold the right of self-government. The Puritans of New England, the Catholics of Maryland, the Quakers of Pennsylvania, and the High-church Anglicans of Virginia, had each impressed a specific type on their descendants; and so, in every one of the colonies, there might be found some peculiar marks of its origin and antecedents, by which it was easily distinguishable from the rest. And whilst they all laid claim to the benefits of the common law, and to the traditional liberties of Englishmen, their provincial constitutions differed very materially from each other, and political power was variously distributed amongst them, according to the several charters and customs by which their local affairs had hitherto been regulated.

The people of New England, with their Puritan principles, and strong democratic tendencies, were fitted to take the lead in the path of revolution. Already in 1760, the town of Boston had resisted the attempt to collect duties on foreign sugar and molasses imported into the colony. It was there that, five years later, the stamp-act was received with closed shops and warehouses, the tolling of bells, the display of colours half-mast high, and all the signs of a city in mourning. It was there that was concocted the scheme to suspend the importation of all articles liable to the payment of imperial imposts. It was there that began the opposition to the quartering of troops, and that the first collision with the soldiers took place in the public streets. It was there that, on a December evening of 1773, the ships from England were boarded by a party disguised as Indians, who broke open the tea-chests, and emptied them into the bay, rather than allow their contents to be subject to taxation. It was at Boston too, that, when their port had been closed, and their charter violated, the inhabitants entered into "a solemn league and covenant" to renounce all intercourse with Great Britain, until the colony should be restored to the full enjoyment of its rights; and, finally, it was the self-constituted assembly of Massachusetts that collected the military stores at Concord, the attempt to seize which, on the part of the British, led to the battle (or skirmish) of Lexington, and to the first bloodshed of the revolutionary war.

But the other colonies had not been slow in following the example of New England. The merchants of New York and Philadelphia had from the first sympathized with Boston, and, although the interests of the landed gentry of Virginia might be less directly concerned, it no sooner became a matter of right and honour (in the claim set up to tax them without their own consent) than the pride of the *Old Dominion*, as it was called, burst into sudden flame, and they showed themselves quite as earnest in defence of their privileges, as any of their Northern brethren. A plan was soon contrived, by means of "corresponding committees," to keep up a regular communication between the different colonies, and to devise measures for the advancement of the common cause. This led, after a while, to the demand for a general convention; and, at length, in 1774, the FIRST CONGRESS assembled at Philadelphia. All the colonies, excepting Georgia, were there represented by delegates, and, from that time, the idea of UNION took possession of the more enthusiastic minds. "All America," said Patrick Henry, the young orator of Virginia, "is thrown into one mass—Where are your landmarks, your boundaries of colonies? They are all thrown down. The distinctions between Virginians,

Pennsylvanians, New Yorkers, and New Englanders, are no more; I am not a Virginian, but an American."

It is certain that this First Congress contained a great number of able, patriotic, and moderate men, who laboured honestly and zealously to effect an arrangement of the disputes with the mother-country, and to vindicate the rights of the colonies, without violating their allegiance to the Crown of Great Britain. "When your lordships," said Chatham, addressing the Peers of England, "look at the papers transmitted to us from America; when you consider their decency, firmness, and wisdom, you cannot but respect their cause, and wish to make it your own. For myself, I must declare and avow, that, in the master-states of the world, I know not the people, or senate, who, in such a complication of difficult circumstances, can stand in preference to the delegates of America assembled in General Congress at Philadelphia."

But, in this as in all revolutions, events travelled faster than the designs and wishes of men. Between the meetings of the First and Second Congress (an interval of only a few months) General Gage, the British Governor of Massachusetts, had ordered the seizure of the stores at Concord, the yeomanry had resisted the soldiers, and the battle of Lexington had been fought. Then all the people of New England at once flew to arms, and Boston was invested by a volunteer force. The Congress, which met at Philadelphia on the 10th of May, 1775, found it no longer possible to confine their proceedings within the legal boundaries of petition and remonstrance. They had to put the colonies into a state of defence, to sanction the raising of a provincial army, and to appoint a commander-in-chief. On the choice they might make for this office would probably depend the only chance of standing their ground, with raw levies, and a half-trained militia, against the disciplined troops of England. It was their great good luck to select a general, whose rare qualities best fitted him for the difficult task, while his extraordinary virtue and moderation secured them from all danger at the hands of their soldier and champion.

GEORGE WASHINGTON (the commander of their choice) was a gentleman of ancient family and independent fortune. His lineage could be traced back, in the old country, to Norman knights, who had settled in the palatinate of Durham soon after the Conquest, and to Cavaliers, who had distinguished

themselves in the King's cause in the Civil War ;
but his immediate ancestors belonged to the landed
gentry of Virginia, and resided on their estates in
the hospitable fashion of that country. He lost his
father when only eleven years of age, and was left
to the care of an excellent mother, who brought up
her children with strict discipline, but warm affection, and inspired them with the highest sentiments
of integrity and honour. The instruction he received
in the ordinary schools of the colony appears to
have been of a very limited kind, and his literary
acquirements were at no time extensive ; but he
early adopted habits of order and exactness, which
accompanied him through life, and were of the utmost value to him on many important occasions.
He seems to have learned most from intercourse
with his fellow-men, and he doubtless derived much
general information from his elder brother Lawrence,
who had been educated in England, had served with
distinction in the West Indies, and had taken part
in the attack on Carthagena, under Admiral Vernon
and General Wentworth. In physical exercises—
such as running, leaping, wrestling, and riding—he
soon became a proficient, and many tales are related
of his boyish prowess. But what chiefly marked his

school-days (as it did all the rest of his career) was that inflexible sense of truth and justice, which commanded universal respect and confidence, and made him, even in his childhood, the chosen arbiter in every juvenile dispute. ·

One of his neighbours, and the owner of immense landed property in Virginia, was Thomas, Lord Fairfax, an amiable, but eccentric English nobleman, whom a disappointment in love had induced to abandon his country, and to bury his rank and talents in the wilds of America. He was a great foxhunter, and his attention was probably first attracted to young Washington, by the boy's skilful and daring horsemanship. Be that as it may, he took him into his special favour, and being just then in want of a bold and trustworthy agent, to whom he could confide the difficult and hazardous survey of his vast possessions beyond the Blue Ridge, he selected this youth of sixteen for the purpose. In the beautiful Valley of the Shenandoah, then a wilderness, only inhabited by wandering Indians, or lawless backwoodsmen scarcely more civilized, Washington acquired his first experience of enterprise and adventure. He accomplished his task to the perfect satisfaction of his employer, and through his influence

was appointed to the office of public surveyor. He
spent three or four years in expeditions of a similar
character, amongst all sorts of strange scenes and
people, and the knowledge he thus gained, as well ·
as the toils and hardships he surmounted, must have
tended to mature and strengthen him both in mind
and body.

But a struggle with France was at hand, for the
possession of the Valley of the Ohio, and Washington soon found employment in the military service
of the colony. In the wild, half Indian warfare
that followed, he acquitted himself with great credit,
rose to the rank of colonel, and, although not always
successful, received the thanks of the Virginia House
of Burgesses for his conduct. In the subsequent
campaign of 1755, when war had been regularly
declared, and troops had arrived from England, he
served as a volunteer on the staff of General
Braddock, and was present in the disastrous expedition, in which that unfortunate veteran lost his life.
It is said, that, if Washington's advice had been
listened to, the catastrophe would have been averted ;
but Braddock, though a good and brave soldier, had
been trained in the usages of European war, and was
too old to adapt himself to the new circumstances, in

which he was so unexpectedly placed. He persisted in marching into the desert, as he would have moved an army on the great highways of Europe, encumbered with baggage and artillery, and all the equipage of a camp. Too confident in the excellence of his troops, he neglected the precautions which Washington constantly urged upon him, and refused to throw his scouts in advance, to explore the dangerous country before him. On the contrary, he marched forward "as at a review in St. James's Park." The consequence was a surprise, followed by a panic, and a total rout. His grenadiers found themselves suddenly assailed by an unseen foe, who mowed down their ranks from behind trees and bushes, and against whom their ordinary tactics were of no avail. In vain they formed in close order, and attempted to charge with bayonets—in vain the artillery-men stood for a while to their guns—in vain the officers rushed to the front, and devoted themselves to certain death. They were shot down one by one from the covert, into which it was impossible to penetrate, whilst the smoke of the rifles, and the horrid yells of the Indians, alone indicated where the invisible enemy lay hidden. The unhappy general, after having five horses killed under him, was at length struck down by a bullet, and was most unwillingly borne away from the fatal field. He died four days after, overwhelmed with mortification and despair; but in his last moments, with brave and honourable feeling, he did justice to the sagacity of Washington, apologized to him for having rejected his advice, and, if tradition is to be believed, left his faithful servant, and his favourite charger, to the care of the young American.

All through that disastrous fight, Washington had done everything in the power of man to retrieve the fortune of the day. He exposed himself to the utmost danger; two horses were shot under him, and his coat was riddled with bullets; but he escaped unwounded. When he saw that all was lost, he exerted himself to bring off the poor remains of the shattered army, and then rode forty miles in search of supplies and reinforcements. He returned in time to the Great Meadows to receive the last words of Braddock, and to read the funeral service over his grave. He then continued the retreat, and reached home in safety; but the events of that brief campaign left a deep impression on his mind, as well as on the public opinion of the colonies. "It gave us the first suspicion," says Franklin, "that our exalted ideas of the prowess of British regular troops had not been well founded." To Washington, at least, it taught the lesson, how such troops might best be encountered by an army of bush-rangers and volunteers.

During the rest of the war with France, he was intrusted, though still very young, with the command of the militia of his native colony, and rendered many important services, the last of which was the capture of Fort Duquesne on the Ohio. But the national struggle was now nearly at an end. The victory on the Plains of Abraham, so dearly purchased by the blood of the gallant Wolfe, was immediately followed by the surrender of Quebec, and subsequently by the capitulation of Montreal and all Canada. The French dominion was destroyed on the Continent of America, and the supremacy of England in those regions appeared to be for ever established.

Then Washington retired to the privacy of domestic life. During his late campaigns, he had, whilst halting at the house of a Virginian gentleman, made the acquaintance of a charming young widow, named Martha Custis, and seems to have at once fallen in love with her. They were soon after engaged, and, on his return from the reduction of Fort Duquesne, they contracted a marriage, which proved a very happy one. Although their union was not blessed with offspring, the lady had two children by her first marriage, and on them Washington bestowed the fondest paternal care. He was now twenty-seven years of age; he had seen enough of war and adventure; and his sole wish was to settle down quietly on his estate, to devote himself chiefly to agricultural pursuits, and to lead a tranquil and useful life in the society of his friends and neighbours. He fixed his abode at the beautiful seat of MOUNT VERNON, on the banks of the Potomac, once the favourite residence of that brother Lawrence, from whom he had learned so much in his youth, and whose early death he had since mourned with a true and deep affection. There, in the midst of the woods and hills, with a noble river washing the borders of his land, possessed of an ample fortune, already honourably distinguished amongst his countrymen, and with a mind too healthy to cherish idle dreams of ambition, he hoped to spend in peace the fruitful and prosperous years. He little knew the work that was prepared for him—the toils he was to undergo, the perils he was to encounter, the glory he was ultimately to achieve.

It should not be forgotten by those who have been

accustomed to associate nothing but rude images of democracy with their idea of the American Republic, that its chief founder was truly and essentially what in England we term a *gentleman,* and what some people would call an *aristocrat.* Not only by birth and fortune, but by tastes, habits, opinions, and character, he belonged to a privileged class, and all the descriptions we have of him leave the strong impression, that personally he much resembled an Englishman of the higher ranks. The calm, un-ruffled bearing, so dignified and self-sustained—the reserved, and somewhat stately manners, yet full of real kindness and old-fashioned courtesy—the plain, but handsome dress, always suitable to the time and occasion—the utmost simplicity in his own mode of living, combined with a princely style of house-keeping, and the largest hospitality to strangers— even the passion for field-sports, and the love of dogs and horses—all show a family-likeness to his English ancestry. He was much beloved by his servants, whom he regarded almost as his children, but from whom he always exacted respect and obedience. He was himself an early riser, would often light his own fire, and was content with the most frugal fare; but he gave great banquets to the neighbouring gentry, had his chariot-and-four with rich liveries for Mrs. Washington and her visitors, and kept his barge on the Potomac, rowed by negroes in check shirts and velvet caps. Regular and systematic in all his transactions, he expected the same punctuality from others, and whilst he treated his guests of every degree with a natural and cordial politeness, which put them perfectly at ease, there was that about him which forbade intrusion, and checked all undue familiarity. It may astonish some of our Reformers to learn, that he was a strict preserver of game; and once, when a sturdy poacher had been making sad havoc on the banks of the river, Washington pursued him into the water, dragged him and his canoe to the shore, wrested from him the gun with which he was armed, and inflicted such personal chastisement, as deterred him from again trespassing in those quarters. It is also amusing to find that Washington was at this time fond of dancing, and, although grave and ceremonious as Sir Charles Grandison, a popular partner with the fair sex. And whilst he thus cultivated the social pleasures at Mount Vernon, he performed the duties of a magistrate with much zeal and judgment, attended the House of Burgesses of which he had been elected a member, and managed the affairs of his estate with business-like accuracy and despatch. And when to all this it is added, that he had been bred up as a loyal subject of the Crown, and a devout member of the Church of England, and that he was at all times remarkable for the moderation and sobriety of his views, it is obvious that such a man must have felt many painful misgivings, before he consented to embark on the stormy sea of revolution.

The truth is, that Washington, along with many other wise and good men, most earnestly desired to prevent the disputes with England from coming to extremity. It must be remembered that no less than fourteen years elapsed, between the first resistance of Boston to the sugar-duties, and the first meeting of Congress at Philadelphia. During that long period of suspense, innumerable efforts were made to effect a reconciliation with the mother-country, and no one was more anxious than Washington for the success of these endeavours. It was only slowly and gradually that he became convinced of the hopelessness of any satisfactory arrangement, and even then he hesitated, before counselling an appeal to arms. But when once blood had been shed, and he saw his native land fairly committed to the contest, he resolved, with whatever reluctance and sorrow of heart, to take his full share in the dangers and responsibilities of the crisis. No thought of the peaceful years he had spent on the banks of the Potomac—of the wife, and friends, and much-loved home, and genial pursuits and prosperous fortune, which must now all be risked on the ·hazard of a die—could hold him back for a moment from what he considered the call of honour and duty. "Unhappy it is to reflect," he writes, "that a brother's sword has been sheathed in a brother's breast, and that the once happy and peaceful plains of America are to be either drenched with blood, or inhabited by slaves. Sad alternative! But can a virtuous man hesitate in his choice?"

It was in this mood that he joined the Congress of 1775. When the time came to appoint a commander-in-chief, many eyes were turned upon him, as the person whose high character and military experience entitled him to the first claim. Difficulties arose, however, from the jealousy which even then had arisen amongst the colonies, and from the unwillingness of New England to confide the army to a Virginian. It would seem that John Adams, of

Massachusetts, had the merit of deciding the Congress on this memorable occasion; and if so, it was the most important of all the services he rendered to his country. The dissentient members were persuaded to withdraw their opposition, and Washington was unanimously elected to the command. He accepted it on the sole condition, that he was not to receive any pay or emolument. " I beg leave to assure the Congress," he said, " that, as no pecuniary consideration could have tempted me to accept this arduous employment at the expense of my domestic ease and happiness, I do not wish to make any profit of it. I will keep an exact account of my expenses. Those, I doubt not, they will discharge, and that is all I desire."

Washington was now forty-three years of age, tall and handsome, majestic in deportment, and full of manly vigour. When he appeared on horseback, every one was struck with his martial air and carriage. The long interval of repose at Mount Vernon had in no way diminished his aptitude for military affairs, and he set about his arrangements with a promptness and decision, which astonished the few veterans with whom he was brought in contact. Amongst these was General Charles Lee, an English soldier of fortune, who had spent his life in camps, and engaged in a variety of adventures. Having served his own country in both hemispheres, and being discontented with his promotion, he had visited first the court of Frederick the Great, and then that of Stanislaus Augustus, obtained employment in the Polish army, held a command of Cossacks in the war between Russia and Turkey, and otherwise distinguished himself in different parts of Europe. Restless and dissatisfied, he now offered his sword to the Americans, and was appointed to the rank of major-general. His colleagues were Artemas Ward a native of Massachusetts, who had served under Abercrombie in the French war; Philip Schuyler, a member of one of the oldest Dutch families of New York, who had gained his experience in the same school; and Israel Putnam, of Connecticut, who was well versed in all the devices of Indian strategy. At Washington's request, the post of adjutant-general was bestowed on Horatio Gates, an English ex-major settled in Virginia, with whom he had formed an acquaintance in Braddock's fatal campaign, and who, like Lee, provoked by what he considered the neglect of his merits, was prepared to turn his arms against the land of his birth.

Whilst the American Congress was thus occupied in organizing an army, large reinforcements had arrived at Boston from England, under the command of Generals Howe, Burgoyne, and Clinton. The investing force, on the other hand, composed of the Massachusetts levies and of volunteers from New Hampshire, Rhode Island, and Connecticut, attempted to seize the neighbouring heights, and to intrench themselves in that position. This led to the battle of Bunker's Hill, in which the American yeomanry first showed that they could contend with British soldiers more equally than had been anticipated; for, although they were ultimately dislodged, and their works carried with the bayonet, it was only after hours of hard fighting, and when they had repulsed repeated attacks, with serious loss to the enemy. The news of this battle reached Washington on his way to the camp, and when, in answer to his eager inquiries, he was informed that the volunteers had stood their ground without flinching, sustained the fire of the English, and reserved their own until they could deliver it at close quarters, he gave a sigh of relief, and exclaimed : " The liberties of the country are safe !"

It is no part of the plan of the present work to

enter into the details of the American War of Independence. It will, therefore, be enough to state in
general terms, that, when Washington arrived before
Boston, he found an army, brave indeed, and full of
enthusiasm, but half clad, ill-provided, inefficiently
armed, and almost wholly undisciplined. One of
the first discoveries he made was, that there were
but thirty-two barrels of gunpowder in store, and
that nearly his whole stock of ammunition was contained in the cartridge-boxes of the men. He had
to bring order out of chaos; to reduce a mixed and
intractable multitude to subordination; to clothe and
arm them, and supply them with everything they
required; to create a commissariat and military
chest; and, finally, to instruct his officers in their
several duties, to obtain for them the respect of the
troops, and to inspire them with confidence in himself. No less powerful intellect, no less resolute will,
would have sufficed for the task. He was aided in
it by an excellent soldier, whose friendship he at
this time acquired, and whose faithful and valuable
services continued through all the worst periods of
the war. This was Nathaniel Greene, of Rhode
Island, who, although the son of a Quaker miller,
had early applied himself to the study of military

tactics, had become a self-taught master of the art, and, having taken great pains to discipline the militia of his native colony, had brought to the lines before Boston the best-trained corps in the army. He was now a brigadier-general, and was soon selected by Washington for one of his most trusted advisers.

The siege of Boston lasted nearly a year, with various fortune. But all the efforts of the British failed in breaking the net which Washington had cast around them, and at length, in March, 1776, the Americans obtained and held possession of Dorchester Heights, which commanded a large portion of the town and harbour. Through the exertions of Henry Knox, an artillery-officer, who was destined hereafter to play a distinguished part, they had been supplied with mortars and heavy cannon, as well as powder and shot, and were now in a condition to bombard the place, and render it untenable by the enemy. Under these circumstances, General Howe resolved to evacuate the town, and to embark his soldiers on board the fleet, threatening to destroy Boston if he were molested in his departure. Washington was too wise to afford him any pretext for executing this menace, and contented himself with closely following on his retreat, and immediately securing the abandoned works. The next day, he entered Boston in triumph; and it was soon noised abroad, through Europe as well as America, that an army of husbandmen, led by militia-officers, had beaten the choice troops and veteran generals of Great Britain, and forced them to surrender the place which had been the first cause of the war. Every one was loud in praise of Washington, the Congress voted unanimously their thanks for his services, and a gold medal was struck in his honour. But *he* knew better than most men, that the real struggle was only then beginning, and that the time for congratulations and rejoicings was yet far distant. General Howe had sailed for Halifax; but it was merely to await the arrival of his brother, Admiral Lord Howe, who was on his way from England with a fleet and strong reinforcements. It was impossible to say where the next blow would fall. Washington could only guess; but his prescient sagacity told him, that it was of the utmost importance to secure New York and the Hudson. Thither he hastened, with whatever troops could be spared from the other points of danger, and proceeded at once to fortify the approaches to the city and river. It was not long before the event proved the correctness of his judgment.

And now, having introduced the great central figure, which necessarily overshadows every other name in American history, it is time to turn to the more immediate subject of the present narrative.

CHAPTER II.

ONE day, while Washington was preparing for the defence of New York, his friend, General Greene, on his way to head-quarters, had occasion to pass through a field where some volunteers were at drill. |His attention was at once attracted by a company of artillery, which seemed to be handled with unusual skill by its commander—a mere boy, small in stature, and of slender frame, but rapid in all his movements, and with an air of remarkable intelligence. The general stopped to speak to him, and was convinced, by a few words of conversation, that he had met with a youth of no ordinary abilities. He desired to cultivate his acquaintance, and made some inquiries about him. He was told that the name of the young captain was ALEXANDER HAMILTON, and that he was a student of King's College.

Already in his short life (for he was only nineteen years of age) Hamilton had seen some notable changes of fortune. Born in the West Indies, on the 11th of January, 1757—a native of the mountain-island of Nevis, one of the many rich and fair possessions of the British Crown—he spent his childhood amid the luxuriant beauty and balmy air of the tropics. Yet he had early known poverty and privation. His father was a Scottish gentleman, descended from a branch of the great house of Hamilton, which plays so distinguished a part both in history and romance; but, being a younger son, and having embraced the profession of a merchant, he had emigrated to the West Indies in search of wealth. There he had married a lady of the name of Faucette, a member of one of those Huguenot families, who, banished from France by the revocation of the Edict of Nantes, carried their virtues and their love of freedom to happier climes, and have been the progenitors of so many illustrious men. Alexander was the only child of this marriage that survived to maturity; and, while yet of a very tender age, the death of his mother, and the ruin of his father through commercial speculations, left him entirely dependent on friends for support and education. He was removed to the island of Santa Cruz, where some of his mother's relations afforded him such elementary instruction as lay within their reach ; and, when only twelve years old, he was placed as a clerk in the counting-house of Mr. Nicholas Cruger, an opulent merchant. He disliked the employment, and sighed for leisure to engage in more congenial studies ; yet he showed such capacity for business, that, before he had completed his fourteenth year, the head of the firm could leave him in sole charge of the establishment during a temporary absence. He found time, moreover, to cultivate mathematics and chemistry, to improve his knowledge by general reading, and to form his style by the practice of composition. An account, which appeared in a newspaper, of the terrific hurricane that desolated the Leeward Islands, in 1772, attracted universal notice by its literary merit, and was traced to the pen of the youthful Hamilton. It was thought a pity that so much natural talent should not be developed by education, and it was resolved to withdraw him from the counting-house, and to send him to pursue his studies at New York. Had that tempest not raged, and that article not been written, a great name would probably have been wanting in the history of the United States.

Provided with the necessary funds, and with letters of introduction to persons of repute, Hamilton embarked on board a vessel, which was nearly destroyed by fire on the voyage to Boston. He arrived there, however, in safety, and proceeded thence to his place of destination. Having delivered his credentials, he soon found friends to interest themselves in his welfare, and, acting by their advice, he first entered a grammar-school at Elizabethtown, New Jersey, and then, after about a year's preparation, became a member of King's College, New York. This was an institution chartered by George II. "with the good design of promoting a liberal education, and to make the same as beneficial as may be," not only to the inhabitants of the province, "but to all our colonies and territories in America." And here the young student was, for the first time, surrounded by an atmosphere suitable to his tastes and powers. He worked hard at the college-course, easily mastered all the ordinary exercises, and soon added the study of anatomy, having then some intention of adopting the profession of medicine. He distinguished himself as a speaker at the local debating-club, wrote serious poetry, as well as doggerel verses of a satirical character, and, while he acquired a high reputation for ability, he was extremely popular with his fellow-students, and generally regarded as a lively and pleasant companion. It is stated on the authority of the friend who shared his room, that he was also very regular in his religious observances, not only attending public worship, but always praying on his knees night and morning—a habit which was probably rare with the young men of his age. The same friend relates, that Hamilton's firm belief in the truths of Christianity, and the eloquent and weighty arguments he advanced in their favour, greatly tended to confirm his own wavering faith.

But the political differences, which had arisen between the colonies and the mother-country, were now becoming a subject of universal interest, and drew off the minds of men from every other question. It was natural, that a youth like Hamilton, at an age when the boyish imagination is so readily kindled at the name of liberty, should be an enthusiastic champion of the popular cause. In this, he no doubt resembled the majority of his fellow-collegians. But what was peculiar to himself was the skill, the force, and the judgment, with which he defended his position. At an open-air meeting in New York, he had attended to hear the speakers;

when, suddenly impressed with the conviction, that they had left the most important points untouched, this unknown stripling of seventeen presented himself to the assembly, and proceeded to address them in a strain of unpremeditated eloquence. For a short time, he seemed to be somewhat embarrassed by his novel situation; but, rising gradually with his theme, he astonished his audience by the originality of his views, the cogency of his arguments, and the manly style of his oratory. Not long after, an attack appeared upon Congress, under the signature of a *Westchester Farmer*, and in answer to this and a subsequent publication, Hamilton (now just eighteen) wrote two pamphlets of such remarkable power, that they were at once ascribed to some of the leading men in the colonies, and people long refused to believe, that works of so much merit were the unaided productions of the young inexperienced West Indian. Yet, decided as were his opinions, and strenuous his exertions, on the side of the revolutionary movement, he had already learned to temper his zeal with a wise forbearance, and never to lose sight of the paramount duties of humanity and justice. When an excited mob attempted to seize the person of Dr. Cooper, the loyal president of King's College,

Hamilton threw himself between them and their intended victim, and gave the worthy clergyman time to escape; and when the house of a Tory printer had been assailed and rifled, it was Hamilton who first denounced this outrage on the liberty of the press, and called on the citizens to pursue and arrest the plunderers. It would have been well for America, if her advocates of popular rights had always been equally fearless in resisting popular violence.

As the prospect of war became more imminent, the young orator and pamphleteer determined to fit himself for a soldier. In him there was none of that idle kind of enthusiasm, which thinks to attain the end while neglecting the means. He at once set resolutely to work to study fortification, gunnery, and the various branches of the military art, besides devoting much time to martial exercises and the practice of arms; so that, when a volunteer force was raised at New York, he readily obtained the command of a company of artillery. It was here, that, as before mentioned, he attracted the attention of General Greene, who invited him to his quarters, treated him with marked kindness, and soon recommended him to the notice of Washington. But some little time elapsed before he was brought into personal relations with his illustrious chief.

Meanwhile, the Congress had taken the final step in the process of separating from England. Even after the war had begun, many had continued to believe in the possibility of an accommodation, and it was only after long debate and doubt, that the representatives of America determined to commit themselves irrevocably to the policy of independence. It was Thomas Jefferson, of Virginia, who was commissioned to prepare the important document, that was to proclaim to the world the termination of the old sovereignty. " When," runs this celebrated manifesto, " in the course of human events, it becomes necessary for one people to dissolve the political bands which have connected them with another, and to assume, among the powers of the earth, the separate and equal station, to which the laws of Nature and of Nature's God entitle them, a decent respect to the opinions of mankind requires, that they should declare the causes which impel them to the separation." It then proceeds to enumerate the rights, which it supposes Great Britain to have violated, and to describe the fruitless endeavours of the colonies to obtain redress ; and it concludes by solemnly declaring "that these United Colonies are, and of right ought to be, FREE AND INDEPENDENT STATES; that they are absolved from all allegiance to the British Crown, and that all political connexion between them and the state of Great Britain is, and ought to be, totally dissolved; and that, as free and independent states, they have full power to levy war, conclude peace, contract alliances, establish commerce, and do all other acts and things which independent states may of right do."

The Declaration of Independence was adopted on the 4th of July, 1776, and the anniversary has ever since been commemorated by Americans with great rejoicings in all parts of the world. They have more than fulfilled the prediction of John Adams, who believed that it would be solemnized "with pomp and parade, with shows, games, sports, guns, bells, bonfires, and illuminations, from one end of this continent to the other, from this time forth for evermore." Unhappily, they have too often forgotten, in the hour of prosperity and success, the sober and earnest spirit with which their fathers devoted to the common cause "their lives, their fortunes, and their sacred honour." They have needed the calm self-control of a Washington to restrain the exuberance of their exultation; even as, on the first appearance of that world-famous document, he rebuked his soldiers for indulging in unseemly and riotous demonstrations. "The General hopes and trusts," he wrote, "that every officer and man will endeavour so to live and act, as becomes a Christian soldier, defending the dearest rights and liberties of his country."

And, indeed, it was no time for any kind of rejoicing. Scarcely had the Declaration of Independence been published, when the storm of war burst with redoubled violence on the shores of America. A British fleet forced the entrance of the Hudson, a British army landed on Long Island, and, after a disastrous battle, and a retreat under cover of a fog, Washington was compelled to abandon New York, and to fall back upon the heights of Harlem. It was there that, while fortifying his camp and going his round of inspection, he was struck with the skilful construction of some earthworks by a young officer of artillery. He entered into conversation with him, and found it was the same Alexander Hamilton, to whom General Greene had already directed his attention. The chief invited the youthful engineer to his tent, and soon discovered how many rare qualities were united in his person. From that moment dates the long intimacy which was destined to exercise so marked an influence on the fortunes of the future republic.

It had become apparent, that the Americans were not yet in a situation, either by numbers or discipline, to contend successfully with the enemy in the open field, and that their true policy was to hold him in check, or draw him on in detachments, as circumstances might suggest, and to take advantage of their superior knowledge of the country, to harass and perplex him, without risking a general engagement. This cautious policy, which was often attacked and sneered at, until it was justified by the results, was now adopted by Washington, and acquired for him the name of the *American Fabius.* As the enemy advanced, he retreated to White Plains, and it was here that Hamilton first had the opportunity of distinguishing himself in action. With two field-pieces, planted on a ledge of rock, he had the honour of offering an obstinate resistance to a large force of British and Hessians, and, although ultimately driven from his position, excited the admiration of the whole army, by his cool courage, and the precision and steadiness of his fire. In the subsequent winter-campaign (one of the most critical of the

war)—in which Washington had to retreat from post
to post, and river to river, with his ragged and
weather-beaten troops often exposed to the extremity
of cold and hunger, and supposed to be on the eve
of total destruction, till he turned suddenly on the
enemy, and gained the battle of Trenton—the conduct
of Hamilton, on every occasion of difficulty and
danger, confirmed and fully established his high
military reputation, and earned for him from his
comrades in arms the epithet of the *Little Lion*.
Two descriptions of his personal appearance at this
time remain on record, and may not be uninteresting
to the reader.

"Well do I recollect the day," says one, "when
Hamilton's company marched into Princeton. It
was a model of discipline; at its head was a boy,
and I wondered at his youth; but what was my
surprise, when, struck with his slight figure, he was
pointed out to me as that Hamilton, of whom we
had already heard so much!"

"I noticed," says another veteran, speaking of the
retreat through the Jerseys, "a youth, a mere stripling, small, slender, almost delicate in frame, marching
beside a piece of artillery, with a cocked hat pulled
down over his eyes, apparently lost in thought, with

his hand resting on the cannon, and every now and then patting it as he mused, as if it were a favourite horse, or a pet plaything."

It was this campaign, which enabled Hamilton not only to prove his own merits as a soldier, but also to form a true estimate of the character of his chief. He saw him contending with every variety of peril and annoyance, not the least of which was the ill-concealed envy of some of his principal officers. Already, a party had arisen, to oppose and thwart the designs of the great leader, on whose genius and virtue depended the safety of America. Already, it was whispered in the camp, that *retreating was the fashion*, and that the frequent changes of position were the result of *indecision of mind*. An attempt was made to set up a rival, in the person of General Charles Lee, whose rashness and obstinacy soon after led to his own capture by the enemy. Washington had the mortification of knowing, that some of those in whom he had placed unlimited confidence, were engaged in these unworthy intrigues, and, although nothing could shake his calm resolution and mag-nanimity, he was yet deeply sensitive to the treachery and unkindness of friends. Through all this period of trial, Hamilton seems to have taken the side of his general, and, notwithstanding his youth, he had no doubt considerable influence with his companions in the service. Of the campaign itself he has left his testimony, that it presented the striking spectacle of a powerful enemy, "straitened within narrow limits by the phantom of a military force, and never permitted to transgress those limits with impunity"—and that, throughout that memorable winter, "skill supplied the place of means, and disposition was the substitute for an army."

In the early part of 1777, when the American head-quarters were fixed at Morristown, and Hamilton's little company had been reduced, by the vicissitudes of the war, to twenty-five men only, he received an invitation from Washington to join the staff. Having accepted the offer, he was appointed aide-de-camp, with the rank of lieutenant-colonel, and, although he found older and more experienced officers in the military family of the chief, he soon became the most valued and trusted of them all. It is greatly to their credit and his, that no jealousy or ill-temper seems ever to have disturbed his intercourse with his fellows. From the first, his popular manners made him a favourite with the other members of the staff; and Colonel Harrison in particular, who was known as the *Old Secretary*, at once gave him his friendship, and treated him with unfailing and almost paternal kindness. Washington himself admitted him to the closest intimacy, and nothing can be more indicative of the terms on which Hamilton was with his commander, than the fact, that the latter used often to address him by the endearing appellation of "My Boy!"

The duties of an aide-de-camp must vary indefinitely with various circumstances. In some cases, during intervals of quiet, they amount to little more than assisting the general in his hospitalities and social relations. In others, they consist of confidential services, on which may depend the event of a battle, or the safety of a state. In the present instance, what Washington chiefly required was the pen of a ready writer, to aid in his multifarious and important correspondence. He had to be in constant communication, not only with the Congress, whose commission he held, but with the authorities of the different States, from which his army was recruited— with his own officers, frequently at a distance from head-quarters—with the English generals, on matters of exchange, treatment of prisoners, and the like— and, at a later period, with military allies, and the

representatives of foreign governments. He made
no pretension to literary skill, and, although what he
wrote was always sensible and to the purpose, he
was too nobly modest and ingenuous, not to be
conscious of a certain deficiency in style. Besides,
the labours of his high post were so many and
onerous, its responsibilities so pressing, as to render
it impossible, that he should give much time to the
composition of letters and papers. It was, therefore,
of the utmost moment, that he should have a
Secretary gifted with the necessary talents, and on
whose judgment and integrity he could place full
reliance. The first, who had served him in that
capacity—Colonel Joseph Reed—had left him for
other employment in the army; Colonel Harrison,
a true and good man of average ability, had not
sufficient grasp of mind, to take in at one view a
vast diversity of matter; and in Hamilton alone was
found that singular mixture of genius and industry
which fitted him to render the exact assistance
required. Quick in seizing ideas, patient in mastering
details, endowed with lucid clearness of thought,
and rich in the resources of language, he was eminently suited to interpret between Washington and
the world. It would now be useless to attempt to

discriminate what were the several shares of the general and his aide-de-camp, in the preparation of the state-papers which issued from the head-quarters of the American army; but it is no disparagement to the glory of the great commander to say, that the hand of Hamilton is visible throughout these despatches; and there is good reason to believe, that not only the finished documents, but often the rough drafts, and the first conception, were entirely his own. It was no light charge to intrust to a youth of twenty, and the manner, in which he accomplished the work, is not among the least of his titles to lasting and honourable fame.

CHAPTER III.

SOME time before Hamilton joined the staff, Washington had thus addressed the Congress: —" I give in to no kind of amusements myself, and consequently those about me can have none, but are confined from morning till evening hearing and answering the applications and letters of one and another, which will now, I expect, receive a considerable addition ; as the business of the Northern and Eastern departments, if I continue here, must, I suppose, pass through my hands. If these gentlemen had the same relaxation from duty as other officers have in their common routine, there would not be so much in it; but to have the mind always upon the stretch, scarce ever unbent, and no hours for recreation, makes a material odds. Knowing this, and at the same time how inadequate the pay is, I can scarce find inclination to impose the necessary duties of their office upon them."

Plenty of work, therefore, was waiting for the pen of Hamilton, and scarcely was he installed in his office, when he had to conduct a most important correspondence on the subject of the treatment of prisoners. At first, England had naturally claimed to regard the Americans as rebels, who, when taken in arms, must be entirely dependent on the mercy of their captors. But, as the war continued, both humanity and self-interest called for a modification of these views. Washington had always insisted that the prisoners taken by either party should be placed on a footing of perfect equality, and had threatened retaliation for any breach of the ordinary customs of war. In Admiral Lord Howe and his brother, General Sir William Howe, he had found courteous and high-minded opponents, anxious to avoid unnecessary harshness, and to mitigate the evils inherent in such a contest. Yet many points of difference had arisen, and it was long before the belligerents came to a perfect understanding on these and similar questions. Hamilton now took up the thread of the negotiation, with the special design of promoting an early exchange of prisoners ; and it was admitted on all hands that his letters were models of good sense, moderation, and dignity.

Even where they failed in attaining their immediate object, they commanded the respect of friends and enemies, and raised the American character in the eyes of the world.

Hamilton was next employed in writing instructions to the different generals for the ensuing campaign, and in communicating the commander's plans and wishes to Congress and the State governments. He had to combat many fears and objections, and especially to insist on the necessity of keeping up the army, and furnishing it with supplies. He had moreover to contend with the intrigues which were constantly undermining Washington's influence, and interfering with his conduct of the war. The rivalry between States, and the jealousy of particular officers, often showed themselves in a manner dangerous to the common cause, and Washington's recommendations were too frequently neglected or over-ruled. It was against his opinion that General Gates (who had originally owed his place in the army to Washington's favour) was now put forward in opposition to the brave and chivalrous General Schuyler, and ultimately superseded him in the command of the Northern division. Yet, while his advice was thus set at nought, the patriot-hero had to compose the feuds occasioned by the disregard of his counsels, and to repair the mischief which he had vainly endeavoured to prevent. In all this he found Hamilton's services of the utmost value, and the wisdom and magnanimity of the chief never appear to greater advantage, than when they take form and substance in the words of the *Young Secretary.*

But the time for action was again approaching. Philadelphia was menaced by the enemy, and, however unwilling to risk a general engagement, Washington felt that he must strike a blow in defence of the capital. Accordingly, he fought the battle of the Brandywine, and, after a severe struggle, was defeated, and compelled to abandon the city to its fate. Congress adjourned to Lancaster, having first invested Washington with extraordinary powers for the emergency; and, before the English arrived at Philadelphia, Hamilton was despatched thither to procure contributions of blankets, clothing, and other stores, to remove the horses, and to send the vessels up the Delaware, so as to prevent their falling into the hands of the enemy. He executed this delicate mission with great success, giving as little offence as possible to the inhabitants, and addressing a letter to the ladies, which seems to have reconciled them to the necessity of parting with their fleecy treasures.

It was at the battle of the Brandywine that another young officer, whose name was afterwards well known in both hemispheres, first had an opportunity of showing his prowess. Amongst the foreigners, who had lately joined the American army as volunteers, was the Marquis de Lafayette, a French nobleman of about Hamilton's age, who had left his pleasant home and gentle bride, and all the gaieties of the proudest court in Europe, to serve a cause with which he had no direct concern, but which had inspired his romantic fancy with an ardent enthusiasm. He belonged to a small class of high-born men with popular sympathies, who in that age were anticipating the speedy advent of a millennium of political freedom, and cherishing dreams of human perfection, from which ere long they were destined to be rudely awakened. At all times of his life he was probably deficient in the wisdom and foresight of a statesman, and at a subsequent period in his career he exhibited an amount of weakness and infatuation, which brought the most serious calamities on his king and country; but there can be little doubt of his honesty and singleness of purpose: and when, as in 1777, he appeared suddenly on the scene, with his youth, his rank, his engaging manners, his generosity, and his courage, it is no wonder that he speedily gained the love and admiration of his new comrades. Washington invited him to share his quarters with his usual frankness and urbanity. "I cannot promise you the luxuries of a court," he said; "but as you have become an American soldier, you will doubtless accommodate yourself to the fare of an American army." And, for several years from that date, Lafayette lived in the most intimate relations with the general and his family, and a friendship sprang up between him and Hamilton, which left many pleasing recollections to both of them.

After fighting another battle at Germantown, which nearly proved a victory, Washington retreated to White Marsh, and occupied himself in providing for the defence of the forts on the Delaware. Meanwhile, Gates had been more fortunate in the Northern campaign. Aided by the magnanimous Schuyler, whom he had supplanted in the command, and by Benedict Arnold (a brave and adventurous soldier, whose services had been poorly requited) he succeeded in forcing Burgoyne to capitulate at Saratoga. It was a brilliant achievement, and very beneficial to the

American cause, but it seems to have filled the mind of Gates with a strange presumption. He neglected to inform the commander-in-chief of his success, and left him to hear of the event by public rumour alone. Moreover, he gave no account of how he intended to dispose of his victorious troops, and Washington was at this time in great need of reinforcements. It was therefore resolved, in a council of war, to send Hamilton to Gates with a letter from Washington, of which the following is an extract:—"By this opportunity I do myself the pleasure to congratulate you on the signal success of the army under your command, in compelling General Burgoyne and his whole force to surrender themselves prisoners of war—an event that does the highest honour to the American arms, and which, I hope, will be attended with the most extensive and happy consequences. At the same time, I cannot but regret that a matter of such magnitude, and so interesting to our general operations, should have reached me by report only, or through the channel of letters not bearing that authenticity which the importance of it required, and which it would have received by a line under your signature stating the simple fact."

Besides this dignified rebuke, Hamilton was the

bearer of instructions, in virtue of which he was to represent to General Gates the situation of the main army, and to urge on him the necessity of immediately detaching a portion of his forces to the assistance of his chief. On reaching Albany, he found Gates most unwilling to comply with Washington's wishes, ready to make any excuse for detaining the troops, and supported in his views by many of his officers, and by the New England States. It was a difficult position for a young man like Hamilton, thus brought into direct collision with a general flushed with conquest, in the midst of his popularity and triumph. But he never hesitated in the straight line of duty. Having advanced every argument he could think of, in favour of sending the required reinforcements, and finding that Gates would only agree, and that most reluctantly, to spare the weakest of three brigades at his disposal, he at once addressed him in language which could not be misunderstood or disregarded. "Knowing that General Washington wished me to pay the greatest deference to your judgment," he wrote, "I ventured so far to deviate from the instructions he gave me, as to consent, in compliance with your opinion, that two brigades should remain here instead of one. At the same

time, permit me to observe, that I am not myself
sensible of the expediency of keeping more than one,
with the detached regiments in the neighbourhood of
this place. . . . When I preferred your opinion to
other considerations, I did not imagine you would
pitch upon a brigade little more than half as large
as the others, and finding this to be the case, I
indispensably owe it to my duty *to desire, in his
Excellency's name, that another may go instead of the
one intended, and without loss of time."*—And to
General Putnam, who also hesitated to send forward
some troops, which had been ordered to join the
main army, he wrote still more emphatically, as
follows :—" I cannot forbear confessing, that I am
astonished and alarmed beyond measure, to find that
all his Excellency's views have been hitherto frus-
trated, and that no single step of those I mentioned
to you has been taken, to afford him the aid he
absolutely stands in need of, and by delaying which
the cause of America is put to the utmost conceivable
hazard. . . . I now, sir, in the most explicit terms,
by his Excellency's authority, *give it as a positive
order from him,* that all the Continental troops under
your command may be *immediately* marched to

King's Ferry, there to cross the river, and hasten to reinforce the army under him." ?

This bold and determined attitude, which was probably little expected in one so young, had the desired effect; and he now lent his personal aid in pushing on the reinforcements as fast as possible. It was when exhausted by his efforts, and suffering under severe illness, that he had the satisfaction of receiving the unqualified approbation of his chief. " I approve entirely," wrote Washington, " of all the steps you have taken, and have only to wish, that the exertions of those you have had to deal with had kept pace with your zeal and good intentions."— And when Putnam complained of Hamilton's *injurious reflections*, Washington answered : — " The urgency of Colonel Hamilton's letter was owing to his knowledge of our wants in this quarter, and to a certainty that there was no danger to be apprehended from New York, if you sent all the Continental troops that were then with you, and waited to replace them by those expected down the river. I cannot but say there has been more delay in the march of the troops than I think necessary ; and I could wish that in future my orders may be immediately complied with, without arguing upon the propriety of them. If any accident ensues from obeying them, the fault will lie upon me, and not upon you."

It was indeed high time for Washington to assert his authority. A cabal had been formed to deprive him virtually of his command; and, notwithstanding the victory of Saratoga, this was perhaps the darkest hour for America of the whole war. Whilst Howe, reinforced by Lord Cornwallis, was advancing against him, and Forts Mifflin and Mercer fell into the hands of the enemy, Washington, waiting in vain for the expected succours, which might have enabled him to change the fortune of the campaign, was exposed to every kind of intrigue and calumny. In Congress, as well as in the army, he was attacked with bitter and shameless ingratitude, and every art was used to exalt General Gates at his expense. General Conway, an Irishman by birth, who had been for some years in the service of France, appears to have taken a prominent part in these plots. It was he who wrote to Gates:—" Heaven has determined to save your country, *or a weak general and bad counsellors would have ruined it!*"—which passage, coming to the knowledge of Washington, was by

him sent back to Conway without further comment.
Yet, although this incident was a matter of notoriety,
Conway was soon after appointed to the important
office of inspector-general, and Gates himself was
made President of the Board of War, with the evident
intention of checking, if not superseding, the commander-in-chief. As Washington retired to his
dreary winter-quarters at Valley Forge, about twenty
miles from Philadelphia, with his poor, half-famished
army, ragged and shoeless, and marking their footsteps with their blood—left almost entirely without
money, clothing, or provisions, and unable to obtain
any assistance from Congress, who now seemed rather
inclined to counteract his measures—his rivals were
taunting him with incapacity, and expressing their
well-feigned astonishment, that he did not keep the
open field. Sadly and wearily must he have looked
round on the forlorn prospect ; but his great soul
never failed him, and neither neglect, nor insults,
any more than toil and danger, could move the iron
resolution, which was yet to triumph over all difficulties.

In this conjuncture, however, the pen of Hamilton
was once more of essential service. Scarcely recovered from his late indisposition, we find him

again at Washington's side, engaged in a correspondence, that exposed and confounded the machinations of his enemies. Lafayette too, whom the conspirators had sought to seduce to their faction, rejected all their offers, and stood firmly and consistently by his chief. And, whatever might be the case with general officers, and members of Congress, nothing could shake the faith of the soldiers in their leader. They loved, and honoured, and trusted him, in the midst of their own sufferings and privations, and thereby paid an unconscious tribute to the moral influence of wisdom and virtue. In the end, the cabal was utterly defeated, and most of its adherents sank into obscurity and oblivion; but, while it lasted, it was fraught with incalculable dangers, and tried to the utmost the temper and judgment of Washington, as well as the fidelity and devotion of his friends.

To Hamilton, it was already apparent, that a marked degeneracy had taken place in Congress. It was no longer the same body which, at its first meeting, commanded the admiration of Chatham. The spirit of intrigue had infected its members; favouritism and injustice, caprice and indecision, improvidence on the one hand, and false economy on the other, began to characterize all their proceedings. The inquiring mind of Hamilton sought to ascertain the reasons for this change. " America once had a representation," he writes to Governor Clinton, " that would do honour to any age or nation. The present falling off is very alarming and dangerous. What is the cause ? and how is it to be remedied ? are questions that the welfare of these States requires should be well attended to. The great men, who composed our first council—are they dead, have they deserted the cause, or what has become of them ? Very few are dead, and still fewer have deserted the cause ; they are all, except the few who still remain in Congress, either in the field, or in the civil offices of their respective States ; the greater part are engaged in the latter. The only remedy, then, is to take them out of these employments, and return them to the place where their presence is infinitely more important. Each State, in order to promote its own internal government and prosperity, has selected its best members to fill the offices within itself, and conduct its own affairs. Men have been fonder of the emoluments and conveniences of being employed at home ; and local attachment, falsely operating, has made them more provident for the particular interests of the States to which they

belong, than for the common interests of the confederacy. This is a most pernicious mistake, and
must be corrected. However important it is to
give form and efficiency to your interior constitutions and police, it is infinitely more important to
have a wise general council; otherwise, a failure
of the measures of the Union will overturn all your
labours for the advancement of your particular good,
and ruin the common cause. You should not beggar
the councils of the United States, to enrich the
administration of the several members. Realize to
yourselves the consequences of having a Congress
despised at home and abroad. How can the common
force be exerted, if the power of collecting it be
put in weak, foolish, and unsteady hands? How
can we hope for success in our European negotia-
tions, if the nations of Europe have no confidence
in the wisdom and vigour of the great Continental
government?"

Thus early had the difficulties of a federal organization forced themselves on the notice of that keen
observer; and already was the young soldier occupied with the problems of the future statesman.
Meanwhile, the year 1778 had opened in clouds
and darkness on the encampment at Valley Forge.

Famine and pestilence were in the American army; and the numbers of the effective troops were so greatly reduced, that it seems almost certain, that, had they been vigorously attacked by the English, they must have suffered a disastrous defeat. Yet they struggled on through the winter, without yielding to despair, and the month of May brought them the important intelligence, that a treaty of defensive alliance had been concluded between France and the United States. The news revived the drooping spirits of the Americans, and was received, throughout the country, with solemn thanksgivings and public rejoicings.

It might, indeed, have been anticipated. From the first, France had secretly encouraged the revolution; and, long before the breaking out of actual war, had been preparing to use the colonies as an instrument of aggression against Great Britain. It now rests on the unquestionable evidence of original documents, that, as far back as 1766, the Duke de Choiseul was sending agents to America, "for the purpose of putting the king in a condition to be able to undertake useful operations against his enemies;" and that he constantly impressed on the French ambassadors in London, to keep him regularly informed on American affairs, with a view to the ultimate dismemberment of the British empire. The same policy seems to have been taken up by the Count de Vergennes in 1775, though at first with considerable caution. While assuring the English government, "that the king's inclination, as well as a sense of justice, would prevent his majesty from ever favouring the troubles in America," he had a secret agent at Philadelphia, in direct communication with Franklin and the leaders of the colonists. This agent was to hold out hopes, without giving any definite promises, so as to leave France at liberty to take advantage of events. And in a paper drawn up by the Count de Vergennes himself, in 1776, to be laid before the king, it is assumed, as a matter of course, that the interests of France and Spain, and those of humanity in general, must be served by the injury and humiliation of England; and it is recommended, that the English ministry be kept in ignorance of the intentions of the French government, but that the insurgents be clandestinely supplied with money and military stores, and that France proceed to arm as quietly and circumspectly as possible.

There can be no doubt that this treacherous and

unworthy policy was inspired solely by hatred of
England, and not in the slightest degree by love of
American freedom. Yet a claim has often since
been made on the gratitude of America, as though
she were under lasting obligations to the chivalrous
generosity of France. The truth is, that the French
government, which had never forgiven the loss of
Canada, saw an opportunity of taking revenge on
an old rival, and had not the virtue or magnanimity
to forego it. The Americans profited by assistance
which was to them of the utmost value; but the
wisest amongst them detected the motives of their
new allies, and received the services rendered with
the caution and suspicion they deserved.

However, as far as England was concerned, France
had now thrown off the mask, and a French fleet
was on its way to America. Meanwhile, Sir William
Howe had been recalled, and Sir Henry Clinton was
left in command at Philadelphia. He resolved to
evacuate the city, and to remove his army to the
neighbourhood of New York. Washington had intelligence of the march, and hastened to follow on
his track. General Charles Lee, who had lately
been released from his captivity (having been ex-
changed for General Prescott), and who appears to

have returned to his duty as wrong-headed and impracticable as ever, was strongly opposed to attacking the enemy on this occasion. With his consent, therefore, the advance was confided to Lafayette ; but scarcely had this arrangement been made, when Lee altered his mind, claimed the command of the vanguard as senior officer, and prevailed upon Washington to send him forward to the front. He came up with the enemy near Monmouth Court House, and, in accordance with the instructions of his chief, commenced the engagement by falling on the rear of the British, while Washington pushed on to support him with the main body of the army. Hamilton, who had been incessantly passing to and fro between the generals, with orders and messages, was just reporting Lee's position to Washington, and the latter was standing with his arm thrown over his horse, halting for a few minutes at a place where two roads met, when, to his great surprise, he was joined by some fugitives from the front, who announced that the vanguard was in full retreat. Spurring rapidly forward, he reached a rising ground, when he beheld Lee approaching with the rest of his division. It was one of the few times in his life when Washington's indignation was thoroughly aroused, and in such moments he is said to have been terrible in his anger.

"What is the meaning of all this, sir?" he exclaimed, as Lee rode up to him. "I desire to know the meaning of this disorder and confusion."

Lee hesitated, and attempted to explain that he had been deceived by contradictory intelligence, and that he did not choose to beard the whole British army in such a situation.

"I have certain information," cried Washington, "that it was merely a strong covering party."

"It was stronger than mine," replied Lee, "and I did not think proper to run the risk."

"I am very sorry," rejoined Washington, "that you undertook the command, unless you meant to fight the enemy."

"I did not think it prudent to bring on a general engagement," persisted Lee.

"Whatever your opinion may have been," said Washington, "I expected my orders would have been obeyed."

When Hamilton was afterwards asked, whether Washington was not provoked to cursing at this interview, he gave the memorable answer : " Washington was careful of his words. He had no time to curse. He had to retrieve the day."

Hamilton's own exclamation at the moment had been : " Let us all die here, rather than retreat ! " —and when, at the voice of their great commander, the troops rallied on the heights, and once more formed in face of the enemy, it was the young aide-de-camp, who galloped here and there to bring up the artillery, and led a charge with the bayonet, which afforded time to complete the order of battle. The English were ultimately repulsed, and Washington lay that night on the field, with Lafayette beside him, at the foot of a tree. Hamilton was thoroughly exhausted, for he had ridden all day in the heat, bare-headed ; his horse had been shot under him, and he was much hurt by the fall. When morning dawned, the Americans found to their astonishment, that Sir Henry Clinton had decamped with his army in the darkness, and was already many miles on his way to New York.

The part which Lee took in this affair was never fully explained. It was the subject of a long investigation by a court-martial, which pronounced, that he had made " an *unnecessary*, and in some instances a *disorderly* retreat," but which seems to have acquitted him of all suspicion of cowardice or treachery. His conduct may probably be ascribed to a perverse waywardness of disposition, rather than to any deliberate design. He was sentenced to be suspended for a year, and, at the end of that time, he wrote so insolent a letter to Congress, that he was finally dismissed from the service. He retired to his estate in Virginia, and lived a solitary life in the midst of his dogs and horses; but he was bitter in his enmity to Washington, and often assailed him with sarcasm and invective. The latter bore these attacks with a noble patience; and when, after Lee's death, he was consulted as to the publication of the general's manuscripts, which might contain matter hostile to himself, he simply answered : " I can have no request to make concerning the work. I never had a difference with that gentleman but on public grounds; and my conduct towards him on this occasion was such only as I felt myself indispensably bound to adopt, in discharge of the public trust reposed in me. If this produced in him unfavourable sentiments of me, I can never consider the conduct I pursued with respect to him either wrong or improper, however I may regret, that it may have been differently viewed by him, and that it excited his anger and animadversions. Should there appear in General Lee's writings anything injurious or unfriendly to me, the impartial and dispassionate world must decide how far I deserved it, from the general tenour of my conduct."

An impartial posterity has long ago decided between Washington and his opponents; but, during his life, he was constantly exposed to malice and detraction. It was one sure sign of his greatness, that he was never moved from a settled purpose by calumny or clamour; but it was another, and still rarer quality of his mind, that he did full justice to the merits even of his most vindictive assailants. In the case of Lee, for instance, he always acknowledged the good points of that eccentric soldier, and, if he mentioned him at all, spoke of him without asperity. Lee, on the contrary, retained his prejudices to the last. He left directions by his will, that he was not to be buried in any church or churchyard, or within a mile of any meeting-house, for the whimsical reason "that he had kept so much bad company while living, that he did not choose to continue it when dead." And, with this misanthropical jest, he passes away from history—a man, who had seen many wars,

F

and done good service in his time—but who failed in the main through his impatient self-will, and the caprices of an ungovernable temper.

Within a few days of the battle of Monmouth Court House, a French fleet arrived at the mouth of the Delaware. Washington at once despatched Hamilton, to confer with the Count D'Estaing, the commander of the expedition. The first design was to attack New York, and, when this was found not feasible, the next attempt was directed against Rhode Island. But some delay had taken place, and, just as the French and Americans were prepared to act together before Newport, a British fleet suddenly appeared in the offing. It was Admiral Lord Howe, who, though inferior in force, had not hesitated to put to sea on hearing of the French movements. A battle was expected, but, after manœuvring for two days, the fleets were separated by a violent tempest, and the ships on both sides were so much shattered and disabled, that, while Howe returned to New York, the French admiral bore away for Boston, to repair the damage he had sustained. The Americans, thus left alone in front of Newport, accused their allies of deserting them, and were soon after themselves obliged to retreat. The utmost exasperation prevailed in the army, and the new alliance appeared to be already in danger. Count D'Estaing was justly offended by the tone adopted towards him, and especially by a protest of American officers, in which his conduct was declared to be "derogatory to the honour of France." He replied, that such a paper imposed on him "the painful, but necessary law of profound silence," and he no doubt felt deeply wounded by insults, which his position as a commander forbade him personally to resent. In these delicate circumstances, it needed all the wisdom of Washington, and all the tact and urbanity of Hamilton, to prevent a rupture. The latter was constantly employed in communicating with the French, and nothing can be better than the courteous and conciliatory style of his letters. He seems to have quite captivated D'Estaing, who, writing to Washington on the subject of a private mission he was about to send to him, says :—" I entreat you not to confide the secret to any person except Colonel Hamilton. His talents and his personal qualities have secured to him for ever my esteem, my confidence, and my friendship."

Having soothed the irritated pride of the French commander, Washington was next occupied with a

still more important matter. Lafayette had proposed to return home, with the view of concerting
with the cabinet of Versailles a magnificent project
for the conquest of Canada, by the combined forces
of France and the United States. It was a complicated scheme, including simultaneous attacks on
Detroit, Niagara, Oswego, Montreal, and Quebec.
Before finally sanctioning the proposal, Congress
referred it to the consideration of the commander-
in-chief. On this, Washington again had recourse
to the pen of Hamilton, and a letter was addressed
to the President of the Congress, in which, though
signed by the general, and doubtless embodying his
views, it is impossible not to trace the peculiar
manner and turn of thought of the aide-de-camp.

"I do not know, sir," it says, "what may be your
sentiments in the present case; but, whatever they
are, I am sure I can confide in your honour and
friendship, and shall not hesitate to unbosom myself
to you on a point of the most delicate and important
nature. The question of the Canadian expedition,
in the form it now stands, appears to me one of
the most interesting that has hitherto agitated our
national deliberations. I have one objection to it,
untouched in my public letter, which is in my esti-

mation insurmountable, and alarms all my feelings for the true and permanent interests of my country. This is the introduction of large bodies of French troops into Canada, and putting them in possession of the capital of that province, attached to them by all the ties of blood, habits, manners, religion, and former connexion of government.

"I fear this would be too great a temptation to be resisted, by any power actuated by the common maxims of national policy. Let us realize for a moment the striking advantages France would derive from the possession of Canada; the acquisition of an extensive territory abounding in supplies for the use of her islands; the opening a vast source of the most beneficial commerce with the Indian nations, which she might then monopolize; the having ports of her own on this continent, independent of the precarious good will of an ally; the engrossing the whole trade of Newfoundland, whenever she pleased, the finest nursery of seamen in the world; the security afforded to her islands; and, finally, the facility of awing and controlling these States, the natural and most formidable rival of every maritime power in Europe. Canada would be a solid acquisition to France on all these accounts, and because of the numerous inhabitants, subjects to her by inclination, who would aid in preserving it under her power against the attempt of every other.

"France, acknowledged for some time past the most powerful monarchy in Europe by land, able now to dispute the empire of the sea with Great Britain, and if joined with Spain I may say certainly superior—possessed of New Orleans on our right, and Canada on our left, and seconded by the numerous tribes of Indians in our rear from one extremity to the other, a people so generally friendly to her, and whom she knows so well to conciliate—would, it is much to be apprehended, have it in her power to give law to these States.

"Let us suppose, that when the five thousand French troops (and under the idea of that number twice as many might be introduced) had entered the city of Quebec, they should declare an intention to hold Canada, as a pledge and security for the debts due to France from the United States; or, under other specious pretences, hold the place till they can find a bone for contention, and in the meanwhile excite the Canadians to engage in supporting their pretensions and claims; what should we be able to say, with only four or five thousand men to carry on the dispute? It may be supposed, that France would not choose to renounce our friendship by a step of this kind, as the consequence would probably be a reunion with England, on some terms or other, and the loss of what she had acquired in so violent and unjustifiable a manner, with all the advantages of an alliance with us. This, in my opinion, is too slender a security against the measure, to be relied on. The truth of the position will entirely depend on naval events. If France and Spain should unite, and obtain a decided superiority by sea, a reunion with England would avail very little, and might be set at defiance. France, with a numerous army at command, might throw in what number of land forces she thought proper, to support her pretensions; and England, without men, without money, and inferior on her favourite element, could give no effectual aid to oppose them. Resentment, reproaches, and submission seem to be all that would be left us. Men are very apt to run into extremes. Hatred to England may carry some into excess of confidence in France, especially when motives of gratitude are thrown into the scale. Men of this description would be unwilling to suppose France capable of acting so ungenerous a part.

I am heartily disposed to entertain the most favourable sentiments of our new ally, and to cherish
them in others to a reasonable degree. But it is a
maxim, founded on the universal experience of mankind, that no nation is to be trusted further than it
is bound by its interests ; and no prudent statesman
or politician will venture to depart from it. In our
circumstances, we ought to be particularly cautious ;
for we have not yet attained sufficient vigour and
maturity to recover from the shock of any false
step into which we may unwarily fall.

"If France should even engage in the scheme, in
the first instance, with the purest intentions, there
is the greatest danger, that, in the progress of the
business, invited to it by circumstances, and perhaps
urged on by the solicitations and wishes of the
Canadians, she would alter her views.

"As the marquis (Lafayette) clothed his proposition, when he spoke of it to me, it would seem to
have originated wholly with himself; but it is far
from impossible, that it had its birth in the cabinet
of France, and was put into this artful dress to
give it the readier currency. I fancy that I read
in the countenances of some people, on this occasion,
more than the disinterested zeal of allies. I hope

I am mistaken, and that my fears of mischief make me refine too much, and awaken jealousies that have no sufficient foundation.

"But upon the whole, sir, to waive every other consideration, I do not like to add to the number of our national obligations. I would wish, as much as possible, to avoid giving a foreign power new claims of merit for services performed to the United States, and would ask no assistance that is not indispensable."

This wise and statesmanlike paper sufficiently shows, that the sagacious minds, which had most laboured to protect the French alliance from unjust and injurious suspicions, were fully alive to its real dangers. Indeed, in some respects, it had already proved less advantageous than was expected. While it had roused the pride of England to new efforts, it had produced a perilous feeling of security in America, and led to a relaxation of the national energies. Washington found it more difficult than ever to recruit his army, or to obtain the necessary supplies, and during some of the winter months, which he spent in Philadelphia, he was a witness of the violent party feuds which had broken out in Congress, and were distracting the attention of the leaders from the great interests of the country. The state of the finances, too, was most alarming ; and several members of the legislature were engaged in transactions, which laid them open to the charge of pecuniary dishonesty. Indignant at some of the abuses that happened to fall within his knowledge, Hamilton wrote a set of essays under the name of *Publius*, which seem to have scattered dismay through the ranks of the intriguers, and to have roused the people to a sense of the risk incurred by the corruption of their representatives.

"The station of a member of Congress," he says, in the course of these essays, "is the most illustrious and important of any I am able to conceive. He is to be regarded not only as a legislator, but as a founder of an empire. A man of virtue and ability, dignified with such a trust, would rejoice that fortune had given him birth at a time, and placed him in circumstances, so favourable for promoting human happiness. He would esteem it not more the duty, than the privilege and ornament of his office, to do good to all mankind. From this commanding eminence, he would look down with contempt upon every mean or interested pursuit.

"To form useful alliances abroad, to establish a

wise government at home, to improve the internal
resources and finances of the nation, would be the
generous objects of his care. He would not allow
his attention to be diverted from these, to intrigue
for personal connexions to confirm his own influence,
nor would he be able to reconcile it, either to the
delicacy of his honour, or to the dignity of his pride,
to confound in the same person the representative
of the commonwealth, and the little member of
a trading company. Anxious for the permanent
power and prosperity of the State, he would labour
to perpetuate the union and harmony of the several
parts. He would not meanly court a temporary
importance, by patronizing the narrow views of local
interest, or by encouraging dissensions either among
the people or in Congress. In council or debate, he
would discover the candour of a statesman, zealous
for truth, and the integrity of a patriot, studious of
the public welfare ; not the cavilling petulance of
an attorney, contending for the triumph of an
opinion, nor the perverse duplicity of a partisan,
devoted to the service of a cabal. Despising the
affectation of superior wisdom, he would prove the
extent of his capacity by foreseeing evils, and con-
triving expedients to prevent or remedy them. He
would not expose the weak sides of the States, to

find an opportunity of displaying his own discern-
ment by magnifying the follies and mistakes of
others. In his transactions with individuals, whether
with foreigners or countrymen, his conduct would
be guided by the sincerity of a man and the politeness
of a gentleman; not by the temporizing flexibility
of a courtier, nor the fawning complaisance of a
sycophant."

So high was the conception, which Hamilton had
formed of the duties and character of a senator!
And so far below it had the reality already fallen!

It is not possible, however, within the limits of
the present work, to describe all the services which
Hamilton rendered to the American cause, during
the period of his residence in the military family of
his chief. Throughout the campaigns of 1779 and
1780, in which Washington acted principally on the
defensive, the general and his aide-de-camp were in
constant, daily, familiar communication with each
other, and labouring incessantly together for the promotion of the common interest. Passing over the
details of these campaigns, there is one incident, the
saddest and most tragical of the war, which, from the
part Hamilton took in it, requires a brief notice here,
and will form the subject of a separate chapter.

CHAPTER IV.

MAJOR ANDRÉ.

THE city of New York being in the hands of the English, it was a prime object with Washington to secure the Highlands of the Hudson; and, with this view, the important position of West Point had been strongly fortified. A rocky promontory here commands the river, which is little more than a quarter of a mile in width, as it turns aside from its course before that natural obstruction. The enemy was as anxious to gain the post as the Americans were to defend it, for upon its possession would probably depend the safety of the country beyond—the event of, at least, one campaign, and, as some thought, the ultimate fortune of the war.

It was in the summer of 1780, that Washington, yielding to the solicitations of Benedict Arnold, confided to his valour and loyalty this momentous charge. No braver soldier had drawn a sword in the cause of independence; and his daring exploits, in the early part of the struggle, had extorted the admiration of friends and foes. There can be little doubt, that it was chiefly to him and Schuyler that Gates was indebted for his victory at Saratoga. Yet his services had not met with the gratitude they deserved; and he had the mortification of seeing his claims passed over, and the representations of Washington, in his behalf, neglected by Congress. Unable to emulate or understand the patient magnanimity of his chief, he seems to have cherished angry and bitter feelings, which were yet to ripen into schemes of violence and revenge. Moreover, he had indulged in habits of luxury and extravagance, which involved him in pecuniary embarrassments, destroyed his sense of honourable independence, and exposed him to fatal temptations. While in command at Philadelphia, he had lived in the most expensive style, engaged in questionable speculations, and incurred debts to a large amount. The envy and ill-will he provoked by his ostentation, found a vent in all sorts of charges against him. He had lately married Miss Margaret Shippen, a beautiful young lady, whose family was suspected of hostility to the American cause; and this was enough to give rise to reports injurious to himself. He at first treated these accusations with scorn; but when they took the form of special complaints to Congress, he demanded a court-martial to inquire into his conduct. After a full investigation, the only charges that could be proved to his disadvantage were a few venial irregularities, which sink into insignificance by the side of his brilliant services. Yet he was sentenced to be reprimanded by the commander-in-chief; and, although Washington performed the unpleasant task with the utmost delicacy, and tempered the reproof with many flattering compliments, Arnold could not forget that his country had been much quicker to blame than praise. In addition to all this, he was annoyed by delays in the settlement of his accounts, and felt deeply aggrieved that, while his private debts were pressing upon him, he failed to obtain the money, which he believed to be due to him from the nation.

It was in this frame of mind that he addressed himself to the French Minister, M. de Luzerne, requesting a loan to extricate him from his difficulties, and hinting that it might be for the interest of the King of France, to secure the attachment of an American general in his position The Frenchman very properly replied, that for the envoy of a foreign power to advance money under such circumstances, would be to *buy*, and not to *secure* the desired support; and that his master, having entered into the league with the United States from motives of justice and policy, could have no objects to serve that were not based on mutual interest and good-will. He was therefore compelled to decline General Arnold's request, with many expressions of esteem for his character, and admiration of his achievements.

It was the gambler's last stake. From that moment, Arnold was not only a disappointed, but a desperate man. He contrived, however, to conceal his purpose; and, while he engaged in a treasonable correspondence with Sir Henry Clinton, he impressed Washington with the belief, that he was most anxious for an opportunity of proving the injustice of his enemies, by again rendering some signal service to his country. He obtained the command of West Point, and fixed his head-quarters àt Robinson House, a country-seat on the opposite bank of the river.

In the month of September, 1780, Washington had visited Hartford, to hold a conference with Count Rochambeau and other French officers, and on his return to the Hudson, accompanied by Lafayette and

Knox, it was arranged that they should look in at West Point, and breakfast with Arnold at his quarters. They sent notice of their intention to Robinson House, and started early in the morning for that place, but, when within about a mile of their destination, Washington turned aside to examine some redoubts. Lafayette observed that Mrs. Arnold would be waiting breakfast, but the general answered, with a smile: "Ah, Marquis! you young men are all in love with Mrs. Arnold. Go you to breakfast, and tell her not to wait for me. I must ride down to the river, but will be with her shortly."

Lafayette and Knox, however, declined to leave their commander, and Hamilton, accompanied by Major M'Henry, rode on to Robinson House, with Washington's apology to Mrs. Arnold, and a request that the breakfast might not be delayed.

The two young officers sat down to table with the family. They were charmed with their amiable hostess, but could not help remarking that Arnold himself was silent and gloomy. He might well be so. Only forty-eight hours before, he had returned from an interview with a British emissary, whom he had met in a lonely spot, beneath the solemn stillness of a midnight sky, to concert a scheme for the betrayal of West Point to the enemy. The conditions had been agreed to, and the plot was ripe for execution, when this unexpected visit of Washington seemed likely to interfere with the plan. Before breakfast was ended, Arnold's doubts were changed into a fearful certainty. A messenger arrived with a letter, stating that a British agent had been captured on his way to New York, having papers about him of so dangerous a character, that the officer into whose hands they had fallen had forwarded them at once to Washington.

Arnold saw that all was over, but did not lose his presence of mind. He beckoned Mrs. Arnold from the breakfast-room, and told her, in a few words, that he must fly for his life. While she sank fainting on the floor of her chamber, he hastened down stairs, and informed his guests that he had to meet the commander-in-chief at West Point. Then, mounting the horse of the messenger who had brought the letter, he galloped down to the river, threw himself on board his barge, and effected his escape to the British sloop-of-war, *Vulture*, which lay anchored a few miles below.

Meanwhile, Washington arrived at Robinson House, and, being told that Arnold had gone to meet him at

West Point, proceeded thither in search of him. Not finding him at the fortress, he was returning in some surprise to the house, when he saw Hamilton approaching with hasty step and anxious countenance. He drew the general aside, and spoke to him in a low voice. The packet containing the fatal papers had been sent after Washington from place to place, and, being deliverd in his absence, was opened by Hamilton as his confidential officer. The general received it from his aide-de-camp, read the papers in silence, and then handed them to Lafayette and Knox, with the simple remark : " Whom can we trust now ? "

His first thought was to intercept the flight of the traitor, and he at once despatched Hamilton in pursuit. The latter rode with all speed to Verplanck's Point, where batteries commanded a lower portion of the river ; but Arnold had passed the spot in safety, and was already on board the *Vulture*. Then Hamilton, having written to General Greene (apparently on his own responsibility) to detach a brigade immediately to secure West Point from a surprise, returned to Robinson House. He seems to have been deeply touched by the grief and despair of Mrs. Arnold. " Everything affecting," he says, " in female tears, or in the misfortunes of beauty—everything pathetic in

the wounded tenderness of a wife, or in the appre-
hensive fondness of a mother—and (till I have reason
to change the opinion, I will add) everything amiable
in suffering innocence—conspired to make her an
object of sympathy to all who were present. She
experienced the most delicate attentions, and every
friendly office, till her departure for Philadelphia."

But Hamilton's humane and chivalrous feelings
were soon to be strongly aroused in favour of another
victim. The English emissary, whose capture had led
to the discovery of the plot, was at once perceived to
be an officer of distinction, and had himself lost no
time in writing to Washington as follows :—

" I beg your Excellency will be persuaded that no
alteration in the temper of my mind, or apprehension for my safety, induces me to take the step of
addressing you, but that it is to secure myself from
the imputation of having assumed a mean character
for treacherous purposes or self-interest. It is to
vindicate my fame that I speak, and not to solicit
security.

" The person in your possession is Major John
André, Adjutant-General of the British army.

" The influence of one commander in the army of
his adversary is an advantage taken in war. A corre-

spondence for this purpose I held, as confidential
with his Excellency Sir Henry Clinton. To favour it,
I agreed to meet, upon ground not within the posts
of either army, a person who was to give me intelligence. I came up in the *Vulture* man-of-war for
this effect, and was fetched from the shore to the
beach. Being there, I was told that the approach
of day would prevent my return, and that I must
be concealed until the next night. I was in my
regimentals, and had fairly risked my person.

"Against my stipulation, my intention, and without my knowledge beforehand, I was conducted
within one of your posts. Thus was I betrayed into
the vile condition of an enemy within your posts.

"Having avowed myself a British officer, I have
nothing to reveal but what relates to myself, which
is true on the honour of an officer and a gentleman.

"The request I have made to your Excellency
(and I am conscious that I address myself well)
is, that in any rigour policy may dictate, a decency
of conduct towards me may mark that, though
unfortunate, I am branded with nothing dishonourable—as no motive could be mine but the service of
my king, and as I was involuntarily an impostor."

This characteristic letter would at once excite the

interest of brave men in the fate of the prisoner;
and when he was brought to West Point, and it
was found that he was a young, amiable, and accomplished gentleman, most fascinating in manners,
agreeable in conversation, and full of the enthusiasm
and high spirit of his profession, the sympathy for
him was greatly increased. And with it came the
sad conviction, that by entering the American lines,
and carrying on a secret intercourse with Arnold,
he had placed himself in the position of a spy, and
was liable to a felon's fate.

Sir Henry Clinton claimed the release of André,
on the ground that he had visited Arnold at the
request of that officer, then in command at West
Point—that he had landed under the sanction of
a flag of truce, and that he had been stopped when
travelling with Arnold's passports. But, unfortunately, neither the invitation, nor the flag, nor the
passports—all of which would have been good in
any ordinary transaction between the parties—could
avail, where the *intention* of the American com-
mandant had been known from the first to his
visitor. A board composed of fourteen general-
officers, with Greene at their head—having examined
the prisoner, who frankly admitted all the facts

relating to himself, but declined to implicate any one else—reported after brief deliberation, that Major André must be considered a spy from the enemy, and, according to the law and usage of nations, ought to suffer death.

When his sentence was announced to him, André remarked, that, since it was his lot to die, there was still a choice in the mode, which would make a material difference to his feelings; and it was with this view that he addressed the following appeal to Washington :—

"Sympathy towards a soldier will surely induce your Excellency and a military tribunal, to adapt the mode of my death to the feelings of a man of honour. Let me hope, sir, that if aught in my character impresses you with esteem towards me— if aught in my misfortunes marks me as the victim of policy, and not of resentment—I shall experience the operation of these feelings in your breast, by being informed that I am not to die on a gibbet."

No one acquainted with the benevolence of Washington's character can doubt, that it must have cost him many a pang, not only to leave André to his fate, but to refuse him even his last request. He acted on the conviction that it was necessary to make an example, which should deter others from engaging in these secret plots, and, as on many other occasions, he sacrificed his own feelings to a sense of duty. Nor can it be disputed, that he was justified in what he did, by the established principles of military law. Yet it may be questioned whether, in this instance, the course, which a romantic generosity would have counselled, might not in the end have proved the best and wisest. No incident of the war made such a painful impression in England as the execution of André, and none left behind it such bitter and lasting memories; while to have spared his life would have at once been acknowledged as an act of clemency, would have appealed to all that is noblest in the English character, and would have done more than almost any other conceivable event, to bring about a speedy and complete reconciliation between the two hostile branches of the British race. And, even if this could not be, it would have been in every way expedient to have saved him from the last indignity. No gallows could attach a felon's shame to the brave young soldier, acting under the orders of his chief, and in the service of his country; and his doom, instead of covering him with ignominy, and striking terror in the breasts of others, only excited a storm of mingled pity and indignation. It was a cruel because it was a wholly useless piece of severity.

Such at least was the opinion of Hamilton. From the first moment he saw him, he took the warmest interest in André, and did all in his power, if not to avert, at all events to mitigate his doom. He was frequently with him, and paid him every kindly attention that the most generous sympathy could suggest. He seems to have gained his friendship, and to have felt a sincere affection for him. " There was something singularly interesting," he says, " in the character and fortunes of André. To an excellent understanding, well improved by education and travel, he united a peculiar elegance of mind and manners, and the advantage of a pleasing person. It is said, he possessed a pretty taste for the fine arts, and had himself attained some proficiency in poetry, music, and painting. His knowledge appeared without ostentation, and embellished by a diffidence that rarely accompanies so many talents and accomplishments." André opened his heart to Hamilton without reserve, and the latter was much impressed by the elevation of his sentiments. " There is only one thing that disturbs my tranquillity," said the captive.

" Sir Henry Clinton has been too good to me ; he has been lavish of his kindness. I am bound to him by too many obligations, and love him too well to bear the thought, that he should reproach himself, or that others should reproach him, on the supposition of my having conceived myself obliged by his instructions to run the risk I did. I would not for the world leave a sting in his mind that should embitter his future days." He then asked permission to write to Sir Henry on this subject, as well as to convey his last wishes with regard to his mother and sisters. Hamilton readily obtained compliance with this request, and other alleviations in the condition of the prisoner ; but when he came to speak of the sentence itself, all his efforts were encountered by a stern, implacable resolution. For the first time, apparently, the general and his aide-de-camp were directly opposed to each other on a matter of importance, and the whole affair seems to have left a sore and dissatisfied feeling on the mind of the younger man.

" Poor André suffers to-day," he writes, on the morning of the execution. " Everything, that is amiable in virtue, in fortitude, in delicate sentiment, and accomplished manners, pleads for him ; but hard-hearted policy calls for a sacrifice. He must die. I send you my account of Arnold's affair, and, to justify myself to your sentiments, I must inform you, that I urged a compliance with André's request to be shot, and I do not think it would have had an ill effect; but some people are only sensible to motives of policy, *and sometimes, from a narrow disposition, mistake it.*

"When André's tale comes to be told, and present resentment is over, the refusing him the privilege of choosing the manner of his death *will be branded with too much obstinacy.*

"It was proposed to me to suggest to him the idea of an exchange for Arnold; but I know I should have forfeited his esteem by doing it, and therefore declined it. As a man of honour, he could not but reject it; and I would not for the world have proposed to him a thing, which must have placed me in the unamiable light of supposing him capable of a meanness, or of not feeling myself the impropriety of the measure. I confess to you, I had the weakness to value the esteem of a dying man, because I reverenced his merit."

All the chivalry of Hamilton's character speaks in the last paragraph. It is true, that Arnold was safe under the shelter of that British flag, which never

yet betrayed the fugitive who trusted to its protection, and that no English general would have consented to purchase the life of friend or brother, by
delivering up the renegade whose proffered services
he had once accepted. But Hamilton felt that there
was dishonour in the very proposal, and that he
should forfeit the esteem of André by even mention-
ing it to him. He measured the nobleness of the
victim by his own lofty standard.

On that fatal morning, there was a gloomy silence
in the camp, and, excepting the brigade on duty,
officers and soldiers retired to their tents. It was
the natural and spontaneous delicacy of true valour.
Having breakfasted, and dressed himself with care
in the full uniform of a British officer, André walked
calmly to the place of execution. There was a
serene smile on his lips, but, when he came in sight
of the gibbet, he asked with some emotion : " Must
I then die in this manner ? " Being told it was
inevitable, he said : " It will be but a momentary
pang ; " and, springing upon the cart, he made the
necessary preparations with admirable composure.
He was informed, that the last moment was at hand,
if he had anything more to say. " Nothing," he
answered, " but to request you will bear witness, that

I meet my fate like a brave man." It was the dying thought of a soldier, who felt that he had to maintain the martial honour of his country.

The tale has been told a thousand times, and still affects us, almost as it affected our grandfathers. In America, as in England, the name of André still awakens a sensation of sorrowing pity. " It was among the extraordinary circumstances that attended him," says Hamilton, " that, in the midst of his enemies, he died universally regretted, and universally esteemed." And with regard to Hamilton himself, nothing is more fitted to endear his memory to gentle hearts on both sides of the Atlantic, than the generous humanity he displayed in the case of the unfortunate André.

CHAPTER V.

THE struggle had now lasted for upwards of five years, and still there seemed to be no sign of a speedy termination of the contest. Both France and Spain were in alliance with America, Holland was threatening to join the coalition, and the States of Northern Europe had united in an armed neutrality against the naval pretensions of Great Britain; but still the invincible pride of England refused to yield. On her own element, Rodney maintained her supremacy; from the rock of Gibraltar, her flag waved defiance to the world; and she clung with desperate tenacity to what remained of her dominion on the continent of America. When the prolonged resistance to the independence of the colonies is ascribed (as it often is) to the obstinacy of George III., it should not be forgotten that, throughout the greater part of the war, the king fairly represented the opinions of the majority of the nation. There was, indeed, a minority, brilliant in eloquence and talent, who, from the first, had taken the side of the Americans; but even these were slow to acquiesce in the dismemberment of the empire, and the main body of the people looked upon the surrender of their transatlantic possessions as tantamount to disgrace and ruin. We have since learned, indeed, that a kindred race may be more valuable as friends and customers than as subjects, and that a sovereignty which can only be preserved by force is not worth preserving at all: but the lesson was hard to learn; and the knowledge of that fact should make us tolerant in our judgment of others, who, in our own day, have striven, with equal stubbornness, and hitherto with as doubtful fortune, to uphold the integrity of an empire against states resolved to be independent.

Meanwhile, the Americans had to suffer many privations, and were by no means exempt from reverses. Charleston had been taken by the English; and, in North Carolina, Lord Cornwallis had surprised and defeated Gates, whose military reputation was rapidly declining. Besides all the old difficulties, Washington had to contend with a mutiny in his army, arising from the neglect of Congress to provide pay for the men, and also from a breach of faith in detaining them beyond their term of enlistment. But, in fact, the Confederacy was altogether disorganized; and the finances were in such a condition that it was almost impossible to raise money for any purpose. Hamilton, who saw more clearly than most men the full danger of the situation, was also one of the first to divine the causes of the existing evils, and to suggest a remedy. He traced the weakness and insolvency of the Congress in a great measure to the want of a central authority, and to the loose way in which the States were held together, without any settled government for the whole Confederacy. And already his busy and versatile mind had sketched the plan of a Constitution for the Union. "At the age of three-and-twenty," says an able American writer, Mr. George Ticknor Curtis, "he had already formed well-defined, profound, and comprehensive opinions on the situation and wants of these States. He had clearly discerned the practicability of forming a confederated government, and adapting it to their peculiar conditions, resources, and exigencies. He had wrought out for himself a political system, far in advance of the conceptions of his contemporaries."

And, until a definite Constitution could be agreed upon, he suggested, as measures of primary importance—1st. An army raised for the war, and not for any shorter term. 2d. A foreign loan, to extricate the Congress from the immediate pressure of insolvency. 3d. Full powers to the same body, to deal with all matters, of war, peace, trade, and finance, that concerned the common interest. 4th. The appointment of executive officers, instead of boards, to administer the several departments of the public service. 5th. The establishment of a national bank, to regulate the issue of notes, and to place the currency of the country on a solid basis.

Yet all this activity of mind did not prevent his attending to interests of a more tender nature. He was at this time paying his addresses to Miss Eliza Schuyler, second daughter of the gallant general of that name, and in December, 1780, he was married to the lady of his choice, at her father's house in Albany. She is described by a French traveller as a charming woman, who united to grace and beauty " all the candour and simplicity of an American wife." By this marriage, Hamilton became permanently established as a resident in the State of New York.

H

And now an event occurred which has occasioned much discussion, and which certainly cannot be recorded without regret. A misunderstanding arose between Washington and his favourite aide-de-camp, which led to the resignation by the latter of his place on the staff. Hamilton's account of the affair is contained in a letter to General Schuyler :—

" Since I had the pleasure of writing you last, an unexpected change has taken place in my situation. I am no longer a member of the general's family. This information will surprise you, and the manner of the change will surprise you more. Two days ago the general and I passed each other on the stairs ; he told me he wanted to speak to me. I answered, that I would wait upon him immediately. I went below, and delivered Mr. Tilghman a letter to be sent to the Commissary, containing an order of a pressing nature.

" Returning to the general, I was stopped on the way by the Marquis de Lafayette, and we conversed together about a minute on a matter of business. He can testify how impatient I was to get back, and that I left him in a manner which, but for our intimacy, would have been more than abrupt. Instead of finding the general, as is usual, in his room, I met him at the

head of the stairs, where, accosting me in an angry
tone—' Colonel Hamilton,' said he, 'you have kept
me waiting at the head of the stairs these ten minutes.
I must tell you, sir, you treat me with disrespect.'—
I replied without petulancy, but with decision : ' I am
not conscious of it, sir ; but since you have thought
it necessary to tell me so, we part.'—' Very well, sir,'
said he, ' if it be your choice,' or something to this
effect, and we separated. I sincerely believe my
absence, which gave so much umbrage, did not last
two minutes.

" In less than an hour after, Tilghman came to me
in the general's name, assuring me of his great confidence in my abilities, integrity, usefulness, &c., and
of his desire, in a candid conversation, to heal a
difference which could not have happened but in
a moment of passion. I requested Mr. Tilghman to
tell him—1st, that I had taken my resolution in a
manner not to be revoked ; 2d, that, as a conversation could serve no other purpose than to produce
explanations mutually disagreeable, though I certainly would not refuse an interview if he desired it,
yet I would be happy if he would permit me to
decline it ; 3d, that, though determined to leave the
family, the same principles which had kept me so

long in it would continue to direct my conduct towards him when out of it; 4th, that, however, I did not wish to distress him or the public business, by quitting him before he could derive other assistance by the return of some of the gentlemen who were absent; 5th, that, in the meantime, it depended on him to let our behaviour to each other be the same as if nothing had happened. He consented to decline the conversation, and thanked me for my offer of continuing my aid in the manner I had mentioned.

" I have given you so particular a detail of our difference, from the desire I have to justify myself in your opinion. Perhaps, you may think I was precipitate, in neglecting the overture made by the general to an accommodation. I assure you, my dear sir, it was not the effect of resentment; it was the deliberate result of maxims I had long formed for the government of my own conduct.

" I always disliked the office of an aide-de-camp, as having in it a kind of personal dependence. . . . It has often been with great difficulty that I have prevailed upon myself not to renounce it; but while, from motives of public utility, I was doing violence to my feelings, I was always determined, if there should ever happen a breach between us, never to consent to an accommodation. I was persuaded that, when once that nice barrier which marked the boundaries of what we owed to each other should be thrown down, it might be propped again, but could never be restored."

There is something so singular in this transaction, as to appear almost inexplicable. It is difficult to believe, that the intimate and endearing relations of those four memorable years could have been thus suddenly interrupted from so inadequate a cause; and, considering the difference in rank and age of the parties concerned, it is impossible to deny, that the conduct of the younger man (on his own showing) was marked by a haughtiness, not to say presumption, which even *his* great talents and services could not justify. On the other hand, Washington appears to much advantage, in his readiness to make the first advances towards reconciliation, and in the prompt and generous assurance of his unaltered esteem for Hamilton. Schuyler (a punctilious and chivalrous gentleman) was evidently of opinion, that the general's friendly explanation ought to have been accepted, for he thus writes in reply to his son-in-law :—

" Long before I had the least intimation that you

intended that connexion with my family, which is so very pleasing to me, and which affords me such extreme satisfaction, I had studied your character, and that of the other gentlemen who composed the general's family. I thought I discovered in all an attention to the duties of their station; in some a considerable degree of ability; but (without a compliment, for I trust there is no necessity of that between us) in you only I found those qualifications, so essentially necessary to the man who is to aid and counsel a commanding general, environed with difficulties of every kind, and those, perhaps, more and of greater magnitude than any other ever had to encounter—whose correspondence must be extensive, always interesting, and frequently so delicate, as to require much judgment and address to be properly managed. The public voice has confirmed the idea I had formed of you; but what is most consoling to me, and more honourable to you, men of genius, observation, and judgment think as I do on the occasion. Your quitting your station must, therefore, be productive of very material injuries to the public; and this consideration, exclusive of others, impels me to wish that the unhappy breach should be closed, and a mutual confidence restored.

You may both of you imagine when you separate, that the cause will remain a secret; but I will venture to speak decidedly, and say it is impossible. I fear the effect, especially with the French officers' with the French minister, and even with the French court. These already observe too many divisions between us. They know and acknowledge your abilities, and how necessary you are to the general. Indeed, how will the loss be replaced?

" It is evident, my dear sir, that the general conceived himself the aggressor, and that he quickly repented of the insult. He wished to heal a difference, which would not have happened but in a moment of passion. It falls to the lot of few men to pass through life, without one of those unguarded moments, which wound the feelings of a friend. Let us then impute them to the frailties of human nature, and, with Sterne's recording angel, drop a tear, and blot them out of the page of life. I do not mean to reprehend the maxims you have formed for your conduct. They are laudable; and yet, though generally approved, times and circumstances sometimes render a deviation necessary and justifiable. This necessity now exists in the distresses of your country. Make the sacrifice. The greater it is, the more glorious to you. Your services are wanted. They are wanted in that particular station, which you have already filled so beneficially to the public, and with such extensive reputation."

These arguments would in general have had great weight with Hamilton, but, in the present instance, they failed of their effect. He adhered to his resolution; and, at this distance of time, we can only account for it by supposing, that there were other causes for the step he took than the slight altercation on the stairs. It may have been, as some have suggested, that even the strong and well-balanced mind of Washington, harassed by constant annoyance, had given way to an irritability that made the situation of his aide-de-camp peculiarly irksome. Or, as others have thought, Hamilton, desirous of obtaining a separate military command, and so of distinguishing himself on a wider field, may have taken the first opportunity of parting from Washington. But neither of these theories is quite consistent with the characters of these two illustrious men. It seems more probable, that some previous offence had been given, perhaps unconsciously; and it may well be, that, in such an affair as that of André, vehement remonstrance on the one side, and stern refusal on the other, may have led, for a time, to coldness and estrangement. But, whatever the cause of the difference, it is satisfactory to know, that it did not ultimately impair that noble friendship. A day was to come when Washington again found in Hamilton his most tried and faithful counsellor, and, to the hour of his death, he never spoke or wrote of him but in terms of affectionate esteem.

It was in the month of April, 1781, that Hamilton retired from the staff, and, in the July following, he obtained the command of a battalion. In the brief interval of repose, he had occupied himself in writing a series of essays, called the *Continentalist*, with the view of impressing on the people the necessity of those reforms in their government which he had already suggested. But the time had now arrived for decisive action on the part of the American army. After a campaign in North Carolina, Lord Cornwallis had entered Virginia, and was encamped on York River. Washington still remained in the neighbourhood of New York, where Sir Henry Clinton was in daily expectation of being attacked by him, when tidings reached the American general, that the Count de Grasse, with a French fleet and army, was on his way to the Chesapeake.

Washington at once saw that the blow must be struck in Virginia. With great secrecy and despatch, having first garrisoned West Point and the posts on the Hudson, he led his troops southwards. The English were not aware of his departure, until he was far upon the road, and it was too late for Sir Henry Clinton to oppose any obstacles to the march. Passing through Philadelphia and Baltimore, Washington heard, on his way, of the safe arrival of the French, and that York River was blockaded by their fleet, while Lafayette had effected a junction with their land forces. Awakened to a sense of his danger, Cornwallis attempted to retreat to the Carolinas, but it was no longer possible. He found himself surrounded by enemies, and had no choice but to fall back on his intrenchments at Yorktown.

On the 28th of September, the combined armies proceeded to invest the place, and their first parallel was opened on the 6th of October. On the 9th and 10th, three French and three American batteries poured a continuous and heavy fire on the besieged, and, on the 11th, the second parallel was opened within three hundred and sixty yards of their works. Cooped up in his defences, with an army reduced to not more than six or seven thousand men, Cornwallis felt that, unless relieved, his case was desperate. He resolved, however, to make a vigorous resistance, and severely galled the Americans from two redoubts, which enfiladed the line of their intrenchments. These redoubts it was determined to carry by storm, and the one was to be attacked by the American light infantry, while the other was assigned to the French grenadiers and chasseurs.

Hamilton had started on the campaign, impatient and eager to distinguish himself. He now saw the opportunity he had so long desired, for, on the day of the assault, his turn of duty had come round. To his great mortification, he found that another officer had been appointed to lead the attack. He instantly appealed to Washington, and claimed his right as the officer of the day. His claim was admitted, and he returned in the highest spirits to his men, repeating: "We have it! we have it!" At eight o'clock in the evening of the 14th of October, two rockets gave the signal for the simultaneous attacks on the redoubts. Hamilton rushed forward at the head of his party, who, without waiting for the sappers to demolish the *abattis*, pushed or pulled them down with their hands, and scrambled over. Placing his foot on the shoulder of a soldier, who knelt on one knee for the purpose, Hamilton was the first to mount the parapet. He stood on it for a moment with three of his men, calling on the others to follow, and then jumped into the ditch. Exposed to a tremendous fire he reached the counterscarp, made his way over every obstacle, and carried the work at the point of the bayonet. So impetuous had been the assault, that the whole affair only lasted a few minutes. And the instant he found himself in possession of the redoubt, his humanity was as conspicuous as his valour. He checked his men in the rush and fury of the onslaught, turned aside a bayonet that was directed against the breast of Colonel Campbell, and so well exerted his authority, that not one of the enemy was injured after the resistance had ceased. The French attacked the other redoubt in a more regular manner, and were much longer about it ; but they also ultimately succeeded in their part of the enterprise.

The next day Cornwallis wrote to Sir Henry Clinton :—" Last evening, the enemy carried my two advanced redoubts on the left by storm, and during the night have included them in their second parallel, which they are at present busy in perfecting.

My situation now becomes very critical; we dare not show a gun to their old batteries, and I expect that their new ones will open to-morrow morning. Experience has shown that our fresh earth-works do not resist their powerful artillery, so that we shall soon be exposed to an assault in ruined works, in a bad position, and with weakened numbers. The safety of the place is, therefore, so precarious, that I cannot recommend that the fleet and army should run great risk in endeavouring to save us."

But, while Cornwallis thus generously warned his countrymen not to expose themselves to imminent danger on his account, he was himself ready to dare the worst, rather than surrender. Having tried a *sortie*, which, though gallantly conducted, was repulsed by superior numbers, he resolved on a desperate attempt to escape. His plan was to leave his sick, wounded, and baggage; to cross over to Gloucester Point, on the opposite side of the river, in the night—to attack the enemy's camp there, and mount his infantry on the captured cavalry horses, and such others as could be collected—and then to push on northwards, and fight his way through Maryland, Pennsylvania, and the Jerseys, to New York. Wild as it appears, the scheme might possibly have succeeded; but, when a portion of the troops had actually crossed over, and a second division was preparing to follow, a violent storm arose, which dispersed the boats, and drove them down the river. The day broke before the passage could be effected, and it was with great difficulty that the advanced party could be brought back again. All hope was now at an end, and to save the lives of the brave troops who had stood by him with dauntless resolution, and only waited his orders to bury themselves with him in the ruins of Yorktown, Cornwallis at length consented to capitulate. Though the terms granted were not dishonourable, it was with difficulty that the British soldiers could be brought to submit to a humiliation, which England, in the long course of her annals, has not often suffered at the hands of any foe. They marched out slowly and sullenly, their drums beating a British march, and threw down their arms with a violence that threatened to break them to pieces. But the officers bowed courteously to each other, whilst both French and Americans looked on without any demonstrations of triumph, and showed their respect for gallant enemies by an expressive silence.

Yet the joy was great and general throughout the Confederacy, and the consternation scarcely less so in the United Kingdom. When Lord North received the news in Downing Street, he considered it as decisive of the contest. "He took it," said Lord George Germaine, who brought him the tidings, "as he would have taken a ball in the breast; for he opened his arms, exclaiming wildly, as he paced up and down the apartment: *O God! it is all over!*"

The part which Hamilton performed in this affair gained him universal honour, and his bearing under it was equally becoming. He received the congratulations of his fellow-soldiers with modest dignity, and it was in these quiet and unpretending terms that he wrote to his wife with reference to his late exploit:—"Two nights ago, my Eliza, my duty and my honour obliged me to take a step in which your happiness was too much risked. I commanded an attack upon one of the enemy's redoubts; we carried it in an instant, and with little loss. You will see the particulars in the Philadelphia papers. There will be, certainly, nothing more of this kind; all the rest will be by approach; and if there should be another occasion it will not fall to my lot to execute it."

Cornwallis having surrendered, and the efforts of General Greene in South Carolina having brought the campaign there to a successful issue for the Americans, Sir Henry Clinton was left to act wholly on the defensive, and the war was virtually at an end. It was true that England might yet renew the struggle ; but it was generally believed that she was weary of so unprofitable a contest, and that, if she could succeed in striking some great blow at her old enemies of France and Spain, she would be willing to let her rebellious children depart in peace. A few months later, Rodney's great victory restored to her the undisputed empire of the sea, the East and West Indies were once more within her grasp, and the vaunted floating batteries of the Chevalier d'Arçon perished in blood and fire beneath the guns of Gibraltar—but Lord North's administration had already fallen before a hostile vote of the House of Commons, and no further operations were attempted on the continent of America. Meanwhile, the Confederacy waited in an attitude of expectation, and Hamilton returned home to Albany to his wife and new-born child. He expressed his intention of retiring from active service, but at the same time announced that he should always be ready at the call of his country to act in any capacity that might be required.

Convinced that the war was drawing to a close, he had already determined to engage in a profession which would enable him to support his family in comfort and independence. It was now the spring of 1782, and the soldier of five-and-twenty (to whom had been committed such important interests as were hardly ever before confided to a man so young) withdrew from the field with no emolument but his fame, and set himself to study the law, in preparation for an entirely new career. Declining the generous offers of Schuyler, and regardless of the advice of friends, who wished him to apply to Congress for some employment worthy of his talents and eminent services, he resolved to trust to himself alone for the advancement of his fortunes. Within four months from the commence- of his studies, he had composed for his own use a *Manual on the Practice of the Law*, which subsequently served as a guide for future students, and became the groundwork of enlarged treatises on the subject. The same vigour of mind, which he had displayed in all other pursuits, enabled him to master with ease the difficulties and subtleties of legal procedure, and in after years he 'attained the position of a leading practitioner at the bar.

But while he was employed in preparing for his new profession, his attention was never wholly diverted from politics. In June, 1782, he is found strongly protesting against the contemplated execution of Captain Asgill, a young British officer, who had been selected by lot from the other prisoners, to suffer in retaliation for the murder of an American captain, named Huddy, put to death by some refugees on the English side. "A sacrifice of this sort," he says, "is entirely repugnant to the genius of the age we live in, and is without example in modern history, nor can it fail to be considered in Europe as wanton and unnecessary. It appears that the enemy (from necessity, I grant, but the operation is the same) have changed their system, and adopted a more humane one; and, therefore, the only justifying motive of retaliation, the preventing a repetition of cruelty, ceases. But, if this were not the case, so solemn and deliberate a sacrifice of the innocent for the guilty must be condemned on the present received notions of humanity, and encourage an opinion, that we are in a certain degree in a state of barbarism.

Our affairs are now in a prosperous train, and so vigorous, I would rather say so violent a measure, would want the plea of necessity. It would argue meanness in us, that at this late stage of the war, in the midst of success, we should suddenly depart from that temper with which we have all along borne with as great, and more frequent provocations." These moderate and humane counsels were soon after backed by the representations of the Court of France, moved by the intercession of the young officer's mother to Queen Marie Antoinette, and Captain Asgill was ultimately set at liberty, and restored to his friends; but in this, as in other instances, Hamilton had the merit of upholding the cause of mercy from the first, and of seeing at a glance that it was identical with the true policy of his country.

He was next appointed Receiver of Continental Taxes in the State of New York—a newly-created office, which he held only for a short time—and, a little later, he was elected a delegate to Congress. He entered that body with a high reputation for ability, which he more than justified in the sequel. General Schuyler, writing to his daughter from Philadelphia, in December, 1782, thus speaks of

his son-in-law:—"Participate afresh in the satisfaction I experience from the connexion you have
made with my beloved Hamilton. He affords me
happiness too exquisite for expression. I daily
experience the pleasure of hearing encomiums on his
virtue and abilities, from those who are capable of
distinguishing between real and pretended merit.
He is considered, as he certainly is, the ornament
of his country, and capable of rendering it the most
essential services, if his advice and suggestions are
attended to. In short, every true patriot rejoices
that he is one of the great council of these States."

The principal questions, which occupied the attention of Congress during this session, were the adjustment of the terms of peace with England, the
reduction of the expenditure of the Confederacy,
the disbanding of the army, and the organization
of a peace establishment. No authentic reports of
the debates exist, but it is well known that Hamilton
took an important part in almost every discussion,
and that his influence was felt and acknowledged
from the commencement. He had clearly before his
mind one grand design—the union of the several
States into a nation, under a free and settled government—and to this end he devoted all his energies.

He was aware that, to effect his purpose, many petty fears, many local jealousies, must be met and conquered; but, above and before all, he was convinced that the Congress must begin by redeeming its credit, and satisfying all who had rightful claims on its justice or its gratitude, if it hoped to establish the Confederacy on sure and lasting foundations.

One of the chief difficulties was the army. After all its hard service, it was about to be disbanded, without any provision for the promised half-pay of the officers, or even for the arrears due to the men. The treasury was empty, and could only be replenished with the consent of the several States; for Congress had no authority to raise taxes, and the concurrence of nine States was required even to contract a loan, or to appropriate public money. The soldiers saw with dismay that, now they were no longer needed, their claims were likely to be postponed to an indefinite future, and they not unnaturally resolved to ask for justice, while they had yet arms in their hands, and were able to enforce their demands. Meetings were held, and language was uttered in the army, which filled the peaceable citizens with alarm, and it needed all the firmness, the moderation, and the popularity of Washington to avert the danger. He addressed the officers in terms which found a way to their hearts, and implored them by every consideration of honour and patriotism, not to sully the glory they had acquired, by any violent or mutinous conduct. He pledged himself to exert whatever abilities he possessed in their favour; but he conjured them to rely on the plighted faith of their country, and to place full confidence in the purity of the intentions of Congress. He produced a letter he had received, to prove the good disposition of the governing body, and when, after reading the first paragraph, he paused to take out his spectacles, and excused himself with the remark, "that he had grown gray in their service, and now found himself growing blind," every heart was touched, and every eye moistened. He finished by persuading them to wait the result of the deliberations in Congress, and not to take any measures that might "open the floodgates of civil discord, and deluge their rising empire in blood."

While Washington was thus labouring to control the impatience of the army, and at the same time representing their grievances to Congress, Hamilton was pleading their cause in the bosom of that assembly. Renouncing his own claim to half-pay

from motives of delicacy, he fought the battle of
his fellow-soldiers with dauntless and resolute perseverance. The debates were long and stormy, and
Hamilton, who had nothing to conceal, wished them
to be open to the public; but in this he was over-
ruled by the majority, and the delegate from Rhode
Island observed, "that if the member wished to
display his eloquence, he should address the people
from the balcony." No taunts or opposition, however, could silence the gifted orator in his advocacy
of the claims of justice. The decision was indeed
delayed, till the troops were on the verge of mutiny,
but Hamilton and the friends of fair dealing at
length prevailed. Nine States were brought to agree
in a tardy and reluctant act of good faith. The half-
pay was commuted into a sum equal to five years'
full pay, for which securities were to be issued, like
those given to the other public creditors, with interest at six per cent. In the resolution making
this grant (which had been prepared by Hamilton)
it was stated, "that Congress was desirous, as well
of gratifying the reasonable expectations of the
officers of the army, as of removing all objections
which may exist in any part of the United States
to the principle of the half-pay establishment—

persuaded that those objections can only arise from the nature of the compensation, not from any indisposition to compensate those whose services, sacrifices, and sufferings have so just a title to the approbation and rewards of their country."

And now the news arrived, that the long-wished-for peace was really concluded. In December, 1782, George III. had already acknowledged the independence of the American Colonies in the speech from the throne. "In thus admitting their separation," he said, "from the Crown of these kingdoms, I have sacrificed every consideration of my own to the wishes and opinion of my people. I make it my humble and earnest prayer to Almighty God, that Great Britain may not feel the evils which might result from so great a dismemberment of the empire; and that America may be free from those calamities, which have formerly proved in the mother-country how essential monarchy is to the enjoyment of constitutional liberty. Religion, language, interest, affections, may, and I hope will, yet prove a bond of permanent union between the two countries. To this end neither attention nor disposition shall be wanting on my part." On the 20th of the following January, the preliminaries of peace were signed at

Paris, and a letter from Lafayette, who had returned to his native country, first brought the tidings of the event to America. The vessel, which carried the letter, reached Philadelphia on the 23d of March, 1783.

The people of the United States have never stood so high in the estimation of mankind as they did at this moment. The internal dissensions which had begun to darken the face of their triumph were not perceptible abroad, their financial difficulties were rightly ascribed to the inevitable results of war, and whatever weakness might be inherent in their Confederacy was unknown or disregarded. It was only remembered that they had ventured all in defence of those liberties which they claimed as their birthright; that, through eight long years, they had maintained the struggle with singular courage, perseverance, and sagacity; that they had raised armies, organized a government, contracted foreign alliances, and finally succeeded in establishing their independence, and taking their place amongst the recognized powers of the world; and that all this had been done with means apparently inadequate, and had not been accompanied with the excesses of revolutionary violence. No wonder that the philanthropists of all countries hailed their success as a great step in the progress of humanity, and looked to their future as full of hope and promise. It seemed as if the problem of centuries was about to be solved by the young Republic of the West, and that the nations were at length to behold the spectacle of a people entirely self-governed, with wisdom and virtue enough to unite all the conditions of order, security, and freedom. It remains to be seen how far the hope has been realized, and the brilliant promise fulfilled.

CHAPTER VI.

THE CONFEDERACY IN DANGER.

SCARCELY was the termination of the war known in America, when Hamilton thus wrote to Washington :—"Your Excellency will, before this reaches you, have received a letter from the Marquis de Lafayette, informing you that the preliminaries of peace, between all the belligerent powers, have been concluded. I congratulate your Excellency on this happy conclusion of your labours. It now only remains to make solid establishments within, to perpetuate our Union, to prevent our being a ball in the hands of European powers, bandied against each other at their pleasure; in fine, to make our independence truly a blessing. This, it is to be lamented, will be an arduous work; for, to borrow a figure from mechanics, *the centrifugal is much stronger than the centripetal force in these States.* The seeds of disunion are much more numerous

than those of union. I will add, that your Excellency's exertions are as essential to accomplish this
end, as they have been to establish independence."

A few days after, Washington replied in these
terms:—"I rejoice most exceedingly there is an
end to our warfare, and that such a field is open
to our view, as will, with wisdom to direct the
cultivation of it, make us a great, a respectable,
and a happy people; but it must be improved by
other means than state politics and unreasonable
jealousies and prejudices, or it requires not the
second-sight to see that we shall be instruments
in the hands of our enemies. . . . My wish to see
the Union of these States established upon liberal
and permanent principles, and inclination to contribute my mite in pointing out the defects of the
present constitution, are equally great. All my
private letters have teemed with these sentiments,
and, wherever this topic has been the subject of
conversation, I have endeavoured to diffuse and
enforce them; but how far any further essay by
me might be productive of the wished-for end, or
appear to arrogate more than belongs to me,
depends so much upon popular opinion, and the
temper and disposition of people, that it is not

easy to decide. I shall be obliged to you, however, for the thoughts you have promised me on this subject, and as soon as you can make it convenient. No man in the United States is or can be more deeply impressed with the necessity of a reform in our present Confederation than myself. No man, perhaps, has felt the bad effects of it more sensibly; *for to the defects thereof, and want of powers in Congress, may justly be ascribed the prolongation of the war, and, consequently, the expenses occasioned by it.* More than half of the perplexities I have experienced in the course of my command, and almost the whole of the difficulties and distress of the army, have their origin here; but still, the prejudices of some, the designs of others, and the mere machinery of the majority, make address and management necessary to give weight to opinions, which are to combat the doctrines of these different classes of men in the field of politics."

The general and his former aide-de-camp were thus fully agreed in the necessity of a change in the constitution, and, indeed, the defects of the Confederacy soon forced themselves on the attention of all sober and thoughtful minds. It had originated in a league

of independent States for a special purpose, and
the first Congress was nothing more than a voluntary meeting of delegates from separate communi-
ties, to concert measures of resistance to the demands
of England. When war became imminent, they
were obliged to raise a continental army, to appoint
a commander-in-chief, and to do other acts of
sovereignty, which are generally supposed to belong
exclusively to a national government. A little
later, the Declaration of Independence expressly
established the principle, that the United States
could enter into treaties, contract alliances, levy
war, or conclude peace, in their corporate capacity.
And on the 17th of November, 1777, Congress
recommended the thirteen States to invest their
delegates with competent powers to subscribe articles
of Confederation and Perpetual Union; but this
recommendation was not finally adopted by all
the States, till after a delay of nearly three years
and a half. New Hampshire, Massachusetts, Rhode
Island, Connecticut, New York, Pennsylvania, Virginia, and South Carolina, ratified the Articles on
the 9th of July, 1778; North Carolina followed on
the 21st of July, Georgia on the 24th of the same
month, and New Jersey on the 26th of November;

but Delaware did not sign till the 5th of May, 1779, and Maryland not till the 1st of March, 1781.

These Articles of Confederation were, in themselves, very vague and unsatisfactory. They declared, as might have been expected, that their object was to establish a permanent Union, for their common defence, the security of their liberties, and their mutual and general welfare. They provided, that the free inhabitants of each State should be entitled to all the privileges of free citizens in the several States; that there should be an open intercourse and commerce between them; that fugitives from justice should be delivered up by one State to another; and that full credit should be given in each State to the records, acts, and judicial proceedings of every other State. But they likewise declared, that each State retained its sovereignty, freedom, and independence, and every power, jurisdiction, and right, not expressly delegated by the instrument itself to the United States in Congress assembled. The Congress was to consist of one Representative Assembly, elected by the several States, in such manner as the Legislature of each State might determine; but no State was to be represented by more than seven, or less than two delegates, and, in deciding any question, each State was to have one vote.

To the Congress, so constituted, was committed the sole right of determining on peace and war, of sending and receiving ambassadors, of entering into treaties and alliances, of dealing with all captures and prizes, of granting letters of marque and reprisal, and of establishing courts for the trial of piracies and felonies on the high seas. It was also invested with power to decide, in the last resort, all disputes between two or more States, concerning boundary, jurisdiction, or any other cause; to regulate the alloy and value of coin, struck by its own authority, or that of the respective States; to fix the standard of weights and measures; to regulate the trade with the Indians; to take the management of the post-offices; and generally to appoint all officers in the service of the United States, and to direct the operations of the forces by sea and land.

But the restrictions which accompanied these powers rendered them almost nugatory. By the same instrument it was provided, that Congress should never engage in a war, nor grant letters of marque or reprisal, nor enter into any treaties or alliances, nor coin money or regulate its value, nor ascertain the sums of money necessary for the public defence and welfare, nor emit bills, nor borrow money on the credit of the United States, nor appropriate money, nor agree upon the number of vessels for the navy, or the number of land and sea forces to be raised, nor appoint a commander-in-chief, *unless nine States should assent to the same.* And, while all expenses for the common defence and welfare had to be defrayed out of a public treasury, this treasury was to be supplied, not by taxes, duties, or imposts levied by the authority of Congress, *but by taxes laid and levied by the Legislatures of the several States*, in proportion to the value of the land, buildings, and improvements within the limits of each State. And although the Articles of Confederation declared that every State should abide by the decision of Congress, on all the questions subject to the control of that body, they contained no provision for enforcing its measures, and practically left every State at liberty to disregard them, unless constrained by the fear of the penalties of civil war.

There was, indeed, one security against the dissolution of the Confederacy, in the existence of a vast territory, as yet unoccupied, but hereafter to be formed into new States and Governments, which was held, as it were, in trust by Congress, for the benefit of the whole Union. It was clear that no single State could withdraw from the Confederacy, without risking its interest in these possessions, and there can be little doubt that this consideration had a powerful influence in binding the States together. Still, whatever may have been the force of this motive, and of those recollections of common danger and glory, which had been left by the events of the war, it soon became apparent, when the pressure from without was removed by the return of peace, that the several members of the league had a strong tendency to fly asunder, and that the constitution they had adopted was far too feeble to serve as a restraining tie.

The proofs of the weakness of the government were too patent to be denied. While Hamilton was urging a provision for the maintenance of a peace establishment of military and naval forces, the mutiny of some eighty soldiers at Philadelphia, and the refusal of the local authorities to call out the militia, obliged Congress to leave that place, and to adjourn to Princeton, in New Jersey. It afterwards removed to Annapolis ; and, as the States could not agree on a seat of government, it seemed likely to become a migratory body, with constantly diminishing numbers and influence. It had so dwindled away, that in December, 1783, on the solemn occasion when Washington came to resign his trust into the hands of the country he had saved, only seven States, represented by about twenty delegates, took part in the ceremony. And when the Treaty of Peace was finally to be ratified by the Legislature, many weeks elapsed before the attendance of the required number of nine States could be procured, and, even then, only three-and-twenty members were present at the ratification.

Such was the body—so powerless, and already grown so neglectful of its duties—that was expected to meet all the difficulties of the transition from war to peace, to maintain the faith of the country with foreign nations, to uphold its credit abroad and at home, and to preserve and perpetuate the Union. Some stood aghast at the prospect, and others attempted to avert the danger by temporary expedients. Hamilton, and Hamilton alone, saw the full extent of the peril, and was prepared to devise a remedy. He entered into a complete

examination of the principles of the existing Confederation, and condemned them as utterly impracticable, and incapable of adaptation or amend-
ment. He held that the only course was for
Congress freely and frankly to inform the country
of the defects under which they laboured, and
which made it impossible for them to conduct the
public affairs with honour to themselves or advantage to the Union; and to recommend to the several
States to appoint a Convention, with full powers
to revise the Confederation, and to adopt and propose such alterations in the constitution and government as should appear necessary, to be finally
approved or rejected by the respective States.

With this purpose, he drew up a set of resolutions
to be submitted to Congress, which afford the most
striking evidence of his far-reaching views, and
contain the first germ of the future constitution
of his country. In them he pointed out that the
Confederation was essentially defective:

1st. In confining the Federal Government within
too narrow limits; in withholding from it efficacious
authority and influence in all matters of common
concern; in embarrassing general provisions by
unnecessary details and inconvenient exceptions,

tending to create jealousies and disputes between the Union and the particular States.

2d. In confounding legislative and executive powers in a single body, contrary to the most approved and well-founded maxims of free government, which require that the *legislative, executive,* and *judicial* authorities should be deposited in distinct and separate hands.

3d. In the want of a Federal Judicature, having cognisance of all matters of general concern in the last resort, especially those in which foreign nations and their subjects are interested ; from which defect the national treaties were liable to be infringed, the national faith violated, and the public tranquillity disturbed.

4th. In vesting the United States in Congress assembled with the power of general taxation for certain purposes, and yet rendering that power nugatory, by withholding from them all control over either the imposition or collection of taxes.

5th. In fixing a rule for determining the proportion of each State towards the common charges, which, if practicable at all, must in the execution be attended with great expense, inequality, uncertainty, and difficulty.

6th. In authorizing Congress to borrow money, or emit bills, on the credit of the United States, without the power of establishing funds to secure the repayment of the money, or the redemption of the bills. And, indeed, in authorizing Congress at all to emit an *unfunded paper* as the sign of value—a resource indispensable in the commencement of the Revolution, but in its nature pregnant with abuses, liable to be made the engine of imposition and fraud, and pernicious to the integrity of government and to the morals of the people.

7th. In not making proper or competent provision for interior or exterior defence.

8th. In not vesting in the United States a general superintendence of trade, equally necessary in the view of revenue and regulation.

9th. In defeating essential powers by provisoes and limitations inconsistent with their nature ; as the power of making treaties with foreign nations, provided that no treaty of commerce shall be made restricting the respective States from imposing duties, "or from prohibiting the importation or exportation of any species of goods or commodities whatsoever."

10th. In granting to the United States the sole

power of regulating the alloy and value of coin struck by their own authority, or that of the respective States, without the power of regulating foreign coin in circulation.

11th. In requiring the assent of nine States to matters of principal importance, and of seven States to all others, except adjournments from day to day—a rule destructive of vigour, consistency, or expedition in affairs, and tending to subject the sense of the majority to that of the minority, by putting it in the power of a small combination to retard, and even to frustrate, the most necessary measures.

12th. In vesting in the Federal Government the sole direction of the interests of the United States in their intercourse with foreign nations, without empowering it to pass all general laws in aid and support of the laws of nations; for the want of which authority the faith of the United States might be broken, their reputation sullied, and their peace interrupted, by the negligence or misconception of any particular State.

The resolutions then go on to declare that, whereas experience has clearly manifested that the powers reserved to the UNION are unequal to the purposes of *the common welfare and defence*—whereas the United States have been too often compelled to make the administration of their affairs a succession of temporary expedients, inconsistent with order, economy, energy, or a scrupulous adherence to the public engagements, and now find themselves, at the close of a glorious struggle for independence, without any certain means of doing justice to those who have fought and suffered, and contributed their property and personal service to the common cause; whereas the security of their funded debt depends on the precarious concurrence of thirteen distinct deliberative assemblies, the dissent of any one of which might leave these States, at this early period of their existence, involved in all the disgrace and mischief of violated faith and national bankruptcy— and whereas it is essential to the happiness and security of these States, that their Union should be established on the most solid foundations, and it is manifest that this desirable object cannot be effected but by a GOVERNMENT, capable, both in peace and war, *of making every member of the Union contribute in just proportion to the common necessities, and directing the forces and wills of the several parts to a general end*—Congress conceive it to be their duty freely to state to their constituents the defects which have been discovered in the Confederation, and solemnly to call their attention to a thorough revisal of the same.

The above is a brief summary of these important resolutions, every line of which deserved the attentive consideration of persons calling themselves statesmen. But, as usual with him, Hamilton was anticipating the progress of opinion. He found that it would be impossible to carry his proposal through Congress, and he was unwilling to risk the injurious effect of its formal rejection. Waiting for the period when his principles would be forced on the nation by the lessons of a bitter experience, he withdrew his resolutions, leaving this endorsement on the draft he had made of them :— "Intended to be submitted to Congress in 1783, but abandoned for want of support."

No doubt, many regarded him as a dangerous innovator, objected to him as a political theorist, or smiled at him as a visionary. "But the temporary expedients of the moment," says Mr. Curtis, in his lucid *History of the Constitution*, "always pass away. The great ideas of a statesman like Hamilton, earnestly bent on the discovery and in-

culcation of truth, do not pass away. Wiser than
those by whom he was surrounded, with a deeper
knowledge of the science of government and the
wants of the country than all of them, and constantly enunciating principles which extended far
beyond the temporizing policy of the hour, the
smiles of his opponents only prove to posterity
how far he was in advance of them."

Perceiving, however, that he could effect little
good for the present, and anxious to maintain his
family by the practice of an honourable profession,
Hamilton determined to retire from Congress. Before the resignation of Washington, or the ratification of the Treaty, he had already returned
home.

It is now generally admitted, that the interval
which elapsed between the Peace of 1783 and the
Convention of 1787 was full of extreme peril to
the Confederacy. While Congress was sinking in
the public estimation, unable to preserve its credit,
or fulfil the national obligations, the jealousies and
rivalries of the States were on the increase, and
patriotism usually took the form of some narrow,
local attachment. The people of America, united
for a season by the great struggle for independence,

seemed about to split into a number of obscure and hostile factions, who only agreed in their devotion to republican forms, and in their antipathy to anything that resembled a strong government. It was observed that the relaxation of authority had been followed by a corresponding change in manners — that the old respect of servants for masters, of children for their parents, of the young for the aged, was on the wane—that politeness and reverence were giving place to a rude and boisterous self-assertion—and, while good men apprehended a moral and social deterioration, merely prudent men looked forward with dismay to the prospect of political anarchy.

CHAPTER VII

WHEN the British evacuated New York in 1783, that city numbered only twenty-five thousand inhabitants. It was, however, already a place of importance, and the return of peace secured for it a speedy accession of wealth and commerce. It was there that Hamilton resolved to fix his residence, and to commence the practice of his profession.

The first cause in which he was engaged exactly suited his character and talents. An action was brought by an American citizen against a British subject, under a local statute, which authorized proceedings *for trespass* by persons who had left their abodes in consequence of the invasion of the enemy, against those who had been in possession of the premises during the war. The statute expressly precluded a justification of the occupancy by virtue of any military order. The case involved many others, and affected a large amount of property; and, under the circumstances of the times, the plaintiff had all the sympathy of a population which had suffered greatly from the war, and now looked for redress and restitution from the laws of their country.

But the treaty with Great Britain had secured an amnesty for acts done during the war; and it was without precedent, that, after the conclusion of peace, suits could be commenced by the subjects of one belligerent against those of another, for injuries committed during the war *by military orders.* It was obvious that the law of nations was here in collision with the local statute, and it became of the utmost urgency to determine whether the court would uphold the State-legislation, against the constitutional powers of Congress to bind all the members of the Confederacy by treaty. It was a question of national faith and honour, and might be attended with the most momentous consequences.

The attorney-general of the State appeared for the plaintiff. The statute was explicit and obligatory. No court of limited jurisdiction could look beyond it. Look where? To the law of nations? That law was unsettled, changeable, affording no certain rule, and ought to have no influence on the government of this State. The war was unjust. By an unjust war the unjust party can acquire no rights. Nor was that court to be bound by the treaty. New York was a sovereign, independent State. Congress had no power to bind the State in this matter, and could not by treaty give away the rights of its citizens. A case like this had never before been heard of. It was without a precedent, and he stood upon the statute.

Then Hamilton rose for the defendant. He began by dilating on the importance of the question, which might affect all the relations of two great empires, be discussed in Europe, produce a good or bad impression of America, and establish precedents that would give a complexion to future decisions, and be handed down to posterity as indicating the character of American jurisprudence. They were told there was no precedent. Then, indeed, it was a new case, and a new case must be determined by the law of nature and the public good. But this case could be decided by the laws of nations. He was asked, Where are they to be found? He answered, that they were the deductions of reason, collected from the principles laid down by writers on the subject, established by the authorized practice of nations, and a part of the law of the land. The laws of nations and the laws of war are part of the common law.

After an able argument, to show how the *general* principles of the law of nations applied to the matter in hand, Hamilton proceeded to address himself to the *special* effect of the treaty, with a view to prove that this action could not be maintained without a violation of the terms of peace. The treaty included an amnesty, which was of its very essence, and which applied to private persons as well as to the public. To say that Congress had no right to bind the State was to reduce the Confederation to the "shadow of a shade." But Congress had an unquestionable right. The sovereignty and independence of the people began by a Federal act; foreign nations only recognized it in the Union; and the Union was known and legalized in the constitution of New York. The Confederation had left to Congress the full and exclusive powers of war, peace, and treaty. The power of making peace is the power of determining its conditions. It is a rule of reason and law, that, to whomsoever any thing is granted, *that* also is granted without which it cannot exist. It is true that the power in this case did not permit the making all possible conditions—such as dismembering the empire, or surrendering the liberties of the people; but it included the power of making all reasonable and usual conditions—such as a remission of damages—for, without it, the state of war would continue.

But could Congress, by treaty, give away the rights of citizens of New York? To this Hamilton answered:—1st. That the citizens of New York had given them power to do it for their own safety.— 2d. That the property of all the individual members of a State is the property of the State itself, in regard to other nations. Hence, an injury from the Government gives a right to take away, in war, the property of its innocent subjects. Hence, also, the claim of damages for injuries done is in the public, who may agree for an equivalent, or release the claim without it. Hence, to make the defendant answerable would be a breach of the treaty of peace. It would be a breach, also, of the Confederation. Congress having made a treaty pursuant to their power, a breach of that treaty would be a violation of their constitutional authority, and a breach of the Confederation. The power of Congress in making treaties is of a legislative kind; their proclamation, enjoining the

observance of a treaty, is a *law*, and a law paramount
to that of any particular State. If it be said that
the sovereign authority may, for reasons of state,
violate its treaties, and that the laws in violation of
them bind its own subjects; it is not true that the
sovereignty of any one State has legally this power,
for it has delegated all power of the kind to
Congress, who are equally to judge of the necessity of breaking, as of the propriety of making
treaties.

If it be said that the accession to the Confederation was an act of the Legislature, and why may
not another act alter or dissolve it?—the answer
is, that the Union was known in the constitution
as pre-existing, and that the act of Confederation
was a modification and abridgment of Federal
authority. But, if this were not the case, the
reasoning would not apply. For the government
of New York, in acceding to the Confederation,
must be considered, not as *a sovereign enacting a
law*, but as *a party to a contract*. It is absurd to
say that one of the parties to a contract may, at
pleasure, alter it without the consent of the others.
It is not denied that a part of an empire may,
in certain cases, dismember itself from the rest.

But this supposes a dissolution of the original compact. While the Confederation exists, a law of a particular State derogating from its constitutional authority *is no law*. But how are the judges to decide? they are servants of the State!—The answer is, that the Confederation having vested no judicial powers in Congress, excepting in prize causes, in all other matters the judges of each State must, of necessity, be judges of the United States, and take notice of the law of Congress as a part of the law of the land. It is conceded that the Legislature of one State cannot repeal a law of the United States. When there are two laws, one not repealing the other, the judges must construe them so as to make them stand together. And, where two laws clash, that which relates to the most important concerns ought to prevail.

"Many of these arguments," he continued, "are on the supposition that the trespass act cannot stand with the laws of nations and the treaty. It may, however, legally receive such a construction as will stand with all; and to give it this construction is precisely the duty of the court. We have seen that to make the defendant liable would be to violate the laws of nations, and to forfeit our character as a civilized people; to violate a solemn treaty of peace, and revive the state of hostility; to infringe the Confederation of the United States, and to endanger the peace of the whole. Can we suppose all this to have been intended by the Legislature? The answer is: *The law cannot suppose it; if it were intended, the act is void!*"

He then proceeded to lay down rules for the construction of statutes, which would render this extremity unnecessary; and, after a minute investigation of the jurisdiction of the court, and of the distinctions to be taken between American citizens and British subjects, claiming the protection of the law of nations, he wound up with a vehement exhortation to preserve the Confederation and the national faith, and concluded in the words of Seneca: "*Fides sanctificissimum humani pectoris bonum est.*"

The above argument, although much abridged, has been given at some length, not only as characteristic of Hamilton, but because it deals with a great constitutional difficulty, which is constantly reappearing in the history of the United States It is this conflict between State rights and Federal authority which has coloured almost every event in the annals of America, influenced the men and measures of the last eighty years, and been the rock on which the republic was ever in danger of splitting. To Hamilton belongs the merit, that he was the first clearly to perceive, and distinctly to point out, the full extent of the danger, and his whole subsequent life was devoted to efforts to remedy and correct the evil. If he did not entirely succeed, it was owing to circumstances beyond the control of any statesman, and to him at least his country is indebted for such a solution of the problem, as secured an interval of comparative repose to more than one generation.

In the present instance, he brought over the judges to his opinion, in spite of local prejudice and popular clamour. The court decided that the Union is known and legalized in the constitution, and adopted as a fundamental law in the first act of the Legislature. "The Federal compact," they said, "hath vested Congress with full and exclusive powers to make peace and war. This treaty they have made and ratified, and rendered its obligation perpetual; and we are clearly of opinion, that no State in this Union can alter or abridge, in a single point, the Federal articles or the treaty."

But this decision, though given in due form of law, was at once called in question. It was first denounced in a great public meeting, as an act of "judicial tyranny;" and then the Legislature of New York passed resolutions, declaring it to be "subversive of all law and good order," and recommending the appointment of judges "who will govern themselves by the known law of the land." A disposition prevailed to set reason and equity at defiance, and to admit no standard of right and wrong but the blind popular will.

The same spirit showed itself in other ways, and, wherever it showed itself, Hamilton was there to confront it. Although the treaty had expressly declared "that no prosecutions should be commenced against any person on account of the part he might have taken in the war, and that no person should, on that account, suffer any future loss or damage, either in person, liberty, or property," the Legislature of New York passed an act, making those inhabitants who had adhered to the enemy, if found within the State, guilty of misprision of treason, and rendering them incapable of holding office, or voting at elections. What made this proceeding doubly odious was, that some of the representatives

of the State had already enriched themselves by
the purchase of the forfeited property of the loyal-
ists, and their motives could hardly escape suspicion,
when they forced through another bill, entitled
" An Act for the speedy Sale of Confiscated Estates."

It was not in Hamilton's nature to restrain his
indignation at such conduct, and this time it was
not as an advocate, but as a private citizen, that
he took up the cause of justice. He addressed a
pamphlet to the people of New York, under the
signature of *Phocion*, in which he called upon the
true friends of liberty to resist the attempts of
persons "who pretend to appeal to the spirit of
Whiggism, while they endeavour to put in motion
all the furious and dark passions of the human
mind. The spirit of Whiggism is generous, humane,
beneficent, and just. These men inculcate revenge,
cruelty, persecution, and perfidy. The spirit of
Whiggism cherishes legal liberty, holds the rights
of every individual sacred, condemns or punishes
no man without regular trial and conviction of some
crime declared by antecedent laws, and reprobates
equally the punishment of the citizen by arbitrary
acts of the Legislature, as by the lawless combinations of unauthorized individuals; while these men

are the advocates for expelling a large number of their fellow-citizens, unheard, untried; or, if they cannot effect this, are for disfranchising them in the face of the constitution, without the judgment of their peers, and contrary to the law of the land."

Inspired by those old words of *Magna Charta*, which to men of English blood carry more weight than a thousand vague and frothy declamations about natural rights, Hamilton proceeds to show the dangers of such acts of arbitrary power. " Nothing is more common," he says, " than for a free people, in times of heat and violence, to gratify momentary passions by letting into the government principles and precedents which afterwards prove fatal to themselves. Of this kind is the doctrine of disqualification, disfranchisement, and banishment, by acts of the Legislature. The dangerous consequences of this power are manifest. If the Legislature can disfranchise any number of citizens at pleasure, by general descriptions, it may soon confine all the votes to a small number of partisans, and establish an aristocracy or an oligarchy; if it may banish at discretion all those whom particular circumstances render obnoxious, without hearing or trial, no man can be safe, nor know when he may be the innocent victim of a prevailing faction. The name of liberty applied to such a government would be a mockery of common sense."

Having proved that the scheme proposed was in direct violation of the treaty, he goes on to ask:— "Can we do by act of the Legislature what the treaty disables us from doing by due course of law? This would be to imitate the Roman general, who, having promised Antiochus to restore half his vessels, caused them to be sawed in two before their delivery; or the Platæans, who, having promised the Thebans to restore their prisoners, had them first put to death, and returned them dead. Such fraudulent subterfuges are justly considered more odious than an open and avowed violation of treaty."

He then considers the supremacy of Congress on the subject, the danger of retaliatory acts on the part of England, and the impolicy of measures which tend to keep alive the seeds of perpetual discord. With regard to an argument which had been used on the other side, that the artisans were interested in excluding the Tories, because they might introduce an injurious competition in their several trades, he replies with a knowledge of principles not very common in his time:—"There is a certain proportion or level in all the departments of industry. It is folly to think to raise any of them, and keep them long above their natural height. By attempting to do it, the economy of the political machine is disturbed, and, till things return to their proper state, the society at large suffers. The only object of concern with an industrious artisan is, that there may be plenty of money in the community, and a brisk commerce to give it activity and circulation. *All attempts at profit, through the medium of monopoly or violence, will be as fallacious as they are culpable.*"

The pamphlet closes with a passage which every free nation should be ready to lay to heart, and which the United States might still study with great advantage to themselves and to the world:

"Were the people of America with one voice to ask:—What shall we do to perpetuate our liberties and secure our happiness?—The answer would be: *Govern well!* and you have nothing to fear either from internal disaffection or external hostility. Abuse not the power you possess, and you need never apprehend its diminution or loss. But if you make a wanton use of it; if you furnish another example, that despotism may debase the government of the many as well as of the few ; you, like all others that have acted the same part, will experience that licentiousness is the forerunner of slavery.

"How wise was the policy of Augustus, who, after conquering his enemies, when the papers of Brutus were brought to him, which would have disclosed all his secret associates, immediately ordered them to ̦be burnt. He would not even know his enemies, that they might cease to hate when they had nothing to fear. How laudable was the example of Elizabeth, who, when she was transferred from the prison to the throne, fell upon her knees, and, thanking heaven for the deliverance it had granted her from her bloody persecutors, dismissed her resentment. The reigns of these two sovereigns are among the most illustrious in history. Their moderation gave a stability to their government which nothing else could have effected. This was the secret of uniting all parties.

" These sentiments are delivered to you in the frankness of conscious integrity, by one who *feels* that solicitude for the good of the community which the zealots whose opinions he encounters *profess ;* by one who pursues not, as they do, the honours or emoluments of his country ; by one who has had too deep a share in the common exertions of this revolution to be willing to see its fruits blasted by the violence of rash or un-principled men, without at least protesting against their designs ; by one who, though he has had in the course of the revolution a very confidential share in the public councils, civil and military, and has as often, at least, met danger in the common cause as any of those who now assume to be the guardians of the public liberty—asks no other reward of his countrymen, than to be heard without prejudice for their own interest."

The tone of these last few lines may, perhaps, remind the reader of the close of Burke's *Reflections on the French Revolution ;* but they were certainly written some six years before the appearance of that celebrated essay.

The pamphlet and its author were at once at-tacked by various writers, and amongst others by a Mr. Isaac Ledyard, under the name of *Mentor.* To this Hamilton replied in a second letter by *Phocion,* which finally demolished the arguments of his opponents. The eloquent and solemn warning with which it concludes is all that can be quoted here :

"Those who are at present intrusted with power in all these infant republics hold the most sacred deposit that ever was confided to human hands. It is with governments as with individuals, first impressions and early habits give a lasting bias to the temper and character. Our governments hitherto have no habits. How important to the happiness, not of America only, but of mankind, that they should acquire good ones?—If we set out with justice, moderation, liberality, and a scrupulous regard to the constitution, the government will acquire a spirit and tone productive of permanent blessings to the community. If, on the contrary, the public councils are guided by humour, passion, and prejudice—if, from resentment to individuals, or a dread of partial inconveniences, the constitution is slighted or explained away upon every frivolous pretext—the future spirit of government will be feeble, distracted, and arbitrary. The rights of the subject will be the sport of every vicissitude. There will be no settled rule of conduct, but everything will fluctuate with the alternate prevalency of contending factions.

"The world has its eye upon America. The noble struggle we have made in the cause of liberty has occasioned a kind of revolution in human sentiment. The influence of our example has penetrated the gloomy regions of despotism, and has pointed the way to inquiries which may shake it to its deepest foundations. Men begin to ask everywhere:— Who is this tyrant, that dares to build his greatness on our misery and degradation? What commission has he to sacrifice millions to the wanton appetites of himself and the few minions that surround his throne?

"To ripen inquiry into action, it remains for us to justify the revolution by its fruits. If the consequences prove that we have really asserted the cause of human happiness, what may not be expected from so illustrious an example? In a greater or less degree, the world will bless and imitate.

"But if experience, in this instance, verifies the lesson long taught by the enemies of liberty—that the bulk of mankind are not fit to govern themselves—that they must have a master, and were only made for the rein and the spur—we shall then see the final triumph of despotism over liberty. The advocates of the latter must acknowledge it to be an *ignis fatuus,* and abandon the pursuit. With the greatest advantages for promoting it that ever a people had, we shall have betrayed the cause of human nature. Let those in whose hands it is placed pause for a moment, and contemplate with an eye of reverence the vast trust committed to them. Let them retire into their own bosoms, and examine the motives which there prevail. Let them ask themselves this solemn question :—Is the sacrifice of a few mistaken or criminal individuals an object worthy of the shifts to which we are reduced, to evade the constitution and our national engagements? Then let them review the arguments that have been offered, with dispassionate candour; and if they even *doubt* the propriety of the measures they may be about to adopt, let them remember, that in a doubtful case the constitution ought never to be hazarded without extreme necessity."

The letters of *Phocion* carried conviction to the minds of all moderate men. For that very reason they excited the intense anger and disgust of the more violent demagogues. These determined to pick a quarrel with Hamilton, to challenge him, and to force him to fight them in succession. Ledyard, the *Mentor* of the controversy, had the

sense and manliness to prevent this stupid outrage.
"No, no, gentlemen," he said; "this can never be.
What! you write as you please, and, because you
cannot refute what *he* writes in reply, you form a
combination to take his life! One challenges, and,
if he falls, another follows!" His remonstrances
put a stop to the design; but the fact of its ever
having been entertained is indicative of the spirit
of the party, to which Hamilton, at all times, offered
his fearless and uncompromising opposition.

It was the same party which distinguished itself
by its endeavours to evade the payment of American
obligations, private as well as public, and so brought
a load of obloquy on the whole Union. The treaty
had provided, that creditors on either side should
meet with no legal impediments to the recovery
of the full value in sterling money of all *bonâ fide*
claims. It was reckoned that, at the commencement
of the war, three millions sterling were due from
the inhabitants of the Colonies to merchants in
Great Britain, and, according to any fair interpretation of the treaty, interest, when agreed to be
paid, or payable by custom, might justly be demanded on such debts. But when, at the return
of peace, the British merchants looked for a settle-

ment of their accounts, they found that the laws of several of the States deprived them of all remedy against their debtors. Some prohibited the recovery of the principal, some of the interest, and others suspended the collection of both, or made land a good payment in place of money. The *patriots*, as they called themselves, strongly resisted any alteration in these laws, and, for some years, a state of things existed which men like Hamilton felt to be scandalous and humiliating. Long after, a young Irish poet, whose sympathies were not generally on the side of power, described in caustic verse—

> "Those vaunted demagogues, who nobly rose
> From England's debtors to be England's foes—
> Who could their monarch in their purse forget,
> And break allegiance but to cancel debt!"

And, although the vast majority of Americans would indignantly repel the imputation, there was certainly enough in the conduct of some of their politicians, to give a colour to the charge, and to make them feel its sting.

But, while Hamilton was thus contending with faction, and haunted by anxious fears for the future of his country, he did not neglect the ordinary

duties of his profession. The young lawyer had
already taken the same high place at the bar which
the young soldier had filled in the life of camps.
His statement of a case is described as at once
clear and exhaustive of the subject, saying all
that could be said, and anticipating every objection ;
and his eloquence would sometimes enchain, for
two or three successive hours, the attention of court
and jury. His figure, though slight and short, was
elegant and graceful, his countenance bright, his
carriage dignified, his manner sweet and engaging.
He was remarkably fluent in speech, he could rise,
on occasion, to lofty flights of rhetoric, and his
arguments bore the impress of the integrity and
benevolence of his character. With him, law was
ever the handmaid to justice, and none could suspect
him of paltering with the truth, or suppose him
capable of taking any mean or dishonourable advantage. Though never a rich man, he was disinterested
and generous in all his professional dealings. When
a merchant of New York, wishing to retain his
legal services for five years, sent him a note for a
thousand dollars, he returned it *as being too much ;*
and when he had successfully defended a member
of the Society of Friends from a charge of libel,

for publicly exposing a person detected in the act of kidnapping free blacks, he refused the proffered fee, with a request that, "as they were both engaged in the cause of humanity, his declining it might not be mentioned."

Hamilton, himself, was opposed to the principle of negro-slavery. He never owned a slave; and when he learned that a domestic he had hired was about to be sold by her master, he immediately purchased her freedom. He once belonged to an association for the gradual abolition of slavery, and proposed a resolution, that every member of the society should begin by manumitting his own negroes. To this the others demurred, and Hamilton discontinued his attendance at their meetings. He was not to be deceived by words, and would certainly never have adopted that cheap and spurious philanthropy, which consists in the unmeasured and indiscriminate abuse of the slave-holder, while feeding on the fruits, and trading with the produce, and growing rich by the indirect employment of slave-labour.

During his first years at the bar, Hamilton was brought into constant intercourse with a man whose name was afterwards fatally associated with his own.

His chief rival in his profession was a young lawyer, about a year his senior, who, like him, had served with distinction in the army, and, at the close of the war, had betaken himself to far different studies. AARON BURR was in many respects an extraordinary person, and, if he fell far below Hamilton in genius and moral qualities, he had some great gifts, which would have secured him a distinguished place in almost any career. He was descended from that rigid Puritan stock, which had taken such deep root in New England from the earliest times. His grandfather, on the mother's side, was Jonathan Edwards, a preacher of wonderful power in his day, and equally remarkable for the narrowness of his theology, and the saintliness of his life. His father, also, was a Presbyterian divine, a famous schoolmaster, and president of the College of New Jersey. But there was nothing in young Aaron which betokened such a descent, if we except, perhaps, the stubborn vigour which he may have derived from the blood of the old Calvinists, and the free command of language, which seems to have been hereditary in his family. Left an orphan in childhood, he grew up a wild, adventurous, intrepid, ungovernable boy. He ran away from his uncle, he ran away

from school—at ten years of age he embarked on
board a ship as a cabin-boy, and, when pursued,
climbed up to the mast-head, and refused to come
down till he had made his own terms—yet, with
all this, he astonished his tutors both at school and
college, by his rapid progress in his studies, whenever he chose to work. As if in recoil from the
strict evangelical views of his relations, he appears
to have embraced, while yet very young, sceptical
opinions in religion, and somewhat lax notions in
morals, and his subsequent experience did not effect
much improvement on these heads. When he
entered the world—brave, handsome, intelligent,
with honeyed speech, and gay, insinuating manners
—he acquired a dangerous influence over the fair
sex, which he exercised with few scruples of conscience. At different periods he was engaged in a
succession of love affairs, and his contemporaries
accused him of leading a life of licentiousness ; but
there is some reason to believe that his own vanity,
as well as the malice of enemies, contributed to
exaggerate the extent of his intrigues and conquests.
Be that as it may, he was a self-willed, self-indul-
gent, susceptible, and impulsive man, endowed with
many of the qualities that women admire and prize,

and he might have trifled away still more of his time in their society, had it not been for another passion which roused him to energetic exertion. In his secret soul he cherished an ambition as restless and daring, as ever found a home in any human bosom.

When the revolutionary war broke out, Burr joined the army as a volunteer, and accompanied Arnold in his bold attempt upon Canada. He marched with him through the wilderness, and travelled a hundred and twenty miles alone through the enemy's country, to convey a message from his chief. He was present in that desperate assault on Quebec, in which the gallant Montgomery lost his life, and, although the campaign was unsuccessful, he returned from it loaded with honour. The distinction he had attained recommended him to the notice of Washington, and for a short time he was a member of the general's military family. But his impatient spirit could not brook the restraints of that position, and he speedily threw up his appointment. Washington seems to have mistrusted him from the first, and Burr always disliked the wise, great man, whose virtues towered so immeasurably above the vulgar standard. Yet Wash-

ington acknowledged to the last Burr's excellence
as a soldier, and when, after four years of hard
service, the latter, who had risen to the rank of
colonel, was compelled by his failing health to retire
from the field, the commander-in-chief expressed
his regret at "the loss of a good officer, and the
cause which made his resignation necessary."

Having rested for some months, and recovered
his health, he married an accomplished lady, named
Prevost, and finding it desirable to recruit his
fortune, which was already much impaired by his
expensive habits, he applied himself to the study
of the law. He settled at New York as a barrister,
in the same year with Hamilton, and, to a super-
ficial observer, there seemed to be a certain resemblance between the two. Both were young, newly-
married, of pleasing person (they were both below
the average height), agreeable in manners, brilliant
in conversation, gifted with rare talents, and possessed of dauntless resolution. Both had earned
their laurels in war, been inmates of the family of
the general, and attained to the same rank in the
army. Both had embraced their new profession
with ardour, and mastered its details with almost
incredible facility. And both, on their first appear-

ance in court, had produced an impression, which marked them out as the future leaders of the bar.

But here the resemblance stops. While Hamilton loved to dwell in the region of great ideas and high principles, and stooped unwillingly to the lower ground of dexterous and skilful advocacy, it was in the latter field that Burr was thoroughly at home. A complete master of his weapons, and careless of the side he took, he enjoyed the combat almost as much as the victory, and seldom hesitated as to the means he employed to achieve a purpose. "Law," said he, "is whatever is boldly asserted, and plausibly maintained;" and, acting on that maxim, he was ever ready to take advantage of the weakness of a judge, or the ignorance of a jury. He had a low opinion of human nature, and turned all its interests and prejudices to account in dealing with his fellow-creatures. He delighted in technicalities, and never failed to catch an opponent tripping in the smallest matter of detail. He neither gave nor received quarter, and, when he had undertaken a cause, he would multiply notices, motions, and appeals, and have recourse to every form of annoyance, until his adversary was wearied out and exhausted. Unlike the flowing style of Hamilton, his eloquence was in general concise, compact, and rapid, and he did not often indulge in figures of speech. Yet, on occasion, he would not scruple to avail himself of a theatrical artifice. It is related, that, being engaged in the defence of a person accused of murder, he became convinced, as the trial proceeded, that the guilt lay between the prisoner and one of the witnesses for the prosecution. He subjected the latter to a searching and relentless cross-examination, and then, as he addressed the jury in the gathering dusk of evening, he brought into strong relief every fact that bore against the witness, and, suddenly seizing two *candelabra* from the table, he threw a glare of light on his face, and exclaimed: " Behold the murderer, gentlemen! " Alarmed and conscience-stricken, the man reeled as from a blow, turned ghastly pale, and fled from the court. The advocate concluded his speech, and the jury acquitted the prisoner.

It would seem that Burr both recognized and admired Hamilton's talents—admired him, perhaps, for some of the qualities in which he was himself deficient, and that he sought and cultivated his friendship. They were often engaged together in the same cause, and must frequently have met in society; but Hamilton, though courteous and conciliatory to all, appears to have held aloof from Burr's more intimate advances. His keen glance had already detected, that this clever and agreeable companion might prove a dangerous ally, and he feared the influence which Burr would sooner or later exercise in politics. He saw that none was more likely to acquire power in a republic, and none more inclined to use it for his own advantage —that he was just one of those able and ambitious adventurers, who would play boldly for high stakes, without much regard for rivals or partners in the game—and that, if the opportunity should arise, he would never hesitate to imperil the most sacred interests for a personal end, seek for gain and glory at any cost, and, in some great and formidable crisis, might ruin, if he could not rule the state.

So the two men remained on terms of mere civility, and Burr looked out for other allies to aid him in his ultimate projects. In those days, there were still certain leading families in the State of New York—the Clintons, the Schuylers, and the Livingstons—who organized parties, and possessed considerable influence. But Burr did not join himself to any of these. He rather endeavoured to play off one against the other, and watched his opportunity to form an independent party of his own. He gathered round him a number of young men, the gay and thoughtless admirers of whatever is bold and specious, who, charmed by his conversation, and proud of his abilities and accomplishments, were pleased to find in their chief no rigid censor of morals. In after years, Hamilton called them *Burr's Myrmidons*, and, through many changes of fortune, they showed extraordinary fidelity and devotion to the hero of their choice. They became indeed a power in the commonwealth, but their objects seem to have been purely personal, and it would be difficult to define what principles they held in common. As for their leader, however it may have suited him to profess extreme democratic views, when they served his purpose in the struggle of parties, no one, who is aware of his contempt for the majority of mankind, can believe that he really held them. The true key to his policy may be found in the words of Hamilton :—"I take it, he is for or against nothing, but as it suits his interest or ambition. He is determined, as I conceive, to make his way to be the head of the popular party, and to climb, *per fas aut nefas*, to the highest honours of the state, *and as much higher as circumstances may permit.*"

The chief colours in this picture have not been borrowed from Burr's political opponents. They are plainly discernible, however ingeniously softened down, in the pages of his latest biographer and apologist, Mr. Parton. It was necessary to form some conception of his peculiar character, to explain the inevitable antagonism between him and Hamilton, which accounts for several transactions in the subsequent life of the latter, and which led in the sequel to its tragical and melancholy close.

Meanwhile, they worked together at the bar, and treated each other with a courtesy, which by some was mistaken for friendship. In 1784, Burr became a member of the Legislature of New York, to which Hamilton was not elected till 1786. But both were preparing for a wider and more important stage; and while Burr was studying those party tactics, which he hoped would raise him to the enjoyment of place and power, Hamilton was slowly elaborating the great principles, on which he desired to establish the fortunes and liberties of his country.

CHAPTER VIII.

GRADUALLY, and almost imperceptibly, the conviction had gained possession of every thoughtful mind in the Union, that the Confederacy could not be maintained on its old footing. It had, indeed, brought the war to a successful issue, but it had signally failed in accomplishing the purposes of peace. It had been unable to meet its engagements, or to fulfil the ordinary obligations of a government. Between 1781 and 1786, Congress had made requisitions on the States for more than ten millions of dollars, and less than two and a half millions had been received by the public treasury. The interest on the debt, the necessary establishments for the safety of navigation and commerce, the payment of civil officers at home, and of the diplomatic service abroad, all remained equally unprovided for. The Congress of 1786 declared, in the most solemn manner, that the crisis had arrived when the people of the United States must decide whether they would preserve the public faith or not. Under the pressure of this appeal, the States seemed inclined to grant to Congress the power of levying a national impost, provided they could all agree to the arrangement; but New York held out obstinately against it, in spite of the efforts of Hamilton. The old difficulties with regard to the treaty were also still in existence; and when Mr. Adams, as Minister at the Court of St. James's, demanded why the British garrisons had not been withdrawn from the military posts in the West, he was assured that, whenever the United States should manifest a real determination to fulfil their part of the treaty, Great Britain would be ready to carry every article of it into complete effect. It was, moreover, found impossible to conclude treaties of commerce with foreign nations, as there was no security for their provisions being executed by the several States. In a word, the government of the Union was fast falling into contempt abroad and at home, and it became evident that, if it did not perish from its own internal weakness, the least accident or convulsion might sweep it entirely away.

At this conjuncture, a great danger arose in that very State which had taken the lead in the early days of the revolution. Massachusetts contained a population at no time submissive to authority, and now become more democratic than at any former period. It was oppressed with a load of debt, both public and private, which could only be met by considerable exertions and sacrifices, and its trade and manufactures had materially suffered by the war. The taxes were heavy, poverty was on the increase, and it soon became a popular doctrine with the more needy citizens, that all ought to share alike in the property which all had aided in defending. Then was seen one of those perilous moments in the history of republics, when the debtor turns his political power against the creditor, and the man who has nothing against the possessor of wealth. Assemblies were held, in which taxes were voted unnecessary, the courts of justice a grievance, and the law and its officers a nuisance. Armed mobs surrounded the court-houses to prevent the administration of justice, and in the autumn of 1786 the insurgents, regularly embodied, bade defiance to the control of the magistrates. A majority in the local House of Representatives seemed inclined to sympathize with the rebels, and no efficient assistance in suppressing the insurrection could be expected from Congress. Fortunately for Massachusetts, her Governor was a man of sense and resolution, named James Bowdoin. He at once called out the militia, and took the requisite steps to put down the disturbances by force. But great alarm had been excited, not only in New England, but throughout the Union, and another example had been given of the extreme weakness of Congress in dealing with such emergencies. It was indeed acknowledged, that the Confederation, as such, had no power to interfere in the case of a State rebellion. "You talk," wrote Washington to a friend in Congress, "of employing influence to appease the present tumults in Massachusetts. I know not where that influence is to be found, or, if attainable, that it would be a proper remedy for the disorders. *Influence is not government.* Let us have a government, by which our lives, liberties, and properties will be secured, or let us know the worst at once."

It was in the midst of all this confusion and terror, that the genius of Hamilton at length saw the way to the accomplishment of his designs. Already, in 1785, the citizens of Virginia and Maryland had appointed commissioners to settle their conflicting rights with

regard to the waters of the Potomac and Pocomoke ;
and these commissioners, during a visit at Mount
Vernon, had concerted a further plan for regulating
the commercial relations between the two States.
This plan included arrangements for maintaining a
naval force in the Chesapeake, establishing a fixed
tariff of duties on imports, and doing other acts in
common ; and, when it came to be discussed in the
Legislature of Virginia, it was resolved to invite the
other States to send deputies to consider the whole
subject of the commerce of the Union. It was
proposed that they should meet at Annapolis, and
circulars to that effect were addressed to the different
States. Hamilton, who believed his opportunity to
be now at hand, urged upon New York the acceptance of the proposal, and was himself appointed one
of her commissioners. Arrived at Annapolis, he
found there the representatives of five States only,
but he was not the less resolved to bring before
them, not only the commercial interests, but the
political condition of the country. He presented a
report, formally proposing to the several States the
assembling of a general CONVENTION, to take into
consideration the position and prospects of the
United States.

He showed in this document that the regulation of trade (the professed object of the present meeting) could not be effected without a corresponding change in the general system of government. The defects in that system were the real cause of the embarrassments both in public and private affairs, and could only be remedied by a complete revision. The Articles of Confederation had provided that no alteration should be made in them, unless agreed to by Congress, and confirmed by the Legislature of every State. It was Hamilton's design to obtain such agreement and confirmation—for he was too wise a man to risk any revolutionary interval between the old government and the new—but he felt that Congress was not the proper body to originate the required reforms. It had fallen into a premature decrepitude, and the chief talent of the country was absent from its debates. He, therefore, suggested that a Convention should be named for the special purpose of *proposing* the necessary changes, and that these should then be submitted to Congress, and to the State Legislatures. The report was adopted by the commissioners at Annapolis, and, not long after, the gathering dangers of the times forced Congress, though unwillingly, to agree to the plan. On the

N

21st of February, 1787, it was resolved, "That, on the second Monday in May next, a Convention of Delegates, who shall have been appointed by the several States, be held at Philadelphia, for the sole and express purpose of revising the Articles of Confederation, and reporting to Congress and the several Legislatures such alterations and provisions therein, as shall, when agreed to in Congress, and confirmed by the States, render the Federal Constitution adequate to the exigencies of Government and the preservation of the Union."

Hamilton had thus gained two most important steps. He had the sanction of Congress for that revision of the Constitution which he believed to be essential to the public safety, and the new movement was thereby placed under the protection of the highest existing legal authority; while the scheme of a separate assembly, elected expressly for the purpose, made it almost certain that, on such a momentous occasion, whatever constructive talent was to be found in America would be discovered and brought forward by the several States.

Since the meeting of that First Congress, which led the way in the struggle for independence, America had seen no such body of men as

now assembled at Philadelphia. Thither came
GEORGE WASHINGTON, from his retirement at Mount
Vernon, where he had hoped "to glide gently down
a stream which no human effort can ascend," called
away from his rural pursuits, and from his much-
loved home, to engage once more in the service of
his country. Thither, from the same fair land of
Virginia, came JAMES MADISON, afterwards President
of the United States, but then a young and rising
politician—industrious, indefatigable, clear, logical,
eloquent — and EDMUND RANDOLPH, Governor of
his native State, who had defended her both in
war and peace, and watched with jealous care to
maintain her special interests. Thither, from Massachusetts, came RUFUS KING, jurist and statesman,
who had doubted the policy of a Convention, but
who, when it was once determined on, resolved to
give it his best assistance. And thither, from South
Carolina, came CHARLES COTESWORTH PINCKNEY,
soldier, scholar, and lawyer—brave, honourable, and
generous—devoted to the views of his brethren in the
Southern States, but prepared to surrender many
opinions, and make many sacrifices, in order to bind
together the scattered members of the Union.

Pennsylvania was peculiarly fortunate in her repre-

sentatives on this occasion. At their head was BEN-
JAMIN FRANKLIN, now in his eighty-second year, the
oldest and most widely known of American public
men, and in some sort combining in his own person
many of the leading characteristics of America. The
poor printer's boy, who had lived on potatoes and
rice, that he might save money to buy books—the
shrewd and skilful tradesman, ever attentive to the
advancement of his business, yet stealing time to
cultivate his mind, and to make discoveries in science
—the philosopher, whose paper kite had drawn the
lightning from the sky—the administrator, who had
passed from the printing-office to the management of
a great public department—the ambassador, who,
finding himself suddenly in the presence of courts and
kings, had proved more than a match for the trained
diplomatists of Europe—the moralist, who touched so
lightly on the follies and vices of his fellow-creatures,
and who never seems to have lost sight of the maxims
of the counter and the shop, even while charming
with his conversation the wits and beauties of Versailles—was certainly no ordinary character. It may
be conceded, that common sense and prudence were
his prime qualities, and that he never rose to what is
sublime and heroic in genius or virtue—that he was

not free from the weakness of vanity, and that he was sometimes, perhaps unconsciously, swayed by narrow, personal motives—yet, after all deductions, it must be acknowledged, that he was a man of great vigour and sagacity of mind, and of much kindness of heart. When he took his seat in the Convention, his venerable age, his long services, his serene and benignant aspect, commanded the respect of all, and imposed a controlling power on the assembly. With him came GOUVERNEUR MORRIS, one of the best and wisest of American patriots, who had early foreseen the dangers of a too unbridled democracy—ROBERT MORRIS, who had made the first attempts at dealing with the complicated difficulties of American finance—and JAMES WILSON, who brought a large share of the acuteness and penetration of his native Scotland, to bear upon the laws, institutions, and government of his adopted country.

There were other men of note in the Convention, such as ROGER SHERMAN of Connecticut, JOHN DICKINSON of Delaware, LUTHER MARTIN of Maryland, JOHN RUTLEDGE of South Carolina, and GEORGE MASON of Virginia—fifty-five members in all, representing twelve sovereign States, for Rhode Island made no appointment. But the whole edifice would have wanted its crowning glory, if New York had not sent HAMILTON, with the treasures of his genius and eloquence. Some few leading Americans were necessarily absent—John Jay was Secretary for Foreign Affairs under the Congress, Thomas Jefferson was ambassador in France, and John Adams in England—but all could be better spared than *he*, who had first conceived the plan of a reform in the constitution, and who alone could carry it to a successful issue. Whilst others were groping their way in the dark, he saw clearly what was to be done, and was ready to take the entire responsibility of his acts, and to urge his views on the acceptance of unwilling minds.

And this man, foremost in an assembly of the most able representatives of the States, and who had already achieved so much in field and council, was yet only thirty years of age. "The very extraordinary early maturity of his character," says Mr. Curtis, " naturally reminds us of that remarkable person, who was two years his junior, and who became Prime-Minister of England at the age of twenty-four. The younger Pitt entered public life with almost every possible advantage. Inheriting a great and celebrated name, educated expressly for the career of a statesman, and introduced into the House of Commons at a moment when power was just ready to drop into the hands of any man capable of wielding it, he had only to prove himself a brilliant and powerful debater, in order to become the ruler of an empire, whose constitution had been settled for ages, and was necessarily administered by the successful leaders of regular parties in its legislative body. . . . The theatre, in which Hamilton appeared, lived, and acted, was one of a character so totally different, that the comparison necessarily ends with the contrast which it immediately suggests. Like Pitt, indeed, he seems to have been born a statesman, and to have had no such youth as ordinarily precedes the manhood of the mind. But, in the American Colonies, no political system of things existed, that was fitted to train him for a career of usefulness and honour; and yet, when the years of his boyhood were hardly ended, he sprang forth into the troubled affairs of the time, with the full stature of a matured and well-furnished statesman. He, in truth, showed himself to be already the man that was wanted. Everything was in an unsettled and anxious state—a state of change and transition.

There was no regular, efficient government. It was all but a state of civil war, and the more clear-sighted saw that this great disaster was coming. He was compelled, therefore, to mark out for himself, step by step (beginning in 1774), a system of political principles, which should serve, not to administer existing institutions with wisdom and beneficence, but to create institutions able to unite a people divided into thirteeen independent sovereignties; to give them the attitude and capacity of an independent nation; and then to carry them on, with constantly increasing prosperity and power, to their just place in the affairs of the world. . . . Mr. Hamilton, therefore, I conceive, proved himself early to be a statesman of greater talent and power than the celebrated English minister, whose youthful success was in the eyes of the world so much more brilliant, and whose early death was no less disheartening; for none can doubt, that to build up a free and firm State out of a condition of political chaos, and to give it a government capable of developing the resources of its soil and people, and of insuring to it prosperity, power, and permanence, is a greater work than to administer with energy and success, even in periods of severe trial, the constitution of an empire whose principles and modes of action have been settled for centuries."

And here it may be well to relate an anecdote, indicative of the high estimation in which Hamilton was held by one of the subtlest intellects of France. When Mr. Ticknor was in Paris, in 1819, Prince Talleyrand said to him, that he had known nearly all the marked men of his time, but that he had never known one, on the whole, equal to Hamilton. The American answered modestly, that the great statesmen of Europe had dealt with larger masses and wider interests. " Mais, monsieur," replied the Prince, " Hamilton avait *deviné* l'Europe."

It would indeed appear, that Hamilton had an almost intuitive knowledge of European politics. He had studied the various forms of government, and considered the relative position of the different nations of the old world, until they had all become familiar to him, and he spoke of them as if from personal experience. The result was, that he preferred the British Constitution to every other, and held it to be the nearest approach to perfection of all governments past or present. Could he have found the materials for establishing such a form of polity in his own country, there can be no doubt, that he would have devoted all his energies to that end. But, entirely free from the mere fanaticism of theory, he was always willing to sacrifice the form to the substance, and to accept those conditions which practically, and under the circumstances, would be most likely to secure the happiness of the people. He saw that some kind of republican government was, at the period of the Convention, the only thing feasible in America, and his object was so to control and modify the democratic element, as to render such a government safe and salutary.

The truth is, that the monarchical and aristocratic institutions of the mother-country had struck no root in the United States. The peculiar situation of the Colonies had not been favourable to the growth of a landed gentry (although the germ of it existed in Virginia and elsewhere), and the events of the war had destroyed the old tradition of loyalty to the throne. The Puritan spirit of the North had more or less affected the whole Union, and the revolution had left behind two leading characteristics—a strong passion for equality, and an unreasoning jealousy of power. Here and there might be found a man, who wished to offer the crown of the young Empire of the West to a son of George III. But Hamilton well knew, that such a prince would have been isolated in the midst of hostile factions, and would have had nothing whereon to rest the foundations of regal authority. There was, indeed, one American, who, had he been less scrupulous and more ambitious, might possibly have established a dynasty; but the thought of personal aggrandizement was wholly foreign to the wisdom and moderation of Washington. Just before the end of the war, many eyes had been turned towards him with some such design, and a veteran officer, Colonel Lewis Nicola, had even addressed him as follows :—" It will, I believe, be uncontroverted, that the same abilities which have led us through difficulties, apparently insurmountable by human power, to victory and glory, those qualities that have merited and obtained the universal esteem and veneration of an army, would be most likely to conduct and direct us in the smoother paths of peace. . . . If all other things were once adjusted, I believe strong arguments might be produced for admitting the title of KING." But Washington at once replied, that he had read these sentiments with surprise and astonishment, and that no occurrence in the course of the war had given him more painful sensations. He was at a loss to conceive what part of his conduct could have given encouragement to an address big with the greatest mischiefs that could befall the country, and more disagreeable to himself than to any other person. "Let me conjure you," he added, "if you have any regard for your country, concern for yourself or posterity, or respect for me, to banish these thoughts from your mind, and never communicate, as from yourself or any one else, a sentiment of the like nature."

And if monarchy was thus hopeless, all institutions based on hereditary distinctions were equally out of the question. At the close of the war, the officers of the army, who had shared together so many dangers and hardships, were anxious to preserve the remembrance of their military brotherhood, and with that view they founded the "*Order of the Cincinnati.*" Called after the famous Roman who retired from war to the peaceful pursuits of agriculture, their object was to maintain the rights and liberties for which they had fought—to promote feelings of national honour and union between the States—to cherish friendship and brotherly kindness towards each other—and to extend relief to such of their comrades, or their families, as might stand in need of it. Their badge was to be a gold medal, suspended from a deep blue ribbon, edged with white; and they proposed that their society (a purely voluntary association) should last during their lives, and be continued by their eldest male posterity. It was also provided that they might admit persons of distinguished talents and patriotism as honorary members. But scarcely had they formed a design so natural, and in many respects so praiseworthy, when a storm of invective was raised against it from all parts of the Union. Massachusetts led the way, Connecticut followed, and on all sides the officers were accused of a plot to elevate the military class above the civil, and to institute an order of hereditary nobility. It was in vain to reason with the popular jealousy; and both Washington and Hamilton, who had taken much interest in the society, advised that the hereditary principle, and the power of electing honorary members, should be abandoned. On these conditions, the old comrades in arms were allowed to meet in peace; but the incident clearly proved, if it ever needed demonstration, how strong was the prejudice in the States against even the shadow of an aristocracy.

A republic was then the only resource; but it by no means follows, that the able leaders of the Convention ever intended to give absolute sovereignty to the mass of the people. They were yet too near to English modes of thought to prefer the realization of a theory to the attainment of a practical good, and they had not learned from history or experience that power is best lodged in the hands of the most ignorant and needy. They knew that, in the old republics, the right of citizenship was a privilege not lightly bestowed—that, in England, the House of Commons was chosen by a limited number of electors —and that, even in the States of the Union, the suffrage was everywhere more or less restricted. They knew that those free governments, which had met with any success in the world, had been restrained by checks, and guarded round with many precautions. They still believed in the words of the sage, that "the wisdom of a learned man cometh by opportunity of leisure," and were not disposed to confide the conduct of the most important affairs to him "that driveth oxen, and whose talk is of bullocks." The modern notion of a pure, untempered democracy, based on Universal Suffrage—that contrivance for giving power to a single despot, or to one class only of the community, and that the lowest, to the exclusion of all the rest—would have found no favour in their sight. They wished to provide for the inviolability of property, the sacredness of law, the protection of minorities, the peace and security of all. To accomplish these ends, they were willing to adopt such expedients as might commend themselves to their judgment, regardless of the abstract idea which either visionaries or philosophers had chosen to form of a republic.

The task was beset with difficulties, and the end by no means certain of attainment. On almost all matters of detail, the members of the Convention differed materially amongst themselves, and they had to contend with the constant pressure of hostile influences from without. That they succeeded in framing a constitution, not perfect indeed, but founded on principles of reasonable compromise, and capable of practical working, is greatly to the credit of their moderation, intelligence, and patriotism.

Washington was unanimously called to the chair, and none could have been more fitted to preside over the debates of a deliberative assembly. The proceedings were all in secret—a precaution perhaps necessary in the disturbed state of the public mind—but

Madison devoted his nights to preserve a record of the discussions. Into particulars of those discussions it is not intended to enter here, but the part which Hamilton took in them was of an importance impossible to rate too highly. He stood in the midst of the jarring elements, like a beneficent genius, ready to evoke order out of chaos ; and the proportion in which his views were adopted or rejected may be almost regarded as the measure of the strength and the weakness of the Constitution.

Various plans were before the Convention. While some were for maintaining the old character of the Confederation as a mere league of independent States, with a Congress composed of a single assembly, invested with a few additional powers, but hardly more effective than those already in existence—the majority recognized the necessity of some kind of national government, and were prepared to admit the principle of the division of the legislative, executive, and judicial functions. But whether the legislature should be composed of one or two houses, how it should be elected, whether the ratio of representation should be based on the wealth or population of the different States, whether the executive should consist of one, three, or more persons, what should be the qualification for office, and how long its term, how the judges should be appointed, and, finally, what were to be the exact limits of the authority delegated to the central government—were all matters of doubt and controversy. Two separate schemes—commonly known as the New Jersey and the Virginia schemes—were already under the consideration of the assembly, when Hamilton rose for the purpose of fully explaining his opinions. Of this speech (one of the most remarkable ever delivered) no accurate report remains, for Madison's notes differ from the brief in Hamilton's own handwriting, and are, in any case, but a meagre sketch of a discourse which held captive the attention of the audience during the whole of a summer's day. There can be little dispute, however, as to the main scope and object of this memorable oration.

He seems to have begun by pointing out the importance of the occasion, which, once let slip, might never again present itself, and would beget despair in the possibility of forming a government by consent. After disposing of the objection, that the Convention had no power to propose a plan differing from the principle of the Confederation, he showed that they had three lines of conduct before them : 1st. To make a league, offensive and defensive, between sovereign States, with treaties of commerce, and an apportionment of the public debt. 2d. To amend the present Confederation, by merely adding such powers to Congress as the public mind appeared ready to grant. 3d. To form a new government to pervade the whole, with decisive powers, and a complete sovereignty. The practicability of the last course, and the mode of accomplishing it, were the real questions before them. They involved an inquiry into the principles of civil obedience, which are the supports of all government.

But those principles did not exist under the Confederation, in favour of a central power. The constant feeling of *interest* was absent; for each State pursued its particular interests, without regard to those of the whole. The conviction of the *utility* and *necessity* of a government was absent; for the central power might dissolve, and yet the order of society would continue protected from anarchy by the institutions of the several States. The *habitual sense of obligation* was unfelt; for it was to the State governments that the people looked for the preservation of order, and the administration of justice, and they only knew the central government by its unwelcome demands for money. *Force* might be of two kinds—coercion by law, and coercion by arms; but the Congress had no machinery to employ the former, and to have recourse to the latter would amount to civil war. There remained then only *influence*, by which he meant not corruption, but the regular and legitimate patronage of a government; and, as the appointment to almost all offices of honour and emolument was vested in the particular States, this support also was lost to the central power.

But no government could maintain itself, which had not in its favour the passions and interests, as well as the reason of its subjects. Passing in rapid review the nations of the old world, he showed that all federal governments had been weak, distracted, and short lived. He showed that there was a perpetual effort in each member of a league to establish its independence of the central authority. He showed that republics were no more exempt than monarchies from intestine discord, that jealousy of commerce begets hostility as well as jealousy of power, and that there had been as many popular as royal wars. He examined the constitution and

history of the Greek Republics, the Germanic Empire, the Swiss Cantons. He glanced from Sparta
to Athens, from Rome to Carthage, from Venice to
the Hanseatic League, and in this grand survey of
the experience of centuries, in which he quoted all
sorts of authorities, from Aristotle to Montesquieu,
from Cicero to Neckar, he laboured to prove that
any government, to be *strong*, must be *sovereign*. It
must not only have a strong soul, but strong organs
by which to operate. It must interest the wants
of men in its support, it must make itself useful
and necessary, it must have the means of coercion.
However it derived its powers, it must ultimately
have the decision of all questions without appeal.

Passing to the different forms of sovereignty that
have existed in the world, he endeavoured to show
by examples, that, if government is in the hands of
the few, they will tyrannize over the many; that,
if it is in the hands of the many, they will tyrannize
over the few. It ought to be in the hands of both,
the separation should be permanent, and they need
a mutual check. He avowed his preference for the
British Constitution over every other. An absolute
sovereignty vested in King, Lords, and Commons—
a monarch, with so much power, that it is not his

interest to risk all to acquire more—a democracy, fairly representing the popular will, combined with an aristocracy capable of resisting popular haste and violence. He admitted that such a combination was not then attainable in America—that the political principles of the people would endure nothing but a republican government, and that it was right and proper, under the circumstances of the country, to give such a government a full and fair trial. But, for that very reason, it was necessary that the government should have all the energy and stability reconcilable with the republican theory. Recapitulating his arguments, that it was impossible to secure the Union by any modification of the present Confederation—that a mere league, offensive and defensive, was full of certain evils and greater dangers—and that to establish a general government (*purely* national, and *wholly* independent of State organization) was extremely difficult, if not impracticable—he came to the conclusion, that they must balance inconveniences and dangers, and choose that system which seemed to have the *fewest* objections.

His own plan was, to vest the legislative power in an Assembly and Senate, subject to a negative—the executive power in a President of the United States

—and the supreme judicial authority in a Court of not less than six, nor more than twelve Judges.

The Assembly was to be chosen by the people for three years, and the number of Representatives was to be distributed amongst the several States, according to population. The Senate was to be appointed by electors chosen for the purpose, but only by persons who had an estate in land ; and the Senators were to hold their office *during good behaviour*, removable only on conviction of some crime or misdemeanour. The President was to be named by electors chosen by electors, according to a somewhat complicated process, intended to secure the fair and complete expression of the popular wishes. He was to hold his office *for life*, removable only by impeachment by two-thirds of the Legislature. He was to have the power to convene and prorogue the two houses, except in case of impeachment, which operated as a suspension until determined— to have a negative on their acts—to take care that the laws be faithfully executed—to command the army, navy, and militia—to have the absolute appointment of the chief officers in the great executive departments—and, with the advice of the Senate, of all other officers, except such as were differently provided for by law—and to be entitled to pardon all offences except treason. The President of the Senate was to be Vice-President of the United States, and to exercise all the powers of the President, in case of his death, resignation, or removal from office, until another should be appointed. In the event of an impeachment, the President, Senators, and other great officers were to be tried by the Judges of the Supreme Court, aided by the Chief Justices of the several States. The Judges of the Supreme Court, and of all courts constituted by the Legislature, were to hold their appointments *for life or good behaviour*.

To such a government, Hamilton would have confided *sovereign* authority. He would have retained the State governments as great municipalities, most important as subordinate agents of the central power, and essential for conducting the local affairs of the various portions of so vast an empire; but he would have had the central government *supreme* in all matters whatsoever, and have made the laws of the Union binding on all its members. He foresaw, with the prescience of a statesman, the inevitable conflicts between the central and local authorities, if both were to continue to exist with a co-ordinate jurisdiction. He would have made use of the State organization, both to constitute his government, and to aid in executing the laws; but he sought to establish a strong, stable, and permanent power, able to command the allegiance of all its subjects, to protect the national interests, and to uphold the national faith. It was with this view, that he approached as near "to the confines of another government" — evidently meaning the British — as the republican principles of America rendered either safe or practicable.

It is of course impossible now to determine, whether such a government would have worked well in the long run. Hamilton was ever the first to maintain, that, in politics, a theory can only be tested by experiment, and must be judged ultimately by its effects on the happiness of mankind. It is, however, a remarkable fact, that Hamilton's scheme differs from the constitution finally adopted, exactly in those points in which the latter has proved most defective. By giving an absolute, instead of a limited sovereignty to the central power, he sought to avoid those collisions between the Confederacy and the States, which have been the fertile source of half the troubles of America; while, by retaining the

State governments in a subordinate position, he hoped that they would apply themselves strictly to the administration of local affairs, serve as a school for the training of public men, and take the place of those great European corporations, which have always been the best safeguards of order, liberty, and law. By vesting the executive power in a Chief Magistrate, chosen indeed by the people, but whose dignity and honour should not be the sport of every breath of popular change, and who should hold his office by a permanent tenure—he sought to make that high post an object worthy of the ambition of the best and noblest, and not to be lightly bestowed by any less solemn sanction than the deliberate exercise of a nation's will. By granting the same tenure of office to one branch of the legislature, he intended to strengthen the hands of the executive for good, while keeping it within the bounds of its legitimate authority, and to control the impatience, while maintaining the rights of the democracy. Both President and Senators would have been responsible—but responsible only to the law, interpreted by an impartial and independent tribunal. The whole life of politicians would not have been wasted in election tactics, and wretched intrigues for power. What other evils might have arisen under this constitution, it is now in vain to inquire. It would at least have given time to adopt a national policy, and to form a generation of statesmen ; and if, after a full and fair trial, it had been found expedient to draw still nearer to the British model, and to substitute the hereditary for the elective principle, the transition need not have been violent, or have involved any sacrifice of the established liberties of the people.

But great as was Hamilton's influence, he could not have carried his plan of government, and indeed he seems rather to have brought it forward as an exposition of his views, than with any serious hope of its being accepted by the assembly. Short of those views, he was ready to labour assiduously in the preparation of the best attainable constitution. With the extreme diversity of opinions in the Convention—with the contending claims of State rights and Federal interests—with some members advocating a single chamber, and even Franklin in favour of a plural executive—Hamilton felt, that the only possible solution of their difficulties lay in *compromise.* In this, the majority agreed with him, and each in turn surrendered some cherished notion, or proposed some modification of another's scheme. After four months of careful deliberation—after many tedious discussions, lasting through the long days from May to September—a Constitution was at length presented to the people of the United States, to be by them either ratified or rejected. The Congress was to consist of two separate chambers—a House of Representatives chosen every second year by the people of the several States, according to the qualifications in each State for election of its own Legislature, and in proportion to the population of each State, reckoning only three-fifths of the slaves—and a Senate composed of two Senators from each State, chosen by the Legislature thereof for six years. No person holding office could be a member of this Congress, which was to meet every year, and to have the power to lay and collect taxes, and provide for the common defence and general welfare of the United States; to borrow money; to regulate commerce; to establish uniform rules of naturalization and laws of bankruptcy; to coin money; to provide for the punishment of counterfeiting the public securities; to establish roads and post-offices; to grant patents and copyrights; to define and punish piracies, and offences against the law of nations; to declare war; to raise and support armies; to provide and maintain a navy; to make rules for the government of the forces; to call out the militia to execute the laws of the Union, to suppress insurrections, and repel invasions; to provide for organizing the militia, and governing such part of them as may be employed in the service of the Union; to exercise exclusive legislation over such district (not exceeding ten miles square) as may become the seat of the government of the United States, and over all forts, magazines, arsenals, and dockyards of the Union; and generally to make all laws which shall be necessary and proper for carrying into execution the foregoing powers. But Congress was not to prohibit the importation of such persons as any State shall think proper to admit (in other words, the *slave-trade*) prior to the year 1808; nor to suspend the writ of Habeas Corpus, unless in case of rebellion or invasion; nor to pass any bill of attainder or *ex post facto* law; nor to lay any direct tax, unless in proportion to the *census;* nor to tax articles exported from any State; nor to give any preference to one State over another by regulations of commerce; nor to draw money from the treasury, but in consequence of appropriations made by law; nor to grant any title of nobility. And, not content with these limitations of sovereignty, it was afterwards expressly provided by a separate article, that the powers not delegated to the United States by the Constitution, nor prohibited by it to the States, are reserved to the States respectively, or to the people.

The executive power was to be vested in a President of the United States, to hold his office for a term of *four years.* He and the Vice-President were to be chosen by electors, appointed in such manner as the Legislature of each State should direct, and equal to the whole number of Senators and Representatives to which the State would be entitled in Congress. The lists of persons voted for were to be sent sealed to the Senate of the United States, and opened in presence of Congress. The person having the greatest number of votes, being a majority of the whole number of electors, was to be President; and if more than one had such majority, and an equal number of votes, then the House of Representatives was to choose one of them by ballot; and if no person had such majority, then the said House was to choose the President from the five highest on the list. And, after the choice of President, the person having the greatest number of votes was to be Vice-President ; and, if two or more remained with equal votes, the Senate was to choose the Vice-President from them by ballot.

The President was to have the power to return any bill to Congress, with his objections to the same ; and it could only become law without his consent, if passed by a majority of two-thirds of both Houses. He was to take care that the laws were faithfully executed, to command the army, navy, and militia, to recommend such measures as he should judge necessary to Congress, to convene both Houses on extraordinary occasions, to receive ambassadors and other public ministers, to grant reprieves and pardons for offences against the United States, and, with the consent of the Senate, to make treaties with foreign powers. He was to nominate, and with the advice of the Senate appoint, all officers of the United States whose appointments should not be otherwise provided for by law. He was to be liable to removal from office, on impeachment by the House of Representatives, and conviction by the Senate, of high crimes and misdemeanours ; and in case of his death, removal, resignation, or inability, the duties of his office were to devolve on the Vice-President, who, until such event occurred, was to be President of the Senate.

The remaining articles provided, that there should be a Supreme Court of the United States, and such inferior courts as Congress might from time to time establish ; that the Judges should hold their offices during good behaviour, and with a fixed compensation ; that the citizens of each State should be entitled to all the privileges of citizens in the several States ; that fugitives from justice, and persons held to service or labour in any State (meaning *slaves*), should be delivered up by any other State into which they might have escaped ; that new States might be admitted into the Union, but not to the prejudice of the rights of any existing State ; that the Union should guarantee a republican form of government to every State ; that the Constitution might be amended by a Convention called by two-thirds of both Houses of Congress, such amendments being ratified by the Legislatures or Conventions of three-fourths of the several States; that all debts and engagements previously contracted under the Confederation should be valid against the new government ; that the Constitution should be the supreme law of the land, binding all judges and officers whatsoever; and that the ratification of the Conventions of nine States should be sufficient for the establishment of this Constitution between the States so ratifying the same.

Such was the CONSTITUTION which the Convention proposed for the acceptance of the people of America. Its authors knew well, and none better than Hamilton, that it was in many respects imperfect. But, like wise and practical men, they were content to sink their differences, to moderate their wishes, and to take whatever good lay within their reach. Some of the delegates continued to protest against the plan, some had withdrawn from the Convention, and Luther Martin confidently predicted that his own Maryland would never accept the Constitution. But the document which embodied the scheme was ultimately signed by a majority of the delegates, and by one or more representatives of *each* of the twelve States present in the Convention. The first name on the list is that of George Washington, who is said to have paused a moment, with the pen in his hand, as he pronounced these words :—
"Should the States reject this excellent Constitution, the probability is that an opportunity will never again offer to cancel another in peace. The

next will be drawn in blood." And in the last speech which Franklin delivered in the assembly, he thus expressed himself:—"I consent, sir, to this Constitution, because I expect no better, and because I am not sure that this is not the best. The opinions I have had of its errors I sacrifice to the public good. I have never whispered a syllable of them abroad. Within these walls they were born, and here they shall die. If every one of us, in returning to our constituents, were to report the objections he has had to it, and endeavour to gain partisans in support of them, we might prevent its being generally received, and thereby lose all the salutary effects and great advantages, resulting naturally in our favour, among foreign nations as well as among ourselves, from our real or apparent unanimity. Much of the strength and efficiency of any government, in procuring and securing happiness to the people, depends on opinion—on the general opinion of the goodness of that government, as well as of the wisdom and integrity of the governors. I hope, therefore, that for our own sakes, as a part of the people, and for the sake of posterity, we shall act heartily and unanimously in recommending this Constitution, wherever our influence may extend, and turn our future thoughts and endeavours to the means of having it well administered." Then, while the members were signing, he turned towards the image of a sun, painted at the back of the President's chair, and said :—" Often and often, in the course of the session, I have looked at it without being able to tell whether it was rising or setting; but now, at length, I have the happiness to know, that it is a rising, and not a setting sun."

Of the delegates from New York, the name of Hamilton is alone attached to the instrument. His two colleagues had withdrawn from the Convention, and left him all the honour and burthen of the day. There is abundant testimony as to how he discharged the duties of his position. " If," said Dr. Johnson of Connecticut, " the Constitution did not succeed on trial, Hamilton was less responsible for it than any other member; for he fully and frankly pointed out to the Convention what he apprehended were the infirmities to which it was liable. And if it answered the fond expectations of the public, the community would be more indebted to Hamilton than to any other member; for, after its essential outlines were agreed to, he laboured most indefatigably to heal those infirmities, and to guard against the evils to which they might expose it."

In thus lending his aid to amend what he could not entirely approve, Hamilton showed the largeness of his mind, and the sincerity of his patriotism. He was not willing to risk anarchy, civil war, perhaps military despotism, in the pursuit of that which can only be attained by TIME and EXPERIENCE. The explanation of his conduct is contained in his own memorable words :—"It may be in me a defect of political fortitude, but I acknowledge that I cannot entertain an equal tranquillity with those, who affect to treat the dangers of a longer continuance in our present situation as imaginary. A *nation* without a *national government* is an awful spectacle. The establishment of a constitution in a time of profound peace, by the voluntary consent of a whole people, is a PRODIGY, to the completion of which I look forward with trembling anxiety."

CHAPTER IX.

THE Convention being dissolved, the plan of the Constitution was laid before the country, and at once excited the most varied feelings of approbation and dissent. In general it was supported by those moderate men, who, like its framers, looked with apprehension at the actual state of affairs, and desired, by any reasonable compromise, to consolidate a practicable government. On the other hand, it was violently opposed by all that class of politicians, who viewed with jealousy the rise of any central power, and whose theory of freedom precluded the notion of authority. Two great parties joined issue on the question of its acceptance or rejection. They took the names of *Federalists* and *Anti-Federalists*. A few years later, after the Constitution had been adopted, the same two parties, with some modifications, continued to divide the people of America; but they were then called *Federalists* and *Republicans.*

These names, like almost all party designations, do not, in themselves, convey any accurate meaning. In one sense all Americans were Federalists, for all believed in the necessity of some Federal tie, to bind together the several States; and in one sense all were Republicans, for they were persuaded that no other form of government was then possible in the Union. But the original distinction between the parties was, that the one sought first to establish and afterwards to strengthen a central government, with sufficient powers to uphold its own dignity and that of the nation; whilst the other strove to circumscribe those powers on every side, and to make them in all respects subservient to the local privileges of the States. As time went on, other causes of difference arose between them, some of the leaders changed sides, old alliances were broken up, and new combinations formed. A day was to come, for instance, when Hamilton and Madison stood in direct opposition to each other. But, for the present, they acted heartily together, and their first object was to secure the acceptance of the Constitution.

One of the most efficient engines employed in accomplishing this purpose was the publication of a series of essays under the name of "THE FEDERAL-IST," which Americans still regard as the greatest and most complete exposition of the principles of their constitutional law. It was the work of Hamilton, Madison, and Jay ; but of the eighty-five essays, of which it is composed, upwards of fifty were written by Hamilton. "It was from him," says Mr. Curtis, "that the *Federalist* derived the weight and the power, which commanded the careful attention of the country, and carried conviction to the great body of intelligent men in all parts of the Union. The extraordinary forecast with which its luminous discussions anticipated the operation · of the new institutions, and its profound elucidation of their principles, gave birth to American constitutional law, which was thus placed at once above the field of arbitrary constructions, and in the domain of legal truth. They made it a science; and so long as the Constitution shall exist, they will continue to be resorted to, as the most important source of contemporaneous interpretation which the annals of the country afford."

The first number of the *Federalist* was written by

Hamilton in the cabin of a sloop, as he glided down the waters of the Hudson on his way to New York, and was published in that city on the 27th of October, 1787. It opens with a remarkable introduction, as full of vigour and boldness as of wisdom and moderation. "Among the most formidable of the obstacles," it says, "which the new Constitution will have to encounter, may readily be distinguished the obvious interest of a certain class of men in every State, to resist all changes which may hazard a diminution of the power, emolument, and consequence of the offices they hold under the State establishments—and the perverted ambition of another class of men, who will either hope to aggrandize themselves by the confusions of their country, or will flatter themselves with fairer prospects of elevation from the subdivision of the empire into several partial confederacies, than from its union under one government.

"It is not, however, my design to dwell upon observations of this nature. I am aware it would be disingenuous to resolve indiscriminately the opposition of any set of men into interested or ambitious views, merely because their situations might subject them to suspicion. Candour will

oblige us to admit that even such men may be
actuated by upright intentions; and it cannot be
doubted that much of the opposition which has
already shown itself, or that may hereafter make
its appearance, will spring from sources, blameless
at least, if not respectable—the honest errors of
minds led astray by preconceived jealousies and fears.
So numerous, indeed, and so powerful are the causes
which serve to give a false bias to the judgment,
that, upon many occasions, we see wise and good
men on the wrong, as well as on the right side
of questions of the first magnitude to society. This
circumstance, if duly attended to, would always
furnish a lesson of moderation to those who are
engaged in any controversy, however well persuaded
of being in the right. And a further reason for
caution in this respect might be drawn from the
reflection, that we are not always sure that those
who advocate the truth are actuated by purer
principles than their antagonists. Ambition, avarice,
personal animosity, party opposition, and many
other motives not more laudable than these, are
apt to operate as well upon those who support, as
upon those who oppose the right side of a question.
Were there not even these inducements to modera-

tion, nothing could be more ill-judged than that intolerant spirit, which has, at all times, characterized political parties. For, in politics as in religion, it is equally absurd to aim at making proselytes by fire and sword. Heresies in either can rarely be cured by persecution.

"And yet, just as these sentiments must appear to candid men, we have already sufficient indications that it will happen in this as in all former cases of great national discussion. A torrent of angry and malignant passions will be let loose. To judge from the conduct of the opposite parties, we shall be led to conclude that they will mutually hope to evince the justness of their opinions, and to increase the number of their converts, by the loudness of their declamations, and by the bitterness of their invectives. An enlightened zeal for the energy and efficiency of government, will be stigmatized as the offspring of a temper fond of power, and hostile to the principles of liberty. An over-scrupulous jealousy of danger to the rights of the people, which is more commonly the fault of the head than of the heart, will be represented as mere pretence and artifice—the stale bait for popularity at the expense of public good. It will be forgotten, on the one hand, that jealousy is the usual concomitant of violent love, and that the noble enthusiasm of liberty is too apt to be infected with a spirit of narrow and illiberal distrust. On the other hand, it will be equally forgotten, that the vigour of government is essential to the security of liberty; that, in the contemplation of a sound and well-informed judgment, their interests can never be separated; and that a dangerous ambition more often lurks behind the specious mask of zeal for the rights of the people, than under the forbidding appearances of zeal for the firmness and efficiency of government. History will teach us, that the former has been found a much more certain road to the introduction of despotism than the latter, and that, of those men who have overturned the liberties of republics, the greatest number have begun their career by paying an obsequious court to the people—commencing demagogues, and ending tyrants."

It was in this frank and manly strain—so unlike the nauseous flattery of later times—that Hamilton always addressed his countrymen. By thus appealing to their good sense and spirit of fairness, he was really paying them a higher compliment, than if he had sought to conciliate their prejudices, or pander to their foibles. And there was yet enough of sound opinion in America, unspoiled by the base and grovelling adulation which has since exalted the popular idols into gods, to appreciate this mode of dealing with great subjects. The influence of the *Federalist* was felt throughout the Union, and left behind it an impression, which all the folly and arrogance of succeeding years have never wholly obliterated.

It is not intended here, to give a detailed account of this memorable treatise. It purports to discuss the utility of the Union—the insufficiency of the Confederation to preserve it—the necessity of a government at least equally energetic with the one proposed—the conformity of the proposed Constitution to republican principles—its analogy to the State constitutions — and the additional security which its adoption would afford to the preservation of a republican government, to liberty, and to property. While it exhausts the subject in hand, it abounds in general reflections of the highest value, and in passages rich with the sterling ore of true political wisdom. It anticipates and answers every objection to the main principles on which the authority of all government must be founded, and its arguments are in many respects as applicable to our own or any other day, as they were to the particular times and circumstances in which they were first written.

The conclusion to which Hamilton came, and which he endeavoured to impart to his fellow-citizens, was, that the proposed Constitution, although not perfect in every part, was upon the whole a good one — the best, perhaps, that the present views and circumstances of the country would permit—and such as promised every species of security which a reasonable people could desire. But he laboured also to impress on their minds, that its success or failure must depend, after all, upon *them*—that institutions are in themselves of little avail, unless worked by the energy, and supported by the virtue of freemen. He wished to have a government strong enough to maintain itself against personal cupidity or ambition; but he looked for no permanent existence of such a government, unless it could command the confidence, acquire the affection, and be sustained by the active co-operation of the main body of the people. " If opposition to the National Government should arise," he says, " from the disorderly conduct of refractory or seditious individuals, it could be overcome by the same means, which are daily employed against the same evil under the State Governments. The magistracy, being equally the ministers of the law of the land, from whatever source it might emanate, would doubtless be as ready to guard the national as the local regulations from the inroads of private licentiousness. As to those partial commotions and insurrections which sometimes disquiet society, from the intrigues of an inconsiderable faction, or from sudden or occasional ill-humours that do not affect the great body of the community—the general government could command more extensive resources for the suppression of disturbances of that kind, than would be in the power of any single member. And as to those mortal feuds, which, in certain conjunctures, spread a conflagration through the whole nation, or through a very large proportion of it, proceeding either from weighty causes of discontent given by the government, or from the contagion of some violent popular paroxysm, *they do not fall within any ordinary rules of calculation.* When they happen, they commonly amount to revolutions, and dismemberments of empire. No form of government can always either avoid or control them. It is in vain to hope to

guard against events too mighty for human foresight or precaution; and it would be idle to object
to a government, because it could not perform im-
possibilities."

It is certain from this, and many similar passages,
that, much as he wished to strengthen the central
government for all ordinary purposes, Hamilton
never contemplated the maintenance of the Union
by force, against the declared opposition of a large
portion of its members. "Every view we may take
of the subject," he says, "as candid inquirers after
truth, will serve to convince us, that it is both
unwise and dangerous to deny the federal government an unconfined authority, in respect to all those
objects which are intrusted to its management. It
will indeed deserve the most vigilant and careful
attention of the people, to see that it be modelled
in such a manner, as to admit of its being safely
vested with the requisite powers. If any plan,
which has been, or may be offered to our consideration, should not, upon a dispassionate inspection, be found to answer this description, it ought
to be rejected. A government, the constitution of
which renders it unfit to be intrusted with all the
powers *which a free people ought to delegate to any*

government, would be an unsafe and improper deposi-
tary of the *national interests*. Wherever these can
with propriety be confided, the coincident powers
may safely accompany them. This is the true
result of all just reasoning upon the subject. And
the adversaries of the plan promulgated by the Convention would have given a better impression of
their candour, if they had confined themselves to
showing, that the internal structure of the proposed
government was such as to render it unworthy of
the confidence of the people. They ought not to
have wandered into inflammatory declamations and
unmeaning cavils about the extent of the powers.
The *powers* are not too extensive for the *objects* of
federal administration, or, in other words, for the
management of our *national interests;* nor can any
satisfactory argument be framed to show that they
are chargeable with such an excess. If it be true,
as has been insinuated by some of the writers on
the other side, that the difficulty arises from the
nature of the thing, and that the extent of the
country will not permit us to form a government,
in which such ample powers can safely be reposed,
it would prove, *that we ought to contract our views,*
and resort to the expedient of separate confederacies,

which will move within more practicable spheres.
For the absurdity must continually stare us in
the face, of confiding to a government the direction
of the most essential national concerns, without
daring to trust it with the authorities which are
indispensable to their proper and efficient management. Let us not attempt to reconcile contradic-
tions, but firmly embrace a rational alternative."

All the ability displayed in the *Federalist*, and all
the exertions of Hamilton and his friends, were
required to secure the acceptance of the Constitution. The struggle was long and arduous. The
adoption of the scheme was not only opposed by
passion and prejudice, but by the strong and earnest
convictions of some men of high talent and character.
"I can say with truth," exclaimed Luther Martin,
addressing the legislature of Maryland, "that so far
was I from being influenced in my conduct by
interest, or the consideration of office, that I would
cheerfully resign the appointment I now hold; I
would bind myself never to accept another, either
under the general government or that of my own
State; I would do more, sir—so destructive do I
consider the present system to the happiness of my
country—I would cheerfully sacrifice that share of

property with which heaven has blessed a life of industry; I would reduce myself to indigence and poverty; and those who are dearer to me than my own existence, I would intrust to the care and protection of that Providence who hath so kindly protected myself—*if on these terms only I could procure my country to reject those chains which are forged for it.*"

In the face of such an opposition it was impossible not to feel anxious. "It is almost arrogance," said Hamilton, "in so complicated a subject, depending so entirely upon the incalculable fluctuations of the human passions, to attempt even a conjecture about the result." What he did was to throw his whole strength into the contest, and to leave no honest means untried to accomplish the end. During the months that elapsed between the dissolution of the Convention and the ratification of the Constitution, his vigilance never slumbered, and his exertions were not relaxed for a moment. Many able men were engaged in that struggle, but none rendered such service as he did to the Federalist cause. He had made it emphatically his own, and was resolved to aid it with all the resources of his genius.

The first State which ratified the Constitution

was the little community of Delaware, on the 7th of December, 1787. The important State of Pennsylvania, influenced by the name of Franklin, and the personal exertions of James Wilson, was the next to follow. Then came New Jersey, Georgia, and Connecticut. But, with the opening of the year 1788, it was felt that the chief battle must be fought in Massachusetts, New York, and Virginia, and that, if even all three were gained over, it would still require one of the remaining States, to make up that mystical number nine on which so much depended. The Convention of Massachusetts met on the 9th of January, and, after long debate, ratified the Constitution on the 7th of February, but only by a majority of nineteen votes, in a house of 355 members. Maryland followed on the 28th of April, in spite of the efforts of Luther Martin, and, before the close of May, South Carolina had given in her adhesion. Eight States were thus gained; but New York, Virginia, and New Hampshire were yet doubtful, and North Carolina and Rhode Island seemed determined to stand aloof. The Convention of Virginia was to meet on the 2d of June, at Richmond, and that of New York on the 17th of the same month, at Poughkeepsie, on the banks of the Hudson. In the one was Madison, in the other Hamilton; and a system of horse-expresses was arranged between them, as well as with the Federalists of New Hampshire, to convey the earliest intelligence of those momentous proceedings to each other.

In Virginia the opposition was led by Patrick Henry, whose fiery eloquence had done so much in exciting his countrymen to resistance, in the commencement of the struggle with Great Britain; in New York the whole interest of Governor Clinton and his friends, and many local, and many personal prejudices, were arrayed against the adoption of the Constitution. There was even a party in the latter State, with sufficient confidence in the growing power and importance of their own community, to be willing to separate altogether from the Union. "Let us turn our eyes," says Mr. Curtis, in the valuable work so often quoted in these pages, "to the pleasant village on the banks of the Hudson, where the Convention of New York was already assembling. Hamilton was there, and was its leading spirit. How vigilant and thoughtful he was, we know— sometimes watching for the messenger who might descend the Eastern hills with reports from New

Hampshire—sometimes turning to the South, and listening for the footfall of his couriers from Virginia —but always preparing to meet difficulties, always ready to contest every inch of ground, and never losing sight of the great end to be accomplished. The hours were slow and heavy to him. The lines of horse-expresses which he had so carefully adjusted, and at whose intersection he stood to collect the momentous intelligence they would bring him, were indeed a marvel of enterprise at that day; but how unlike were they to the metallic lines that now daily gather for us, from all ends of the land and with the speed of lightning, minute notices of the most trivial or the most important events! Still, such as his apparatus was, it was all that could be had; and he awaited, alike with a firm patience and a faithful hope, for the decisive results. Even at this distance of time, we share the fluctuations of his anxious spirit, and our patriotism is quickened by our sympathy.

"Rarely indeed, if ever, was there a statesman having more at stake in what he could not personally control, or greater cause for solicitude concerning the public weal of his own times, or that of future ages, than Hamilton now had. His own

prospects of usefulness, according to the principles
which had long guided him, and the happiness
or misery of his country, were all, as he was deeply
convinced, involved in what might happen within
any hour of these few eventful days. The rejection
of the Constitution by Virginia would, in all probability, cause its rejection by New York. Its rejection by those States would, as he sincerely believed,
be followed by eventual disunion and civil war.
But if the Constitution could be established, he
could see the way open to the happiness and welfare of the whole Union; for, although it was not
in all respects the system that he would have preferred, he had shown in the *Federalist* how pro-
foundly he understood its bearing upon the interests
of the country, into what harmony he could bring
its various provisions, and what powerful aid he
could give in adjusting it into its delicate relations
to the States. He had, too, already conceived the
hope that its early administration might be undertaken by Washington; and with the government
in the hands of Washington, Hamilton could foresee
the success which, to us, is now historical.

"To say that Hamilton was ambitious, is to say
that he was human; and he was by no means free

from human imperfections. But his was the ambition of a great mind, regulated by principle, and made incapable by the force and nature of his convictions of seeking personal aggrandizement through any course of public policy, of which those convictions were not the mainspring and the life. In no degree is the character of any other American statesman undervalued or disparaged, when I insist on the importance to all America, through all time, of Hamilton's public character and conduct in this respect. It was because his future opportunities for personal distinction and usefulness were now evidently at stake, in the success of a system that would admit of the exercise of his great powers in the service of the country—a system that would afford at once a field for their exercise, and for the application of his political principles—and because he could neither seek nor find distinction in a line of politics which tended to disunion—that his position at this time is so interesting and important. As a citizen of New York, too, his position was personally critical. He had carried on a vigorous contest with the opponents of the Constitution in that State; he had encountered obloquy, and misrepresentation, and rancour—perhaps, he had provoked them. He had told the people of the State, for years, that they had listened to wrong counsels, when they had lent themselves to measures that retarded the growth of a national spirit and an efficient general government. The correctness of his judgment was now, therefore, openly and palpably in the issue. His public policy, with reference to the relations of the State to the Union, was now to stand or to fall with the Constitution proposed."

At first, the opposition sought to reject the plan as defective, while they disclaimed all wish to bring about a dissolution of the Union; but when, on the 24th of June, Hamilton received intelligence, that, by the ratification of New Hampshire, the Constitution had been adopted by nine States—the number requisite for its establishment—the question was at once raised whether New York was to remain in the Confederacy, or to stand alone as an independent power. There can be no doubt that there was a party in the Convention prepared for the latter alternative; but Hamilton felt, that, to leave out New York, would be to abandon the heart and centre of the Union, and resolved to combat the project by all the means at his disposal. Anxiously, most anxiously, did he watch for tidings from Virginia; and at length, on the 8th of July, one of his horsemen came spurring to Poughkeepsie with the news, that the land of Washington had ratified the Constitution. The vote had been carried by a majority of ten, and Patrick Henry, yielding to what he could not prevent, had declared that he would still be a peaceable citizen, and wait with hope, "that the spirit which predominated in the Revolution is not yet gone, nor the cause of those who are attached to the Revolution yet lost." A tenth State—the eldest and noblest of the Confederacy — was thus gained over to the side of regular government.

But the Convention of New York still hesitated. Unable to procure the absolute rejection of the Constitution, the Anti-Federalists resolved, that it should only be accepted conditionally. They hampered it with a number of amendments, and proposed, that, if these were not adopted within a certain time, their State should be at liberty to withdraw from the Union. They sought to carry constructive declarations of its meaning, which would have materially interfered with the powers exercised under it. The Federalists were obliged to concede that sundry amendments should be *recommended*, though they would not allow them to be made *conditions*. The final struggle took place on the question of conditional or unconditional ratification, and, after protracted and violent debates, the Constitution was at length adopted on the 26th of July, by thirty votes against twenty-seven.

And so Hamilton had triumphed. He had triumphed against difficulties and prejudices, which, at this distance of time, it is perhaps impossible fully to estimate. And he had the proud satisfaction of knowing, that his success was due to no truckling to popular delusions, no flattery of the popular will, but to the free, bold, uncompromising enunciation of great truths and high principles. And that very people, so often amused or disgusted by the clumsy worship of the demagogues they despise, had learned to honour and appreciate this man. During the last days of the Convention, the streets of New York were filled with an excited crowd, waiting for news from Poughkeepsie, and, as each messenger arrived, it was repeated from mouth to mouth: "Hamilton is speaking! Hamilton is speaking yet!" as though the destinies of the country hung suspended on his words. And when at length the tidings of the ratification reached the city, the bells pealed from the church-towers, the cannon resounded from the forts, and a loud and exulting shout proclaimed, that the popular voice had sanctioned the victory of the Constitution.

On the 5th of August, 1788, the ratification was celebrated at New York with great public rejoicings, and Hamilton was the hero of the festival. " He must have experienced on that day," says Mr. Curtis, to quote once more from a book to which I am anxious to acknowledge my obligations, "the best reward that a statesman can ever find ; for there is no purer, no higher pleasure for a conscientious statesman, than to know, by demonstrations of public gratitude, that the humblest of the people, for whose welfare he has laboured, appreciate and are thankful for his services. Public life is often represented, and often found, to be a thankless sphere for men of the greatest capacity and the highest patriotism ; and the accidents, the defeats, the changes, the party passions and obstructions of the political world, in a free government, frequently make it so. But mankind are neither deliberately heartless, nor systematically·unthankful ; and it has sometimes happened, in popular governments, that

statesmen of the first order of mind and character
have, while living, received the most unequivocal
proofs of feeling, direct from the popular heart;
while the sum total of their lives appears, in history,
to be wanting in evidences of that personal success, which is attained in a constant triumph over
opponents. Such an expression of popular gratitude
and sympathy, it was now the fortune of Hamilton
to receive.

"The people of the city did not stop to consider
on this occasion, whether he was entitled, in comparison with all the other public men in the United
States, to be regarded as the chief author of the
blessings which they now anticipated from the Constitution. And why should they? He was their
fellow-citizen—their own. They remembered the
day when they saw him, a mere boy, training his
artillerymen in their public park, for the coming
battles of the Revolution. They remembered the
youthful eloquence, and the more than youthful
power, with which he encountered the pestilent and
slavish doctrines of their Tories. They thought of
his career in the army, when the extraordinary
maturity, depth, and vigour of his genius, and his
great accomplishments, supplied to Washington, in

some of the most trying periods of his vast and prolonged responsibility, the assistance that Washington most needed.   They recollected his career in Congress, when his comprehensive intellect was always alert, to bear the country forward to measures and ideas, that would concentrate its powers and resources in some national system.   They called to mind how he had kept their own State from wandering quite away into the paths of disunion—how he had enlightened, invigorated, and purified public opinion, by his wise and energetic counsels—how he had led them to understand the true happiness and glory of their country—how he had laboured to bring about those events, which had now produced the Constitution—how he had shown to them the harmony and success that might be predicted of its operation, and had taught them to accept what was good, without petulantly demanding what individual opinion might claim as perfect.

" What was it to them, therefore, on this day of public rejoicing, that there might be in his policy more of consolidation than in the policy of others —that he was said to have in his politics too much that was national, and too little that was local— that some had done as much as he in the actual construction of the system which they were now to celebrate? Such controversies might be for history, or for the contests of administration that were soon to arise. On this day, they were driven out of men's thoughts by the glow of ,that public enthusiasm, which banishes the spirit of party, and touches and opens the inmost fountains of patriotism. Hamilton had rendered a series of great services to his country, which had culminated in the adoption of the Constitution by the State of New York; and they were now acknowledged from the very hearts of those who best knew his motives, and best understood his character.

"The people themselves, divided into their respective trades, evidently undertook the demonstrations in his honour, and gave them an emphasis which they could have derived from no other source. They bore his image aloft upon banners. They placed the Constitution in his right hand, and the Confederation in his left. They depicted Fame, with her trumpet, crowning him with laurels. They emblazoned his name upon the miniature frigate, the Federal ship of state. They anticipated the administration of the first President, by uniting on the national flag the figure of Washington and the figure of Hamilton. All that ingenuity, all that affection, all that popular pride and gratitude could do to honour a public benefactor, was repeated again and again through the long line of five thousand citizens, of all orders and conditions, which stretched away from the shores of that beautiful bay, where ocean ascends into river, and river is lost in ocean—and where commerce then wore her holiday attire, to prefigure the magnificence and power which she was to derive from the Constitution of the United States."

CHAPTER X.

ELEVEN States having now ratified the Constitution, the old Congress, which was still sitting, resolved not to wait for the tardy concurrence of Rhode Island and North Carolina, but to take at once the necessary steps for inaugurating the new government. The *seat* of that government, which had not been determined by the Convention, was one of the first subjects of discussion. A thousand jealousies were raised by this question, which threatened to throw the whole country once more into tumult and confusion. Hamilton again exerted himself to effect a compromise between the contending parties, and it was at length arranged that they should have recourse to a *temporary* settlement. Postponing to a future time the claims of Virginia and Pennsylvania, and the plan for a central capital, to be erected on neutral territory on the banks of the Delaware or the Potomac, it was agreed that the city of New York should be for the present the seat of government. The first Wednesday in January, 1789, was fixed for the appointment of electors; the first Wednesday in February for the election of President; and the first Wednesday in March for the Constitution to come into working order.

As the time drew near, almost every eye in America was turned towards one man, as the destined choice of the nation for its highest office. It had not yet been discovered, that insignificance and obscurity are qualifications for the chief magistrate of a great empire, and so long as tried and honourable service was the test of fitness, no one could for a moment compete with the claims of Washington. He was emphatically the leader, the deliverer, foremost in peace and war—the founder of the commonwealth, the father of his country. Even faction was silenced in his presence, and envy could detect no weak place in the panoply of his virtue. To him all were willing to yield a pre-eminence, which was acknowledged by the voice of the whole civilized world; or if he still had his enemies and detractors, who had dogged his footsteps from the first, and were afterwards found yelping at his heels with cur-like pertinacity, they now deemed it prudent to slink into their holes and corners, and dared not rouse the indignation of a grateful and admiring people.

As free from affectation as from vulgar ambition, there can be no doubt of the sincerity of the wish he expressed to pass the remainder of his days in quiet. His friends, his family, the shades of Mount Vernon, the pursuits of agriculture, the tranquil dignity of private life, these were the true objects of his desire. He was at this time engaged in attending the sick-bed of his aged mother, who had trained him in childhood to obedience and self-control, and from whom he had derived the simplicity and moderation of his character. She had watched his career with tender interest, but with no undue exultation, and valued more the good son and the good citizen than the hero and conqueror. When he was called away from her on this occasion, their parting had the solemnity of a last interview, for they could hardly hope to meet again upon earth. And, no doubt, the old lady felt, as in the years long ago, that although "her George" might have done better "to stop at home and mind his farm," yet, wherever he went, and whatever

R

he undertook, he would "do his duty like a man."

But while the universal expectation had fixed on Washington as the President, it was not so clear to whom the second place in the republic was to be offered. The post of Vice-President has not proved very influential in practice; but, when the Constitution was yet untried, it was impossible accurately to determine how far his powers might extend. At all events, he was to preside in the Senate, and to have the casting vote; and, in case of the death or resignation of the President, he was to replace that great officer in all his functions. It was, therefore, an appointment of high dignity, and might become one of serious importance. In this, as in many other matters, the division of the States led to the first choice. If Virginia was to supply a President, and New York was to be the seat of government, it was necessary to conciliate New England in the selection of a Vice-President.

Just before this time, JOHN ADAMS had returned from his mission to the Old World, and had been received by his fellow-citizens with the respect due to his unwearied exertions in their behalf. He was a native of Massachusetts, the son of a New England farmer, who gave him the advantage of an education at Harvard College. Descended from the Puritans, and at first intended for the ministry in one of their churches, he soon found that he could not accept their Calvinistic tenets, and resolved to devote himself to the study of the law. Born in 1735, he was in the prime of manhood at the commencement of the troubles in America, and at once took a prominent part in public affairs. He was employed by the town of Boston to contest the legality of the Stamp Act, and on all occasions defended the rights of the Colonies, while he strongly deprecated any acts of popular violence. When the collision took place between the king's troops and the citizens, which was afterwards absurdly described as the Boston Massacre, Mr. Adams distinguished himself most honourably by his advocacy of the unfortunate soldiers accused of murder. Having proved that they had only fired in self-defence, he upheld the principles of justice, and the undoubted law of the land, against the excited passions of the people, and succeeded in obtaining a reasonable verdict. Elected to the First Congress, he assumed his full share of the responsibility of their measures, and was engaged during the following years in most of the chief acts of the revolution. Once convinced that a reconciliation with England was impossible, he urged the policy of an open, irrevocable rupture. His influence secured the appointment of Washington to the command of the army, and he was a member of the committee which prepared the Declaration of Independence, although that document was really written by Jefferson. He seems to have participated in the doubts, the fears, and the impatience with which most Americans regarded the inevitable delays of the war, and at one time to have lost confidence in the illustrious chief he had himself recommended to the choice of the country; but there is no pretence for the assertion that he ever wavered in the cause he had embraced. In 1778, he was sent on a mission to France, whence he returned in 1779, and before the close of that year was again despatched to Europe. He negotiated a treaty with Holland, and was afterwards engaged in discussing the preliminaries of peace with Great Britain, and, throughout these transactions, his plain sense and integrity appear in favourable contrast to the refined and tortuous diplomacy of the French Ministers. In 1785, he was appointed envoy to the Court of St. James's, and continued to reside in England till 1788.

The important affairs in which Mr. Adams was concerned abroad, the high place he afterwards filled at home, and the partiality of friends and admirers, who knew and honoured him in the calm retirement of his extreme old age, have left a somewhat exaggerated impression of his abilities. He was undoubtedly a brave, honest, energetic man, indefatigable in the public service, endowed with good talents for business, and holding many sound, practical views on political subjects; but he was not a great statesman, and nothing but ignorance or prejudice could ever have thought of comparing him with Hamilton in that capacity. His letters and journals afford the best key to his character, and in them we may trace the picture of a shrewd, sensible, bustling, irascible person, somewhat obstinate, somewhat dogmatical, with a strong conviction of the value of his own opinions, and rather inclined to force them upon others; but amiable in his private relations, kind-hearted, and devoted to the cause of his country. He was a portly man of moderate stature, with an open countenance, broad forehead, and sparkling eye, and in look and bearing must have much resembled a comely and prosperous Englishman of the middle class. There can be no question as to the many and great services he rendered to America; but his errors of temper and judgment were attended with serious consequences, of which the following pages will supply some striking illustrations.

When the time came for the choice of a Vice-President, and it was generally acknowledged, for the reasons already stated, that a citizen of New England should have the preference, the name of Adams was one of those which at once attracted the public attention. Hamilton was of course consulted, and seems at first to have hesitated. He knew that Adams had declared in favour of the Constitution, and that he would have the support of many Federalists; but he also remembered that the New Englander had formerly shown distrust of Washington, and he feared that he was too democratical in his tendencies. He wrote to friends in Massachusetts to make inquiries on the subject. He was assured that Adams had returned from Europe with his prejudices softened, and his views much modified, and that he was a man of " unconquerable intrepidity, and incorruptible integrity, greatly experienced in

the interests and character of the country." Under
these circumstances, Hamilton resolved to give him
every assistance in securing his election. But another
danger soon presented itself to the sagacious mind
of the Federalist leader. The Anti-Federalists had
started Clinton as a candidate, and threatened to
divide their vote between him and Adams. The
Constitution had provided that two names should be
selected, the one with the largest number of votes
for President, and the one with the next largest for
Vice-President. If the Federalists all voted for
Adams, it might so happen that Washington's election for President would fail. It was necessary, not
only to prevent the possibility of such an occurrence,
but to procure the return of the great chief by such a
preponderating majority, as would clearly prove that
no other name could for a moment be brought into
competition with his. It was, therefore, Hamilton's
opinion, that the Federalists should take care to give
so many less votes to Adams than to Washington
as would secure the above objects; and the electors
of the different States appear to have acted upon his
advice. When the returns were made up, Washington
had sixty-nine votes, or the unanimous voice of all
the States; whereas Adams had thirty-four votes

and the remaining thirty-five were distributed amongst various persons.

Mr. Adams was deeply offended at the course pursued by Hamilton on this occasion, and his grandson and biographer, Mr. Charles Francis Adams, stigmatizes it as a " refinement of policy," and " ominous of imperfect faith." It is difficult to say what is meant by this. Hamilton was no personal friend of Adams, and was in no way pledged to him as a politician. He gave him the preference over other candidates on public grounds alone ; and, in consulting with those who confided in his judgment and patriotism, he had a perfect right to suggest such measures as he thought necessary, to place the paramount claims of Washington above all dispute. In this there was no breach of faith, and nothing that ought to have wounded the most sensitive pride. But Adams was peculiarly susceptible on the subject of his own dignity, and strongly resented what he considered an unjustifiable interference with his votes. It was the beginning of a misunderstanding between him and Hamilton, which afterwards grew to larger proportions, and, in the end, proved very fatal to the interests of the Federalist party.

But, for the present, all else was forgotten in the

triumphant progress of Washington. When the result of the election was known, the whole country prepared to honour the chieftain of their choice. His friends and neighbours escorted him on the first part of his journey. At Baltimore and Philadelphia, he was received by a numerous cavalcade, and passed under laurelled arches, amid the roar of artillery. At Trenton, the scene of his former exploits, young girls dressed in white strewed flowers before him, and the bridge bore the inscription : " The defender of the mothers will be the protector of the daughters." Through all New Jersey, the line he had so often traversed in his weary marches was marked by a series of festivities. As he approached New York, a committee of Congress came out to meet him, and, embarking on board a splendid barge, he entered the bay to the sound of martial music, amid the ringing of bells, the thunder of salutes, and the shouts of an excited multitude. Governor Clinton received him at the landing-place, and General Knox, and other old comrades in arms, welcomed him as he stepped on shore. The streets were hung with flags and garlands, ladies waved their handkerchiefs from the windows, the people crowded on his passage, and tears of joy and enthusiasm were mingled with acclamations. It was one of the brightest, fairest, and most genuine of civic triumphs. And yet, in the midst of it all, Washington had a painful feeling, that he might not be able to satisfy the expectations of his countrymen, and that he might live to witness the reverse of that joyous spectacle.

A few days later, on the 30th of April, 1789, he was finally inaugurated as President. In the morning, the churches were thronged with worshippers, imploring the blessing of heaven on the new government. A procession was formed to attend the President to the Hall of Congress. John Adams, as Vice-President, conducted him to the chair of state; but it was in an open balcony, in full view of the people, that he was to take the oath of office. Clad in a suit of dark brown cloth, with white silk stockings, and a steel-hilted sword, Washington advanced to the table, on which lay a richly-bound Bible on a velvet cushion. Chancellor Livingston administered the prescribed oath, the Secretary of the Senate presented the Bible, and Washington, having solemnly repeated the words, " I swear—so help me God!" stooped down, and reverently kissed the book. Then the Chancellor exclaimed, in a loud voice:

" Long live George Washington, President of the United States !"—a signal-flag rose into the air, the artillery pealed from the batteries, and the renewed acclamations of the populace announced the completion of this simple, but impressive ceremony.

While it lasted, old friends and fellow-soldiers were grouped around their beloved chief; and among the foremost was Hamilton. For this day he had long schemed and toiled, and it must have been with no small satisfaction that he at length saw the fruit of his labours, in the establishment of a regular government, with the greatest of American citizens at its head. It was, indeed, one of those moments of exultation which do not often occur in the life of any man, when success comes to reward the efforts of the past, and even the wisest may be excused for indulging in too sanguine hopes of the future. But however Hamilton might rejoice in what he had already accomplished, he well knew how much remained to be done, before the institutions of his country could repose upon a solid basis.

CHAPTER XI.

SCARCELY was the inauguration over, when Washington's difficulties began. At first, he was beset with visitors, who intruded on his privacy, and left him not a moment to himself. "By the time I had done breakfast," he writes, "and thence till dinner, and afterwards till bed-time, I could not get rid of the ceremony of one visit, before I had to attend to another. In a word, I had no leisure to read or to answer the despatches that were pouring in upon me from all quarters."

It was necessary at once to take some steps to protect him from this annoyance, and to secure the respect due to the dignity of his office. He consulted several persons on the subject, and amongst them Adams and Hamilton. The former advised, that he should, to a great extent, adopt the ceremonial of European courts, and that none should be admitted to his presence, except on proper application to a chamberlain, or other great officer. The latter also was of opinion that it was essential to maintain the dignity of the chief magistrate, but, at the same time, he considered it expedient to offend, as little as possible, the republican prejudices of the country. He counselled that the President should hold a levee once a week, for not more than half an hour; that he should accept no invitations, and only give formal entertainments at certain stated intervals; and that the heads of departments, foreign ministers, and the members of the Senate, should alone have the *general* right of access. Other suggestions were made in different quarters, and at length some sort of etiquette was established. But the most obvious regulations in these matters provoked the jealous spirit of the people, and were soon made use of by hostile factions to injure the popularity of the President.

In the same way, accusations were brought against him of an excessive love of pomp and parade. Nothing could be further from the truth, for Washington was a man of noble and simple tastes. But he rightly thought, that the chief magistrate of a great empire should appear in public with some regard to the decencies of his station, and that to neglect them

would really be to insult the nation he represented.
If, therefore, he drove through the streets of New
York with four horses to his carriage, gave splendid and hospitable entertainments, and received his
guests in a full suit of black velvet, with bag, and
sword, and powdered hair—the usual dress of state
and ceremony in those days—he showed himself
wiser and more consistent than his assailants, who,
by their senseless cavils and objections, only proved
the undue importance they attached to such trifles.
These were the persons who could find, in a sofa at
the President's ball, some fancied resemblance to a
throne ; and such as they have ever since continued
the same system of attack, till they have driven the
best minds of America from office, lowered the
standard of public life, and substituted a class of
nameless adventurers, for the really eminent order
of men, who founded, and might have saved the
republic.

But Washington was soon occupied with more
serious questions than those of etiquette. It was
necessary to organize executive departments, and to
appoint the members of the cabinet. Before anything
could be done, the constitution of the several departments had to be settled by Congress, and, while the

matter was still pending, the President was taken alarmingly ill. For some weeks he was in great pain and danger, and prepared himself for the worst with his accustomed courage and resignation. "Whether to-night or twenty years hence," he said to his physician, "makes no difference. I know that I am in the hands of a good Providence." His illness had, however, the effect of rousing the people to a sense of what they might suffer by his loss, and of silencing for the moment the cabals already formed against him. While slowly recovering, he received intelligence of the death of the venerable mother, who had guided his childhood with so firm and steady a hand, and whom in age he had never ceased to revere. He was deeply affected by the news, and his strength had been much shaken by his late malady; but the public service demanded his immediate attention, and he never postponed the national interest to any private consideration.

It was Madison who proposed in Congress the plan for the establishment of executive departments. After long discussion, bills were passed, instituting the several offices of a Secretary for Foreign Affairs; to be called the Secretary of State, who was also to have the custody of the seals and archives—a

Secretary for War, whose functions included the management of both army and navy—and a Secretary of the Treasury, who was, in most respects, to perform the duties of an English Chancellor of the Exchequer. These appointments were to be made by the President, with the advice and consent of the Senate, but the ministers might be removed by the authority of the President alone. The latter clause led to much debate, and was only carried in the Senate by the casting vote of the Vice-President. The above three officers, with the Attorney-General, were to form the cabinet.

Washington at once confided the War Department to his old comrade in arms, General Knox, and offered the Treasury to Hamilton. He is said to have consulted Robert Morris, the former Superintendent of Finance, as to the second of these appointments, asking with a sigh: "What is to be done with this heavy debt?"—"There is but one man in the United States," answered Morris, "who can tell you, and that is Alexander Hamilton. I am glad you have given me this opportunity to declare to you the extent of the obligations I am under to him."

The President, who well remembered the invaluable services of his aide-de-camp, could fully subscribe to this flattering estimate of his talents. He had lately been in frequent communication with Hamilton, and had consulted him on several grave and delicate questions. He had always cherished a pleasant recollection of their intimacy, and now the old feelings of friendship had strongly revived between them. In his elevated position, Washington needed more than ever a friend he could entirely trust. On every ground, therefore, private as well as public, he was glad to offer this important post to Hamilton; and the latter did not hesitate to accept it, although he well knew its difficulties. When warned of the calumny and persecution, which would inevitably attend his efforts to do his duty in such a position, Hamilton only answered: "Of that I am perfectly aware; but I am convinced it is the situation in which I can do most good."

Soon after, Washington informed him that he intended to nominate Mr. Jefferson, then absent in France, as Secretary of State, and Mr. Edmund Randolph as Attorney-General. The last-named gentleman had formerly served with him in the army, and had since been Governor of his native State of Virginia. As a member of the Convention he had opposed several of the provisions of the Constitution, and refused his signature to the draft; but he afterwards gave his support to its final adoption. Like Knox and Hamilton, Mr. Randolph at once accepted the appointment. Mr. Jay, who had been Secretary for Foreign Affairs under the Congress, was made Chief Justice of the Supreme Court, and no wiser, no more upright judge ever sat in any tribunal.

Hamilton now devoted all his thoughts to the national finances, and was busy in devising schemes to meet the pressing exigencies of the time. He was at once assailed with applications for his interest to obtain appointments, and with questions as to his intentions with regard to the policy to be adopted. Calmly and resolutely he refused to return any answer to these importunities, or to give any information which could by possibility be turned to the promotion of private interests. Even when an old friend made some inquiries as to the value of the debt and other matters, a knowledge of which could hardly be thought injurious to the public, Hamilton replied: " My dear friend, I have received your letter of the 16th instant. I am sure you are sincere when you say you would not submit me to an impropriety. Nor do I know that there would be any in answering your queries. But you remember the saying with regard to Cæsar's wife. I think the spirit of it applicable to every man concerned in the administration of the finances of a country. With respect to the conduct of such men, suspicion is ever eagle-eyed, and the most innocent things are apt to be misinterpreted. Be assured of the affection and friendship of . . . Yours, &c. &c."— It is to be feared that the statesmen of America have not all inherited this refined and sensitive delicacy.

The duties of the Secretary of the Treasury were many and various. Besides originating plans for the improvement and management of the revenue, and for the support of the public credit, he had to prepare and report the estimates, and to superintend the collection, receipt, and disbursement of the public moneys, all authority for transfers or payments being vested in him. He was the exclusive judge of the time and amount of the disbursements, subject only to the check of the Comptroller, who countersigned the warrants, and to the ultimate settlement of the accounts by the Auditor and Comptroller. And it must be remembered that, when Hamilton assumed the office, almost everything was new, strange, and untried in this great department, and that he had to construct the *machinery* with which he was to perform his task.

He began by establishing a system for the collection of the revenue, and the organization of the Treasury, which has since been generally admired for the completeness of its self-acting checks, and on the principle of which all subsequent innovations have been founded. He instituted a strict and regular audit of accounts, to secure that all expenditure should be made in pursuance of legal appropriations, and that the balances of amounts unexpended should be clearly shown. But the great difficulty with which he had to contend was the necessity of taking immediate steps to support the public credit. No really efficient measures had yet been adopted to meet the debts and obligations of the United States. The Foreign Debt, due to France, Holland, and Spain, with heavy arrears of interest —the Loan Office Debt, for moneys lent to government in each State—the Army Debt, for pay and commutation of pensions—the Debt of the Five Great Departments (as it was called), for services and supplies during the war—the old Continental issues, and innumerable obligations for interest and unpaid balances—all had to be provided for. To add to the inextricable confusion of these various claims, some were held to be State debts, and others debts of the Union. Hamilton saw at once that there was but one way to deal effectually with this pressing emergency. It was to assume the State debts as identical with those of the Union, *to fund the whole*, and to make all the national resources available for the security of the public creditor.

In the report which he presented to Congress, he urged the importance of maintaining the national credit, as upon it depended the individual and aggregate prosperity of the citizens of the United States,/ their relief from the embarrassments they now experienced, their character as a people, and the cause of good government. But, besides motives of political expediency, there were arguments for it which rested on the immutable principles of moral obligation. And these derived additional strength from the nature of the debt of the United States. *It was the price of liberty;* and the faith of America had been repeatedly and solemnly pledged for its redemption.

He then proceeded to point out the evils of an

unfunded debt as an object of speculation, diverting capital from more useful channels, and being itself a precarious commodity from its fluctuation and insecurity. Whereas, by funding the debt, and making due provision for it, they would render the obligations of the government in some sort a substitute for money, and promote, instead of discouraging, the great interests of industry.

But while they were all agreed, that the foreign debt ought to be provided for in accordance with the precise terms of the contract, there was a difference of opinion as to the domestic debt. Some urged, that there ought to be a discrimination between the original holders and the present possessors by purchase. This doctrine Hamilton denounced as "unjust, impolitic, highly injurious even to the original holders, and ruinous to the public credit." He then proceeded to the question, whether any difference ought to remain between the creditors of the Union and those of the individual States. He showed that a provision by one authority would be more effectual than by several; that collision and confusion would thus be prevented; that conflicting systems must needs diminish the aggregate revenue; and that the public creditors, receiving

their dues from one source, distributed with an equal
hand, would have a common interest, and would
all unite in supporting the fiscal arrangements of
the government.

"Hence," he argued, "it was the interest of the
creditors of the Union, that those of the States
should be comprehended in a general provision.
Neither would it be just that one class of public
creditors should be more favoured than the other.
*The objects for which both debts were contracted were
the same; indeed, a great part of the State debts had
arisen from assumptions by them on account of the
Union.*"

Therefore he insisted that both should be placed
on the same footing, and he devised a scheme for
the equitable adjustment of accounts between the
Union and the States, to be executed under the
superintendence of commissioners appointed for the
purpose. With regard to the question of interest,
he contended that all arrears then due were entitled
to an equal provision with the principal of the debt.
Assuming the whole to be a capital bearing interest
at six per cent., he proposed a loan for the entire
amount, on five different plans at the option of the
creditor. To provide for the payment of interest

on the same, and also to meet the current expenses, he suggested additional duties on wine, spirits, tea, and coffee. But persuaded that "the creation of debt should always be accompanied with the means of its extinguishment," he likewise proposed that the net revenue of the Post-Office should be vested in commissioners, to be applied by them to the gradual discharge of the debt. And to facilitate all these operations, and assist in the general business of the country, he contemplated the establishment of a National Bank, of which he was prepared to submit a sketch for the consideration of Congress.

When this memorable report was ready to be laid before the Legislature, one of the main defects in the Constitution became apparent. That instrument had provided that no person holding office could be a member of Congress, and the able and eloquent minister, who had conceived and elaborated this great scheme of finance, was precluded from explaining or defending his views, in presence of the assembly which was to decide upon their adoption or rejection. It was, indeed, moved in the House, that the Secretary of the Treasury might be permitted to make his communication in person; but, after a short debate, it was resolved to receive his report in writing—a decision which deprived Congress at the time of most valuable assistance, and established a precedent which has been highly injurious to America.

Nothing can be more absurd than the rule, which forbids a statesman to expound and elucidate his own plans, and prevents him from answering objections and removing difficulties, while it leaves to his opponents the power of putting forth their whole strength to defeat him. Only the extreme jealousy of government, which prevails in a purely democratic society, could have led to the adoption of such a rule. It has forced the chief politicians of America either to refuse office, or to accept it at the cost of their parliamentary influence ; it has alternately robbed the Administration and the Legislature of some of their best men ; it has compelled ministers to have recourse to indirect means, through the press or the platform, to support the policy which they ought to have upheld in Congress ; and it has thus had a direct tendency to degrade both the Cabinet and the Assembly, and to transfer the discussion of all important matters, from the representatives of the people to the agitators of the newspapers and the hustings.

On this occasion, the opponents of the Secretary's measures found an unexpected and formidable champion in James Madison. That gentleman had sided with Hamilton in the Convention, and shared with him and Jay in the labours and honours of the *Federalist*. He had fought manfully for the establishment of the Constitution, had partaken largely of the favour and confidence of Washington, and was peculiarly obnoxious to the Anti-Federalist party. But he now sat in the House of Representatives, in which he was ambitious of the post of leader, and his constituents in Virginia were strongly opposed to some of Hamilton's plans. Agriculturists, and often in need of money, they had been forced to part with their government bonds or certificates at a great sacrifice; and they now resented as an injustice, that the speculators, who had purchased these securities, and who chiefly belonged to the Northern States, should be placed in so much better a position than themselves, and profit by the losses they had sustained. They likewise urged, that the North had the larger share of State debts to transfer to the Federal account, and they protested against additional burdens being entailed on the South, by the assumption of obligations to which they were not already liable.

Madison made himself the interpreter of these views, advocated a discrimination between the original holders of the debt and its present possessors, and resisted the principle of the assumption of the State debts by the Union. Had he succeeded in his opposition, Hamilton's whole scheme must have miscarried, and the credit of America have been ruined for many a day. But the friends of a just settlement of the debt, amongst whom Fisher Ames was honourably distinguished, were fortunately in the majority, and resolutions were at length passed in accordance with Hamilton's report. Once more the statesman had triumphed in the face of unnumbered difficulties, and, however bitter the enmity he had provoked, he felt certain of the ultimate success of his financial measures. That success was yet to come, more brilliant than could have been anticipated, to justify his prescience, and consecrate the work of his genius. " He smote the rock of the national resources," says Daniel Webster, " and abundant streams of revenue gushed forth. He touched the dead corpse of the Public Credit, and it sprang upon its feet. The fabled birth of Minerva from the brain of Jove was hardly more sudden or more perfect, than the financial system of the United States, as it burst forth from the conceptions of Alexander Hamilton."

But, before he finally accomplished his object, another actor appeared upon the scene, who was destined to play an important part in the subsequent history of his life.

CHAPTER XII.

IT has been already said, that the post of Secretary of State was offered to Jefferson, and as he had now arrived in New York, to undertake the duties of his office, it is time to introduce this singular personage to the notice of the reader.

THOMAS JEFFERSON was born in Virginia, on the 2d of April, 1743. He was the son of a planter of considerable wealth, and descended from a family of Welsh origin. He was educated at Williamsburg, and, while at college, appears to have had the reputation of a shrewd, lively, pleasant fellow, who, in spite of his tall, gaunt figure, red hair, harsh features, and freckled face, was welcome in most companies, and somewhat of a favourite with the ladies. He seems early to have adopted a light and easy philosophy, with sceptical views in religion, to have cultivated a taste for literature and music, and to have acquired the habits and address of a man of the world. Within a few years of leaving college, he was called to the bar, and obtained a seat in the Assembly of Virginia, where, fired by the eloquence and enthusiasm of Patrick Henry, and always strongly attracted by a popular cause, he threw himself heart and soul into the struggle with England. But it was less by speeches and open demonstrations, than by schemes concocted in private, and the dexterous management of the " corresponding committees," that he was able to render good service to the Colonies. It is said that, when at school, he used to put forward other boys to ask for whatever he himself wanted ; and he continued through life the same tactics—preferring to remain in the background and pull the wires, rather than engage actively in personal or political combats.

His services were, however, well known ; he was elected a delegate to the General Congress, and, when it was determined to break finally with England, he was appointed one of the committee to prepare the Declaration of Independence. Both Adams and Franklin pressed him to undertake its composition, and, as he was always ready with his pen, he consented to make the draft. It contained some extravagant expressions which Congress had the good sense to omit; but, in the main, his sketch was ultimately adopted, and there can be no doubt, that the mere fact of his having been the author of that celebrated document greatly contributed to the influence which he afterwards exercised over the public mind.

The next task in which he was engaged was one exactly suited to his character. Washington only became a republican from the necessity of the case, and, if Adams was one by conviction, it was with no fanatical attachment to any particular form. But Jefferson was a republican on system, with a philosophical theory to be carried out to its logical conclusions, and in this, as in many other respects, his mind seems to have been cast in a French, rather than an English mould. It was, therefore, with real satisfaction, that he set about remodelling the laws and constitution of his native Virginia, so as to bring them into harmony with his democratic notions. Entails and primogeniture, hereditary distinctions, a powerful gentry, and an Established Church, still existed in that portion of America; and all these were doomed to destruction by this ardent republican. "When I left Congress in 1776," he says, "it was in the persuasion that our whole code must be reviewed, and adapted to our republican form of government; and now that we had no negatives of councils, governors, and kings, to restrain us from doing right, that it should be corrected, in all its parts, with a single eye to *reason*."

Some people might have thought, that reason generally points to the lessons of experience, and that, before destroying an aristocracy which had no exclusive *political* privileges, it would be well to examine the working of the new institutions, and wait to see what checks might possibly be required. But such timid counsels were by no means suited to the impatience of a philosopher like Jefferson. He urged on the Assembly of Virginia the immediate abolition of every law and custom, that had any tendency to favour the preservation of the old hereditary fortunes and families; and he persevered in his efforts, till he succeeded in almost entirely breaking down the aristocracy of the Ancient Dominion. It might have been better for posterity, had he shown equal perseverance in maintaining his views with regard to negro-slavery; but, though always opposed to it in theory, he was more complying on this head, and he left to another age the bitter legacy of a question, which in his time lay within narrow bounds, and admitted of a peaceable solution.

Appointed Governor of his native state, he was surprised by the sudden invasion of a few hundred English soldiers, who were allowed to penetrate to the very heart of Virginia, and very nearly captured both the Governor and the Legislature. Jefferson owed his safety to the speed of his horse, and was accused by his enemies of having displayed, on this occasion, a total want of capacity and courage. But, after all, it is no great reproach to a civilian that he happens to be deficient in martial qualities, and the only objection which can fairly be taken to his conduct is, that he should ever have accepted an office, which in those days was so likely to involve the necessity of military service.

In 1782, he was named as one of the negotiators for peace with England, but the preliminaries were concluded before he could set out on his mission. Two years after, however, he was despatched to Europe to negotiate treaties of commerce with different nations, and, when Dr. Franklin returned to America, he remained in Paris as Minister of the United States. He was here far more in his element than in a position where he was exposed to the

rough criticism of political opponents, or to the still
more troublesome attacks of hostile invaders. Diplomacy was suited to his tastes, and France was just
then the field for the cultivation of his peculiar
opinions. At his house were assembled many of
the members of the reforming party, and his vanity
seems to have been flattered by the deference paid
to his judgment. He was free with his advice on
all subjects, political, religious, scientific, social; and
the polite Frenchmen of that day, still faithful to
their traditional manners, listened and admired with
exemplary good-breeding. The smiles of beauty, the
play of wit, the charm of conversation, the delicacy
of compliment, all conspired to seduce this wanderer
from the wilds of America. He formed an attachment for France, to which he adhered through many
vicissitudes of fortune. Years after, he wrote : " In
a comparison of this with other countries, we have
the proof of primacy which was given to Themistocles after the battle of Salamis. Every general
voted to himself the first reward of valour, and the
second to Themistocles. So, ask the travelled in-
habitant of any nation, in what country on earth
would you rather live ? — Certainly, in my own,
where are all my friends, my relations, and the

earliest and sweetest affections of my life.—Which
would be your second choice ?—France ! "

But it was not only the grace and polish of society
which had so strong a fascination for Jefferson. Here
also he found that love of theory, that fondness for
grand ideas and symmetrical systems, which had for
him an irresistible attraction, and in which he deemed
the "lethargic Englishman" so deficient. And he
came at a time when he might hope to gratify every
vague aspiration, and realize the wildest dreams ;
for it was the eve of the French Revolution, and the
air was charged with the electricity of the impending
storm.

He hailed the advent of that revolution with
delight, and watched its progress with ever-increasing
interest. He had certainly no prejudices to stand in
the way of his sympathy, for he wished " to extirpate
from creation that class of human lions, tigers, and
mammoths, called kings ; " and held it desirable that
" the tree of liberty should be refreshed from time to
time with the blood of patriots and tyrants." Nor
would his religious scruples have been shocked by
the boldest flights of the sceptical philosophy. " It
is not to be understood," he says, " that I am with
Christ in all His doctrines. I am a materialist ; He

takes the side of spiritualism." And in writing to a youth at college, his own nephew, who had consulted him on such matters, he advises him "not to be frightened from this inquiry by any fear of its consequences. *If* it ends in a belief that there is *no* God, you will find incitements to virtue in the comfort and pleasantness you feel in its exercise, and the love of others which it will procure you. *If* you find reason to believe there *is* a God, a consciousness that you are acting under His eye, and that He approves you, will be a vast additional incitement. *If* that there be a future state," &c. &c.— with much more to the same effect. And, whatever his doubts on these important subjects, he had the most superstitious confidence in popular wisdom-- or, at least, in the wisdom of a people enlightened by newspapers—and was even convinced that " those societies (as the Indians) which live without government enjoy, in their general mass, an infinitely greater degree of happiness than those who live under the European governments."

No wonder that so thorough a democrat, and so profound a philosopher, was not fully satisfied with the Constitution, which the labours of Hamilton and his colleagues had bestowed on the United States.

He particularly objected to the re-eligibility of the President. "This, I fear," he says, "will make it an office for life first, and then hereditary. I was much an enemy to monarchies before I came to Europe, and am ten thousand times more so since I have seen what they are. There is scarcely an evil known in these countries which may not be traced to their king as its source, nor a good which is not derived from the small fibres of republicanism existing among them."—It was a great relief to him when he found, that the President of the United States was not to be addressed as His Highness. "I hope," says Jefferson, "the terms of Excellency, Honour, Worship, Esquire, may for ever disappear from among us from this moment. I wish that of Mr. would follow them!"—One almost regrets that Jefferson did not remain in France, and join that Jacobin Club, of which he would have been so distinguished an ornament.

When summoned to the post of Secretary of State in his own country, he does not appear to have shown much alacrity in accepting office. It probably involved too direct an amount of responsibility, to be quite in accordance with the tastes of the wary diplomatist. But Washington desired to found his cabinet on as wide a base as possible, and to include in it the author of the Declaration of Independence, as well as the champion of the Constitution.   Urged to accept the appointment, Jefferson wrote to the President in a tone of extraordinary modesty, expressing doubts of his own abilities, and concluding with these remarkable professions of respect and submission : "Signify to me by another line your ultimate wish, and I shall conform to it cordially.   If it should be to remain in New York, my chief comfort will be to work under your eye—my only shelter the authority of your name, and the wisdom of measures to be dictated by you, and implicitly executed by me." It is unfortunate that he did not always retain the same sense of inferiority to that illustrious man.

It was in November, 1789, that Jefferson arrived in the United States, but, having affairs of his own to settle in Virginia, he did not reach New York till March, 1790.   He came just in time for the great struggle on the financial question, for, although resolutions had been carried in conformity with Hamilton's report, the bills had yet to be passed for executing the proposed plan.   A violent opposition to the measure still existed, especially in Virginia; and North Carolina, which had now joined the Union, threw all her members into the same scale, and thus reversed the former majority. Hamilton saw that his great scheme was once more in danger, and that it was of the utmost importance to gain over Jefferson to its support. The steps he took with this view shall be related in Jefferson's own words :—

"As I was going to the President's one day, I met Hamilton in the street. He walked me backwards and forwards before the President's door for half an hour. He painted pathetically the temper into which the Legislature had been wrought; the disgust of those who were called the creditor States; the danger of the secession of their members, and the separation of the States. He observed that the members of the administration ought to act in concert; that, though this question was not of my department, yet a common duty should make it a common concern; that the President was the centre on which all administrative questions ultimately rested, and that all of us should rally around him, and support, with joint efforts, measures approved by him; and that, the question having been lost by a small majority only, it was probable that an appeal from me to the judgment and discretion of some of my friends might effect a change in the vote, and the machine of government, now suspended, might be again set into motion. I told him that I was really a stranger to the whole subject ; that, not having yet informed myself of the system of finance adopted, I knew not how far this was a necessary sequence ; that, undoubtedly, if its rejection endangered a dissolution of our Union at this incipient stage, I should deem that the most unfortunate of all consequences, to avert which all partial and temporary evils should be yielded. I proposed to him, however, to dine with me the next day, and I would invite another friend or two, and bring them into conference together ; and I thought it impossible that reasonable men, consulting together coolly, could fail, by some mutual sacrifices of opinion, to form a compromise which was to save the Union. The discussion took place. I could take no part in it but an exhortatory one, because I was a stranger to the circumstances which should govern it. But it was finally agreed that, whatever importance had been attached to the rejection of this proposition, the preservation of the Union, and of concord among the States, was more important, and that therefore it would be better that the vote of rejection should be rescinded—to effect which some members should change their votes. But it was observed that this pill would be peculiarly bitter to the Southern States, and that some concomitant measure should be adopted, to sweeten it a little to them. There had before been projects to fix the seat of government either at Philadelphia, or at Georgetown, on the Potomac; and it was thought that by giving it to Philadelphia for ten years, and to Georgetown permanently afterwards, this might, as an anodyne, calm in some degree the ferment which might be excited by the other measure alone. So two of the Potomac members (White and Lee, but White with a revulsion of stomach almost convulsive) agreed to change their votes, and Hamilton undertook to carry the other point. In doing this, the influence he had established over the Eastern members, and the agency of Robert Morris with those of the Middle States, effected his side of the engagement."

On Jefferson's own showing, nothing could be fairer than Hamilton's part in this transaction.

What he says about the necessity of the cabinet's acting together would appear to Englishmen a self-evident proposition, and he was clearly justified in offering to yield the less important question of the site of a capital, to the far higher consideration of maintaining the public faith of the Union. Yet Jefferson afterwards charged Hamilton with trickery and *finesse*, in having induced him to bring about this compromise. " It was a fiscal manœuvre," he says, "to which I had most ignorantly and innocently been made to hold the candle." Of Jefferson's *ignorance* of finance, there can indeed be no doubt. He held opinions on that head, which are not only opposed to great principles, but even to common sense and common honesty. He had a theory, that one generation cannot bind another, and that, as by the laws of mortality the majority of grown men gives place to a new majority every nineteen years, no national contract should extend beyond that period. In other words, each generation was to inherit from its predecessors all the advantages of their wealth, and all the triumphs of their skill and industry, but none of their debts, burdens, or obligations. With his usual caution, he did not bring forward this notable doctrine himself, but endeavoured to persuade Madison to adopt it. "At the first blush," he says, "it may be laughed at as the dream of a theorist; but examination will prove it to be solid and salutary."—Madison was in no way inclined to be made the cat's-paw in such a business, and the theory had to slumber undisturbed in the breast of its ingenious author. But he never abandoned it; and, even at a late period of his life, he reverted to the proposition, that no public debt or contract should be binding for more than nineteen years. Surely, Jefferson may fairly claim the merit of being the father of the great system of *repudiation!*

Was he sincere in these strange and startling paradoxes? It is difficult to answer, for he talked wildly on many subjects, and often shifted his ground. Still, there is a certain thread of consistency which runs through all his opinions, and would rather tend to show that he was in earnest. If so, his views much resembled the exaggerated notions of schoolboys—respectable, as the conceptions of young, ardent, inexperienced minds, dazzled by vague dreams of liberty and popular right—but wholly deficient in the elements which constitute the character of a statesman. And among the less

worthy motives which seem to have influenced his
conduct, it is impossible not to recognize a restless
jealousy of those superior natures, with whom he
was brought in contact, and whose gifts were so
different from his own.

Thus, when he had aided Hamilton to pass his
measures, although in a modified form—with the
understanding that Congress was to meet for ten
years at Philadelphia, and then in a new city to
be founded on the confines of Maryland and Virginia
—he appears almost immediately to have repented
of the help he had given him. He saw that those
measures were attended with remarkable success,
and that Hamilton was likely to become a great
power in the state. At once he began to insinuate
suspicions of his intentions. Might not fiscal
schemes be directed to obtain political influence?
Had he not been duped by the Secretary of the
Treasury, and made a tool for forwarding his ambitious views? Was Hamilton really a republican,
and might not the liberties of the country be in
danger from his monarchical tendencies?

From that moment, Jefferson lost no opportunity
of damaging the colleague before whose genius he
stood rebuked. Too proud to conceal his opinions,

and taking little pains to conciliate the prejudices of the people, Hamilton laid himself open to attack by the frankness and boldness of his speech. Resolved to give the republic a fair trial, and having done more than any other man to secure for it the chances of durability, he still avowed his preference for the British Constitution. In the unguarded freedom of after-dinner conversation, he expressed himself strongly, often carelessly. On one occasion, after the cloth was removed, the talk ran upon the government of the mother-country. "Purge it of its corruption," said Adams, "and give to its popular branch equality of representation, and it would be the most perfect constitution ever devised by the wit of man." "Purge it of its corruption," replied Hamilton, "and give to its popular branch equality of representation, and it would become an *impracticable* government; as it stands at present, with all its supposed defects, it is the most perfect government which ever existed."

This was enough for Jefferson. He spread the report everywhere—but only in whispers, to be spoken aloud by others—that the Secretary of the Treasury was in favour of "a monarchy bottomed on corruption." Either he misunderstood Hamilton, or he wilfully misrepresented his meaning. No candid person would have taken those words literally. It was far from Hamilton's intention to defend or justify corruption—no man had combated it more bravely in all its forms—but he held that there was a legitimate mode of exercising personal or political influence, and that such influence ought not to be destroyed, because it was liable to some abuses. He believed that rank and wealth played a necessary and salutary part in the working of the English system—that even rotten boroughs might have their advantages, in giving a voice to minorities, and opening a road for untried talent—and that to attempt to equalize representation, by any such plan as dividing the country into uniform electoral districts, would be to sacrifice the strength and harmony of the British Constitution, to the whims of pedants, and a passion for mere outward symmetry. If he erred, it was in company with some of the wisest of British statesmen; and, although subsequent experience may have proved, that certain reforms in the institutions of the United Kingdom were safe, practicable, and expedient, there is no reason to suppose that it would have altered the main grounds on which he based his opinions.

But it suited Jefferson's purpose to disfigure and exaggerate all this. He invented new words to describe Hamilton and his friends, with a view of throwing discredit on their loyalty to the republic. He called them *monocrats* and *anglomen*, evidently insinuating that their attachment to monarchy and to England was inconsistent with their duty as American citizens. He did all in his power to foster that stupid and vulgar prejudice against the land of their fathers, which has since become so marked a feature in the character of the American populace. And in this, at least, Jefferson's inclinations went along with his policy. He had always disliked England, and it was natural he should dislike her. The country, whose temperate freedom rests on the foundations of habit, experience, and old tradition, and which cherishes, beyond most other lands, the faith in contracts, the respect for authority, and obedience to the supremacy of law, could expect little sympathy from the hollow theorist, whose only rule was submission to the blind will of the people, and who contemplated making a clean sweep every nineteen years, and beginning the world afresh. And the very same motives, which weighed with Jefferson in his dislike for England, contributed to confirm and strengthen his partiality to France. There he saw a people ready to break loose from all their old moorings, and to venture rashly on the untried sea of change. There he found the novelty and excitement, which, for him, had so irresistible a charm. And there he hailed with delight the progress of that destructive spirit, which, acknowledging nothing stable in the present, and nothing venerable in the past, was eager to pull down all that the world had hitherto held . sacred, in the hope of erecting in its stead the idols of a vain philosophy.

Very different was the view which the really great men of America took of the French Revolution. Already in October, 1789, when affairs in France looked bright and promising, Hamilton had thus written to Lafayette:—

" I have seen, with a mixture of pleasure and apprehension, the progress of the events which have lately taken place in your country. As a friend to mankind and to liberty, I rejoice in the efforts you are making to establish it, while I fear much for the final success of the attempt, for the fate of those I esteem who are engaged in it, and for the danger, in case of success, of innovations greater than will consist with the real felicity of your nation. If your affairs still go well when this reaches you, you will ask why this foreboding of ill, when all the appearances have been so much in your favour? I will tell you. I dread disagreements among those who are now united. . . . I dread the vehement character of your people. . . . I dread the interested refractoriness of your nobles. . . . And I dread the reveries of your philosophic politicians, who appear in this moment to have great influence, and who, being mere speculatists, may aim at more refinement than suits either with human nature or the composition of your nation. These, my dear Marquis, are my apprehensions."

"I assure you," writes Washington, at a somewhat later date, "I have often contemplated, with great anxiety, the danger to which you are personally exposed by your peculiar and delicate situation. . . . The tumultuous populace of large cities are ever to be dreaded. Their indiscriminate violence prostrates, for the time, all public authority, and its consequences are sometimes extensive and terrible. In Paris we may suppose these tumults are peculiarly disastrous at this time, when the public mind is in a ferment, and when, as is always the case on such occasions, there are not wanting wicked and designing men whose element is confusion, and who will not hesitate in destroying the public tranquillity to gain a favourite point."

If Lafayette could have profited by the warning of his former chief, and, instead of coquetting with mobs until they became his masters, had resolutely maintained the public peace at any and every risk, it might have been better for his king, his country, and his own fame.

But, as the revolution proceeded with all its violence and terror, Jefferson could only see subjects for admiration. When the unhappy Louis XVI. was brought back a prisoner to Paris, after the flight to Varennes, Jefferson merely remarks: "Such are the fruits of that form of government, which heaps importance on idiots. . . . It would be unfortunate were it in the power of any one man to defeat the issue of so beautiful a revolution!" And when the September massacres had disgusted the outraged humanity of the whole civilized world, it is thus that this amiable philanthropist explains and extenuates the crime:—"In the struggle which was necessary, many guilty persons fell without the forms of trial, and with them some innocent. These I deplore as much as anybody, and shall deplore some of them to the day of my death ; but I deplore them as I should have done had they fallen in battle. It was necessary to use the arm of the people, a machine not quite so blind as balls and bombs, but blind to a certain degree. A few of their cordial friends met at their hands the fate of enemies. But time and truth will rescue and embalm their memories, while their posterity will be enjoying that very liberty, for which they would never have hesitated to offer up their lives. The liberty of the whole earth was depending on the issue of the contest, and was ever such a prize won with so little innocent blood? My own affections have been deeply wounded by some of the martyrs to this cause, but, rather than it should have failed, I would have seen half the earth desolated. *Were there but an Adam and Eve left in every country, and left free, it would be better than as it now is.*"

The mingled folly and ferocity of this passage would almost lead to a doubt of the sanity of the writer, were it not for the sagacity and self-possession with which, at this very time, he conducted his political schemes. They were, indeed, chiefly directed to injure and supplant his rivals ; but, whatever his objects, he showed no want of capacity in adapting means to ends. No stone was left unturned to throw suspicion on the Secretary of the Treasury, and to excite that popular jealousy which, in democratic societies, is the most insidious and fatal of weapons. The assumption of the State obligations, the funding of the debt, the establishment of the National Bank— all the great measures, in fact, which Hamilton had conceived and carried out—were represented as so many steps in a conspiracy, to obtain power by wholesale corruption, and then to betray the republic. But the author of these charges took care not to bring forward the worst of them in his own name. A paper was started, called the *National Gazette*, edited by Philip Freneau, a clerk in Jefferson's office. It contained the most shameless and virulent attacks on the government—always excepting the Secretary of State—spread the alarm of monarchical and aristocratic plots, accused respectable men of bribery and stock-jobbing, gave currency to every absurd rumour affecting the Federalist leaders, and in general set the example of that unscrupulous style of warfare, which has lowered the American press in the eyes of all candid observers. Neither Washington's exalted virtue, nor the unblemished reputation of Mr. Adams, could shield them from these shafts of calumny; but Hamilton was the principal mark at which they were pointed, and to ruin his influence with the public seemed to be the main design of the journalist.

At first, Hamilton treated such charges with the contempt they deserved. For many months he bore the attacks of the *Gazette* without retaliation, although he well knew the hand from which they originated. He continued to meet Jefferson in the cabinet, and was there always prepared to contest with him, on the broad grounds of national honour and interest, the policy of their several measures. But Jefferson had no relish for such close encounters, and already talked of retiring from office. He had won over Randolph to many of his views, while Knox stood firmly by Hamilton, and Washington saw with regret the growing divisions in his cabinet. The President had wished to unite various shades of opinion in the administration, in order to modify the violence of parties, and facilitate the working of the Constitution; but he had not expected these radical differences, and still less these extremes of personal antipathy. He complained to Jefferson of the gross unfairness of the democratic press, and especially of those articles which tended to excite hatred against the government, and had actually led in Pennsylvania to an illegal combination to resist the spirit-tax. Without identifying himself with these articles, Jefferson endeavoured to excuse them, as directed against the Treasury department only. But Washington refused to accept this explanation, or to separate himself from the acts of his Minister of Finance. " In condemning the administration," he said, " they condemn me ; for, if they thought these were measures pursued contrary to my sentiments, they must conceive me too careless to attend to them, or too stupid to understand them."

Still the attacks went on, and, at length, Hamilton lost patience. In a letter, signed *An American*, he denounced " an experiment somewhat new in the history of political manœuvres in this country ; a newspaper instituted by a public officer, and the editor of it regularly pensioned with the public money in the disposal of that officer."—He asked whether it was possible " that Mr. Jefferson, the head of a principal department of the government, could be the patron of a paper, the evident object of which was to decry the government and its measures ? If he disapproves of the government itself," continues the writer, "and thinks it deserving of his opposition, can he reconcile it to his own personal dignity, and the principles of probity, to hold an office under it, and employ the means of official influence in that opposition? If he disapproves of the leading measures which have been adopted in the course of his administration, can he reconcile it with the principles of delicacy and propriety to hold a place in that administration, and at the same time to be instrumental in vilifying measures, which have been adopted by majorities of both branches of the Legislature, and sanctioned by the chief magistrate of the Union?"

The blow told; for, in spite of an affidavit from Mr. Freneau that he was acting quite independently of the Secretary of State, most people believed in the substantial truth of Hamilton's accusation. Anxious to avoid a violent rupture, which he believed would be detrimental to the public interests, Washington wrote to both the Secretaries, urging them to mutual concessions. Both sent letters in reply, which are very characteristic of the two men. Jefferson repeats the old nonsense, that his difference with Hamilton arose entirely from the attempts of the latter to establish a system adverse to liberty, and "calculated to undermine and demolish the republic, by creating an influence of his department over the members of the Legislature." He adds, that he is about shortly to retire from the administration; that he looks to that event "with the longing of a wave-worn mariner," and that "his main object during the residue of his term will be to wind up the business of his office—reserving until that time his defence under his own name, by a public appeal, which he hopes will not be necessary." And he concludes by declaring that he "will not suffer his retirement to be clouded by the slanders of a man whose history, from the moment at which history can stoop to notice him, is a tissue of machinations against the liberty of the country, which has not only received and given him bread, but heaped its honours on his head."—Hamilton, on the contrary, frankly avows that he has been driven into retaliation by personal attacks, which were intended to make himself and his department odious, and to subvert his measures. He has considered it his duty "to endeavour to resist the torrent, and, as an essential mean to this end, to draw aside the veil from the principal actors." He thinks that events will prove he has judged rightly. "Nevertheless," he concludes, " I pledge my honour to you, sir, that, if you shall hereafter form a plan to reunite the members of your administration, upon some steady principle of co-operation, I will faithfully concur in executing it during my continuance in office. And I will not, directly or indirectly, say or do a thing that shall endanger a feud."

Whilst Hamilton was thus defending himself from the assaults of a colleague, Aaron Burr, his old rival at the bar, was gradually making his way to political distinction. Already in January, 1791, he was elected in opposition to General Schuyler to represent New York in the Senate of the United States. His success appears to have caused some surprise at the time, and was probably the result of a coalition of parties. Be that as it may, it was soon felt on both sides that his support was worth gaining, and Jefferson seems to have courted him assiduously. But Burr's game was to belong to no party for the present, to act independently of all, and to wait for the chapter of accidents. He knew that Washington disliked, and that Hamilton distrusted him ; but circumstances might oblige them to accept his alliance, and he was too able a man not to estimate the value of their moral influence. It would not have been difficult, perhaps, to secure his aid to the President and to the Federalist party; and there can be no doubt that Jefferson would have found in him the most formidable of opponents. He could plot and counter-plot more effectually than the Secretary of State; he had the courage to face the multitude, and the craft to lead them; he exercised a personal fascination over many men, and almost all women. The one obstacle, that stood in the way of his junction with the Federalists, was the invincible repugnance of Hamilton to offer him the right hand of fellowship.

It would be a mistake to suppose that Hamilton undervalued Burr's talents. It was because he rated them highly that he believed him to be so dangerous a man. He would not trust him with power, because he feared its abuse in those bold and dexterous hands. When, therefore, Burr was proposed as Governor of New York in April, 1792, and the votes of the Federalist party would have carried his election, Hamilton refused his sanction, and the candidate was forced to retire. From that time, Burr drew closer to the avowed opponents of the government, and adopted the watch-words of the extreme Republican faction. In the *Answers* to some of Jefferson's charges, which Hamilton addressed to Washington in the August of the same year, there occurs a passage which evidently alludes to Burr: " The only path to a subversion of the republican system of this country is, by flattering the prejudices of the people, and exciting their jealousies and apprehensions, to throw affairs into confusion, and bring on civil commotion. Tired at length of anarchy or want of government, they may take shelter in the arms of monarchy for repose and security. Those, then, who resist a confirmation of public order are the true artificers of monarchy. Not that this is the intention of the generality of them. Yet it would not be difficult to lay the finger upon some of their party, who may justly be suspected. When a man, unprincipled in private life, desperate in his fortune, bold in his temper, possessed of considerable talents, having the advantage of military habits, despotic in his ordinary demeanour, known to have scoffed in private at the principles of liberty—when such a man is seen to mount the hobby-horse of popularity, to join in the cry of danger to liberty, to take every opportunity of embarrassing the general government and bringing it under suspicion, to flatter and fall in with all the nonsense of the zealots of the day—it may justly be suspected that his object is to throw things into confusion, that he may *ride the storm and direct the whirlwind.*"

But a more important election than that of Governor of New York was approaching. Washington's first term of office had nearly expired, and the choice of a President and Vice-President was again in question. Alarmed at the gathering tempests in the political horizon, the universal voice of the country once more silenced the whispers of faction, and all parties united to call the great pilot to the helm. But those, who dared not attack Washington, resolved to oppose the re-election of Adams, and Burr was now mentioned as a candidate for the Vice-Presidency. Other names were in the field, and, in the complication of jarring interests, Burr had reason to hope for the support of Federalist votes. But again Hamilton interposed. "I am mistaken," he said, "if it be not Burr's object to play the game of confusion, and I feel it a religious duty to oppose his career. Mr. Adams is the man who will be supported by the friends of the government. They reason thus :—Mr. Adams, like other men, has his faults and foibles—some of the opinions he is supposed to entertain we do not approve—but we believe him to be honest, firm, faithful and independent, a sincere lover of his country, a real friend to genuine liberty, combining his attachment to that with love of order and stable government. No man's private character can be fairer than his. No man has given stronger proofs of disinterested and intrepid patriotism." The views of Hamilton prevailed, and Adams was re-elected by a small majority.

And now the Secretary of State began to reconsider his resolution to withdraw from office. He had tried a last effort to drive Hamilton from his post, by instigating an inquiry into the affairs of the Treasury, in Congress, and endeavouring to cast imputations on the probity of the rival minister. The result had been a triumphant refutation of every charge, and the House had confirmed the opinion of Boudinot, that the Secretary of the Treasury "was free from even a suspicion of malconduct in the whole transaction." Then Jefferson reflected, that for him to retire would be to leave Hamilton victorious and powerful, and he expressed his willingness, if the President had made no arrangements to the contrary, to continue in the cabinet somewhat longer—" how long he could not say, perhaps the summer, perhaps the autumn." If Washington consented to this proposal, it was, that he still hoped to control the violence of faction, and to prevent a convulsion at home, in the face of the innumerable dangers which threatened the peace of the world.

CHAPTER XIII.

THE FRENCH ENVOY.

THE year 1793 opened under the darkest auspices. The judicial murder of Louis XVI. was followed by the French declaration of war against England, and by the commencement of a contest that was to shake all the corners of the globe. The wise and good men of America beheld with dismay the rise of a new republic, whose creed was atheism, and whose foundations were laid in blood. The king, who had aided them in their struggle for liberty, had perished on the scaffold; the friends, who had fought by their side, were in exile or in prison; the principles they had loved and cherished were degraded by the foul caricature of a mad and impious anarchy. To such men as Washington and Hamilton, the state of France could only be a subject for deep regret, and their chief anxiety was to avert from their own country the evils of so pernicious an example.

Very different was the mood in which Jefferson
watched the progress of events, and received intelligence of each new piece of Jacobin frenzy. He
could see nothing objectionable in the excesses of
republican zeal, and was always ready to extenuate
crimes that were committed in the name of liberty,
equality, and fraternity. Freneau and the *National
Gazette* were employed to excite the popular mind
in favour of France, the execution of the king was
described as "a great act of justice," and the expression of pity for his fate was represented as
"the shriek of a monarchical junto." Every art
was used to stimulate the unworthy prejudice against
England, to stigmatize her as the champion of the
tyrants and despots of Europe, and to sow the seeds
of a lasting enmity between two kindred races of
freemen.

The treaty which France had concluded with the
United States, during the course of the War of
Independence, was entitled "a treaty of alliance
eventual and defensive;" and it now became a
question whether, under its provisions, America
might not be bound to assist France in the present
crisis. "Now is the time," wrote Jefferson to
Madison, "for America to show her gratitude to

her friendly ally, France; now is the time to assist in the struggles of liberty." And if this language could be held by a person in the responsible position of Secretary of State, it is no wonder that the excited populace were ready to put the most forced and violent construction on the national obligations. Hamilton saw the danger that America might be dragged into a war with half the world, for interests that were not hers, and objects which she could not in sober reason approve. It was his opinion that, in acknowledging the French Republic as a government *de facto*, America should reserve to herself the right to consider the applicability of the treaty to the changed situation of the contracting parties. And he urged upon Washington that, before receiving a minister from the French Convention, it would be expedient to publish a Declaration of Neutrality with regard to the war now raging between France and Great Britain.

A stormy, and most important cabinet-council followed. Jefferson opposed the Declaration of Neutrality, but, with his usual cunning, based his objections less on the measure itself, than on the want of power in the President to take such a step without the consent of Congress. In the discussion which ensued, Hamilton tore his arguments to pieces, and scattered them to the winds. The author and interpreter of the Constitution knew too well the just limits of the executive authority to be beaten on such a point. His opinion prevailed, and a proclamation was issued by the President "forbidding the citizens of the United States to take part in any hostilities on the seas, with or against any of the belligerent powers; warning them against carrying to any such powers any of those articles deemed contraband according to the modern usage of nations; and enjoining them from all acts and proceedings inconsistent with the duties of a friendly nation towards those at war."

While these affairs were in progress at Philadelphia, now the seat of government, Edmond Charles Genet, or *Citizen Genet* as he called himself, minister from the French Republic to the United States of America, had landed at Charleston, in South Carolina. He was a brother of Madame Campan, well known as a trusted attendant on Marie Antoinette, and, probably through the interest of his sister, had experienced many acts of kindness from the royal family. He obtained, at an early age, a commission in the dragoons, and was afterwards attached to various legations; but, when the fortunes of his patrons changed, Genet was not the man to follow them to the prison or the scaffold. He discovered, indeed, that his patriotism required him to declare strongly on the other side, and he so far gained the confidence of the revolutionary government as to be selected for the important mission to America. There can be no doubt that his instructions were to take every advantage of the popular feeling, whether sanctioned or not by the chief magistrate, and to use any means, however extraordinary, to implicate the United States in the general war.

He is described as a young man "of a good person, with a fine ruddy complexion, always in a bustle, and more like a busy man than a man of business." He was fond of talking and boasting, and seems rather to have undervalued the penetration of the Americans. "His system is, I think," says one of Hamilton's friends, "to laugh us into the war, if he can." His object in landing at Charleston, instead of at the seat of government, was to receive a popular ovation before presenting his credentials, and, if possible, to involve the American people in his designs. The very day after his arrival, intoxicated by the warmth of his reception, and presuming on the support of the democracy, he began to issue commissions for fitting out privateers against British commerce, and ordered the French Consul at Charleston to establish a Court of Admiralty to adjudicate upon the captures. Thus American vessels, manned by American seamen, were armed and equipped in an American port, under the authority of a foreign minister, to make war upon a friendly nation—and that very minister was to appoint the tribunal that was to decide on the validity of the prizes!

The impudence of these pretensions did not cool the enthusiasm of the populace, and Genet's progress through the country was a continued triumph. His arrival at Philadelphia was celebrated by public rejoicings, in which red caps, and trees of liberty, and fraternal embraces, might have almost made him fancy himself back in Paris. Of course, Jefferson looked on approvingly; but Hamilton was filled with disgust and indignation. "It cannot be without danger and inconvenience to our interests," he says, "to impress on the nations of Europe an idea, that we are actuated by the same spirit which has for some time past fatally misguided the measures of those who conduct the affairs of France, and sullied a cause once glorious, and that might have been triumphant. The cause of France is compared with that of America during its late revolution. Would to heaven that the comparison were just! Would to heaven that we could discern, in the mirror of French affairs, the same humanity, the same decorum, the same gravity, the same order, the same dignity, the same solemnity which distinguished the course of the American Revolution! Clouds and darkness would not then rest upon the issue, as they now do.

"I own I do not like the comparison. When I contemplate the horrid and systematic massacres of the second and third of September; when I observe that a Marat and a Robespierre, the notorious prompters of those bloody scenes, sit triumphantly in the Convention, and take a conspicuous part in its measures—and that an attempt to bring the assassins to justice has been obliged to be abandoned; when I see an unfortunate prince, whose reign was a continued demonstration of the goodness and benevolence of his heart, and of his attachment to the people of whom he was the monarch—who, though educated in the lap of despotism, had given repeated proofs that he was not the enemy of liberty

—brought precipitately and ignominiously to the block, without any substantial proof of guilt as yet disclosed—without even an authentic exhibition of motives, in decent regard to the opinions of mankind; when I find the doctrines of atheism openly advanced in the Convention, and heard with loud applauses; when I see the sword of fanaticism extended to force a political creed upon citizens, who were invited to submit to the arms of France as the harbingers of liberty; when I behold the hand of rapacity outstretched to prostrate and ravish the monuments of religious worship, erected by those citizens and their ancestors; when I perceive passion, tumult, and violence usurping those seats where reason and cool deliberation ought to preside—I acknowledge that I am glad to believe there is no real resemblance, between what was the cause of America, and what is the cause of France—that the difference is no less great than that between liberty and licentiousness. I regret whatever has a tendency to confound them; and I feel anxious, as an American, that the ebullitions of inconsiderate men among us may not tend to involve our reputation in the issue."

But Hamilton was not content with protesting against the follies of the mob. Practical questions were forcing themselves on the attention of the cabinet, and he was ever at his post to support the cause of public faith and the law of nations. Genet's cruisers had brought prizes into port, and one British vessel had been actually captured in American waters. The English minister demanded restitution, and Hamilton was clearly of opinion that it should at once be granted. Jefferson agreed to restore the ship captured in American waters, but demurred to all the rest. He thought the other questions should be left to the ordinary courts. Hamilton argued, on the contrary, that the acts of the French envoy involved a *national* injury and affront, which the *government* of the United States was bound to redress, on pain of being regarded as an associate of France, and a party to the war. "It is the case," he said, "of an infringement of our sovereignty to the prejudice of a third party;" and he held that it must be settled "by reasons of state," as well as by "rules of law." Knox sided with Hamilton, but Randolph adhered to Jefferson's opinion. The cabinet was equally divided, and the point was reserved for further deliberation. But Washington insisted that the foreign ministers should at once be officially informed, that he would take effectual measures "to prevent the future commissioning, equipping, and manning of vessels in American ports, to cruise against any of the belligerent powers."

And now Genet presented his credentials, and was received by Washington with a calm and dignified courtesy. The impetuous Frenchman complained of the coldness of his reception, and sought the congenial sympathy of the Secretary of State. " It is impossible," writes Jefferson, " for anything to be more affectionate, more magnanimous, than the purport of his mission ; " and forthwith he proceeds to make this foreigner his confidant in all his suspicions and jealousies of his colleagues and countrymen. No wonder that Genet looked on Washington as the tool of a *coterie,* and believed he could set him at defiance, by appealing to the people against the President. He determined to adopt a tone unprecedented in the intercourse of a diplomatic agent with a sovereign state, and which neither his native insolence, nor the absurdities of his Jacobin masters will explain, without those " useful hints respecting men in office," which he boasts to have derived from Jefferson.

Pursuant to the President's resolution, two Americans, who had embarked on one of the privateers, were brought on shore and sent to prison. Genet denounced this act in the most extravagant terms. "The crime laid to their charge," he says, "the crime which my mind cannot conceive, and which my pen almost refuses to state, is the serving of France, and defending with her children the common and glorious cause of Liberty!" And he proceeds to demand the instant release of the prisoners. The government refused to comply, but Genet was not discouraged. Availing himself of the temporary absence of Washington from Philadelphia, he caused the *Little Sarah*, a British merchant vessel captured by a French privateer, to be armed, equipped, and manned as a cruiser, and her name to be changed to that of the *Petit Démocrat*. The Governor of Pennsylvania, informed that this vessel was about to put to sea, sent his secretary to Genet to request him to detain her until the return of the President. The Frenchman flew into a violent passion, declared that the President was not the sovereign of the country, threatened to appeal to the people, and added that he expected the arrival of three ships of the line, and that he was prepared to repel force by force. On this menace, the Governor called out a portion of the militia, and communicated the affair to the cabinet. Jefferson at once undertook to arrange matters amicably with the envoy. He endeavoured to persuade him to await the return of the President; and when Genet repeated, that the President was not the sovereign, Jefferson explained to him that the Constitution had left to the executive the carrying out of laws and treaties. The Frenchman only shrugged his shoulders, and said "he would not compliment Mr. Jefferson on such a Constitution!" He declined to give any pledge as to the departure of the vessel; but he assured Mr. Jefferson that she was not in a state of readiness, and was going to fall down the river to complete her equipment. "But let me beseech you," he added, "not to permit any attempt to put men on board of her. She is filled with high-spirited patriots, and they will unquestionably resist. And there is no occasion; for I tell you she will not be ready to depart for some time."—On this, Jefferson expressed himself satisfied, and the Governor dismissed the militia!

When Hamilton heard of what had happened, he took a very different view of the question. He saw that the honour of the country was concerned, and his advice was to plant guns immediately on Mud Island, with orders to stop the departure of the vessel, by firing on her if she attempted to pass. But this obvious precaution was far too simple for Jefferson. He was sure that the vessel would not sail, and, if she did, he conjured up all sorts of imaginary dangers from trying to stop her. She would resist the attempt, and other French ships would arrive and join in the conflict. A war would ensue, the kings of the earth would be gratified by the unnatural spectacle of a contest between two republics, and the hopes of man would receive the last mortal stab from the hands of the friends of liberty! While Jefferson was talking this nonsense, the *Petit Démocrat* dropped down the stream, and ultimately sailed in open defiance of the government. Meanwhile, Washington returned to Philadelphia, and instantly wrote to Jefferson:—"What is to be done in the case of the *Little Sarah?* Is the minister of the French Republic to set the acts of this government at defiance with impunity, and then threaten the executive with an appeal to the people? What must the world think of such conduct, and of the government of the United States in submitting to it?" Jefferson could only reply, that he had received assurances from the French minister that the vessel would not depart before the President's decision.

But, although a cabinet-council was held the next day on the subject, it was too late to take any effective measures to prevent the sailing, and the *Petit Démocrat*, true to her name, proceeded on her cruise in contempt of all lawful authority.

It was in the midst of the excitement caused by these events, that Hamilton had once more recourse to his fertile and powerful pen, and in a series of letters, signed *Pacificus*, entered into a full justification of the policy of neutrality, as understood by himself, and adopted by the President. In the clear and forcible statement and elucidation of sound principles, as distinguished from vague assertions and popular clamour, these letters are only second in importance to the *Federalist*. They were written, he says, to counteract " attempts very dangerous to the peace, and, it is to be feared, not very friendly to the Constitution of the United States ; " and they undertook to answer, one by one, all the objections urged against the Proclamation of Neutrality and its consequences. They showed that the President, being charged with the executive power, was bound to guard against the infringement of the law of nations as well as the municipal law; and that it was his duty to prevent the country's being made responsible for acts done by its citizens, without the privity or connivance of the government, in contravention of the principles of neutrality. The Proclamation was, therefore, a warning to American citizens, and also indirectly a notification to foreign powers of the intentions of the government. And in this there was no usurpation of authority, for, although the legislature had reserved to itself the right to declare war, it was obvious that, until it did so, it was the province and duty of the executive to maintain peace. But it had been objected, that the Proclamation was contrary to treaties with France. It was said, that a defensive alliance existed between the two nations, and that America was bound to assist France in the present war. Now a defensive alliance implies, that the stipulated assistance is only to be given, when one of the allies is engaged in a *defensive*, and not in an *offensive* war. But the nation which commences hostilities, from whatever cause, is held to make an offensive war; and there could be no doubt that France first declared and began war against Austria, Prussia, Savoy, Holland, England, and Spain.

The cause or occasion of the war, and the war itself, are things entirely distinct. The first who

takes up arms, whether justly or unjustly, commences an offensive war; and France, being on the
offensive, could not claim the assistance of the
United States under the treaty. But it was objected
that, although the war might be offensive in point of
form, yet in point of principle it was defensive; that,
in each instance, it was a mere anticipation of medi-
tated attacks, and justified by previous aggressions of
the opposite parties. In answer to this, Hamilton
argued, that a legal and positive obligation must be
construed strictly, by certain rules, and not by vague
matters of opinion; and that the abstract justice of a
war cannot bind any nation to engage in it, when its
formal obligations do not enjoin it to do so. But,
even if this were not the true doctrine, an impartial
examination would prove that France was not blameless in the circumstances which led to the war; that,
if she received, she also gave cause of offence; and
that the justice of the war on her side was, in some
cases, not a little problematical.

Hamilton then proceeded to comment on those
acts of the French nation, which had given such
general and serious cause of alarm in foreign countries—more especially the interference between the
government and people of other states, and the

attempt to excite revolution beyond the limits of France. He showed how *impolitic* it would be for America to involve herself in such a quarrel, unless absolutely forced to it by the letter of her bond. But it was objected that, if not opposed to the treaty, the Proclamation was yet inconsistent with gratitude to France, for services rendered during the war of independence. On this subject of gratitude, Hamilton entered into a strict and searching investigation of the claims thus confidently advanced, and what he thought of them may be gathered from the following passage :—

" France, the rival from time immemorial of Great Britain, had, in the course of the war which ended in 1763, suffered from the successful arms of the latter the severest losses and the most mortifying defeats. Britain from that moment had acquired an ascendant in the affairs of Europe and in the commerce of the world, too decided and too humiliating to be endured without extreme impatience, and an eager desire of finding a favourable opportunity to destroy it, and to repair the breach which had been made in the national glory. The animosity of wounded pride conspired with calculations of interest to give a keen edge to that impatience and to that desire.

"The American Revolution offered the occasion. It early attracted the notice of France, though with extreme circumspection. As far as countenance and aid may be presumed to have been given, prior to the epoch of the acknowledgment of our independence, it will be no unkind derogation to assert, that they were marked neither with liberality, nor with vigour; that they wore the appearance rather of a desire to keep alive disturbances which might embarrass a rival, than of a serious design to assist a revolution, or a serious expectation that it could be effected.

"The victories of Saratoga, the capture of an army, which went a great way towards deciding the issue of the contest, decided also the hesitations of France. They established, in the government of that country, a confidence of our ability to accomplish our purpose, and, as a consequence of it, produced the treaties of alliance and commerce.

"It is impossible to see in all this anything more than the conduct of a jealous competitor, embracing a most promising opportunity to repress the pride and diminish the power of a dangerous rival, by seconding a successful resistance to its authority, with the object of lopping off a valuable portion of its dominions. The dismemberment of this country from Great Britain was an obvious, and a very important interest of France. It cannot be doubted, that this was both the determining motive, and an adequate compensation for the assistance afforded to us.

" Men of sense, in this country, derived encouragement to the part which their zeal for liberty prompted them to take in our revolution, from the probability of the co-operation of France and Spain. It will be remembered, that this argument was used in the publications of the day ; but upon what was it bottomed ? Upon the known competition between those nations and Great Britain, upon their evident interest to reduce her power and circumscribe her empire ; not certainly upon motives of regard to our interest, or of attachment to our cause. Whoever should have alleged the latter, as the grounds of the expectation held out, would have been then justly considered as a visionary or a deceiver. And whoever shall now ascribe to such motives the aid which we did receive would not deserve to be viewed in a better light.

" The inference from these facts is not obscure. Aid and co-operation, founded upon a great interest pursued and obtained by a party rendering them, is not a proper stock upon which to engraft that enthusiastic gratitude, which is claimed from us by those who love France more than the United States."

Hamilton admitted, however, that France, though acting from motives of policy, had not taken advantage of the situation of America to extort from her any humiliating or injurious concessions, and that she was therefore entitled to claim, not indeed the extraordinary sacrifices proposed, but the friendship, esteem, and good offices of her allies. But then came the question, to whom were these chiefly due—to the unfortunate prince, by whom the assistance was given, or to the nation, of which he was the head? Louis XVI. had at the time the sole power of directing the will of France, the sole legal right of deciding to assist America, and, if there was kindness in the decision, the kindness was his. If the concurrent testimony of the period may be credited, there was no man more personally friendly to the cause of America than Louis XVI. The repeated declarations of Franklin proved this fact. And yet the very men, who were so loud in their expressions of gratitude to France, were ready to consign to the flames all those who gave a sigh of sympathy or regret to the fate of that unhappy monarch. Could it consist with justice or humanity, thus to partake in the angry and vindictive passions excited against him? Was it a crime in him to have been born a prince? Could this circumstance forfeit his title to the commiseration due to his misfortunes as a man?

"But complete justice," continues Hamilton, "would not be done to this question of gratitude, were no notice to be taken of the address which has appeared in the public papers, from the Convention of France to the United States, announcing the appointment of the present minister plenipotentiary. In that address the Convention informs us, *that the support which the ancient French Court had afforded the United States to recover their independence was only the fruit of a base speculation; that their glory offended its ambitious views, and the ambassadors of France bore the criminal orders for stopping the career of their prosperity.*

"If this information is to be admitted in the full force of the terms, it is very fatal to the claim of gratitude towards France. . . . If the organ of the nation, on whose will the aid which was given

depended, acted not only from motives irrelative to
our advantage, but from unworthy motives, or, as
is alleged, from a base speculation; if afterwards
he displayed a temper hostile to the confirmation
of our security and prosperity—he acquired no title
to our gratitude in the first instance, or he forfeited
it in the second. And the people of France, who
can only demand it in virtue of the conduct of
their agent, must, together with him, renounce the
pretension. It is an obvious principle, that, if a
nation can claim merit from the good deeds of its
sovereign, it must answer for the demerit of his
misdeeds.

"The truth probably is, that the base speculation
charged amounts to nothing more, than that the
government of France, in affording us assistance,
was actuated by the motives which have been
attributed to it—namely, the desire of promoting
the interest of France, by lessening the power of
Great Britain, and opening a new channel of commerce to herself; that the orders said to have been
given to the ambassadors of France, to stop the
career of our prosperity, are resolvable into a
speculative jealousy of the ministers of the day,
lest the United States, by becoming as powerful

and great as they are capable of being under an efficient government, might prove formidable to the European possessions in America. With these qualifications, the address offers no new discovery to the intelligent and unbiassed friends of their country. They knew long· ago, that the interest of France had been the governing motive of the aid afforded ; and they saw clearly enough in the conversation and conduct of her agents, while the present Constitution of the United States was under consideration, that the government, of which they were the instruments, would have preferred our remaining under the old form. They perceived also, that these views had their effect upon some of the devoted partisans of France among ourselves ; as they now perceive, that the same characters are embodying, with all the aid they can obtain, under the same banner, to resist the operation of that government of which they withstood the establishment.

"All this was and is seen ; and the body of the people of America are too discerning to be long in the dark about it. Too wise to have been misled by foreign or domestic machinations, they adopted a Constitution which was necessary to their safety and to their happiness ; too wise still to be ensnared by the same machinations, they will support the government they have established, and will take care of their own peace, in spite of the insidious efforts which are employed to detach them from the one, and to disturb the other.

"The information, which the address of the Convention contains, ought to serve as an instructive lesson to the people of this country. It ought to teach us not to overrate foreign friendships, and to be upon our guard against foreign attachments. The former will generally be found hollow and delusive ; the latter will have a natural tendency to lead us aside from our own true interest, and to make us the dupes of foreign influence. Both serve to introduce a principle of action, which, in its effects, if the expression may be allowed, is antinational. Foreign influence is truly the Grecian horse to a republic. We cannot be too careful to exclude its entrance. Nor ought we to imagine that it can only make its approaches in the gross form of direct bribery. It is then most dangerous when it comes under the patronage of our passions, under the auspices of national prejudice and partiality."

These *Letters of Pacificus* had a great effect. They convinced and carried with them the sober and enlightened part of the community, and provoked in proportion the rage and animosity of the agitators. The authorship was not concealed, and the Secretary of the Treasury was attacked with the utmost fury. He was called the "Votary of Despotism," the "Abettor of Carthaginian Faith," the "Arnold of his country." Washington was emphatically warned, that he must disentangle himself from the meshes of enemies and traitors to liberty, on pain of forfeiting the respect and confidence of the people. A public meeting in honour of France was held at Philadelphia, and Genet, growing bolder with this encouragement, caused the walls to be placarded with bills, inviting all able-bodied seamen to enlist in the service of the French republic. In the American sea-ports, the tri-coloured flag floated above the national ensign, French ships lay moored along the coast, and French privateers issued forth to plunder the commerce of friendly nations. Under these circumstances the cabinet again met, and this time Jefferson became alarmed at his own work. Slowly, but surely, the real voice of the country, as distinguished from the shouts of the rabble, was beginning to make itself heard. The bulk of Americans might be deceived by demagogues, or bewildered by theorists, but they had yet too much Saxon blood in their veins to submit quietly to be bearded by an insolent foreigner. The reaction had set in, and Jefferson at once yielded to the stream. It was resolved *unanimously*, that restitution of prizes illegally taken should be made in every case, and that the French nation should be held responsible for damages. It was also determined, that a statement of Genet's proceedings should be laid before the government of France, accompanied by a request for his recall. The Secretary of State was compelled, however reluctantly, to communicate the views of the cabinet to the French Minister.

When the *Letters of Pacificus* first appeared, Jefferson had urged Madison to take up his pen in answer; and that versatile statesman, once the ally of Hamilton in the battle for the Constitution, but now the instrument of the opposite faction, had published a series of essays under the signature of *Helvidius*, directed against the form and substance of the Proclamation of Neutrality. With curious consistency, Jefferson could thus write to Madison only a few weeks after :—" I believe it will be true wisdom in the Republican party to approve unequivocally of a state of Neutrality; to avoid little cavils about who should declare it; to abandon Genet entirely, with expressions of strong friendship and adherence to his nation, and confidence that he has acted against their sense. In this way *we shall keep the people on our side*, by keeping ourselves in the right. I have been myself under a cruel dilemma with him. I adhered to him as long as I could have a hope of getting him right, *because I knew what weight we should derive to our side*, by keeping in it the love of the people for the French cause and nation, and how important it was to ward off from that cause and nation any just grounds of alienation. Finding at length that the man was incorrigible, I saw the necessity of quitting a wreck which would but sink all who should cling to it. It is determined to insist on his recall, and I am preparing a statement of his conduct to be laid before the Executive Council."

But Jefferson, like other magicians, had raised a demon whom it was not so easy to quell. Genet refused to be put down by the changed demeanour of the Secretary of State. He repaired to New York, and began a new career of agitation; he addressed a letter to the President, surpassing in effrontery all his former productions; and he openly accused Jefferson of betraying him, after pretending to be his friend, and "initiating him into mysteries which had inflamed his hatred against all those who aspire to absolute power." It must have been hard for Jefferson to be told, that it was not in Genet's character, "to speak, as many people do, in one way and act in another—to have an official language, and a language confidential"—and it must have been still harder to have all his own principles thrown in his teeth, and to be denounced as an associate of aristocrats, and a tool of the partisans of England!

In the midst of these tumultuous scenes, Hamilton fell ill of yellow fever, and was for some time in extreme danger. He was forced to retire to Albany to recruit his strength, and it was only late in the autumn that he returned to Philadelphia. He found, however, that, during his absence, the policy he had so warmly advocated—the policy of reason, justice, and honour—had been rapidly making progress. The best men of the nation, not yet deprived of all influence in the state, were once more rallying round the President. The *Letters of*

Pacificus had borne fruit, and, when Congress re-assembled, Washington's public censure of the acts of the French minister was received with general approbation.

It was in this position of affairs, that Jefferson was seized with an intense desire for retirement and philosophic leisure. As if to signalize his withdrawal from office, by something more credit-able than his late performances, he produced a very able report on the commercial relations of the country, in which he pointed out the various restrictions and prohibitions that embarrassed the trade of America, and suggested either friendly arrangements with foreign nations to remove them, or else a system of countervailing duties. Allowing for the notions of commercial policy then in vogue, and a certain latent prepossession against England, this document appears to have had considerable merit, and went far to redeem the reputation of its author. It was to have been his last act, but his old friend Genet would not let him depart in peace. The restless envoy now sent him translations of the instructions of the French Government, and desired, that the President should lay them officially before Congress, adding that he would furnish him in succession with copies of other papers for the same purpose. Jefferson wished to escape the responsibility of answering this offensive letter; but Washington expressed a strong wish that the reply should bear the signature of the Secretary of State, and it was sent accordingly, in these terms:—"I have it in charge to observe that your functions, as the missionary of a foreign nation here, are confined to the transaction of the affairs of your nation with the Executive of the United States; that the communications, which are to pass between the executive and legislative branches, cannot be a subject for your interference; and that the President must be left to judge for himself what matters his duty or the public good may require him to propose to the deliberations of Congress. I have, therefore, the honour of returning you the copies sent for distribution, and of being with great respect, sir, your most obedient and most humble servant."— Such was the end of that famous political friendship, and of all those wonderful raptures of international enthusiasm!

The parting words of Jefferson to Washington were: "I carry into my retirement a lively sense of your goodness, and shall continue gratefully to remember it."—Mr. Randolph succeeded him as Secretary of State, and Mr. William Bradford, of Pennsylvania, became Attorney-General.

But they had not yet done with Genet. It was discovered that he had sent emissaries to Kentucky (then lately admitted as a State of the Union) to enrol American citizens for an attack on the Spanish possessions in the South, and that he was trying to organize a similar expedition in Carolina and Georgia. A cabinet-council was summoned, in which it was determined to supersede his functions, and deprive him of the privileges of an envoy; and Hamilton was charged to prepare a message to Congress in justification of the measure. Before it could be executed, however, news arrived from France that Genet was recalled from his mission, and that all his acts were disavowed by the Committee of Public Safety, then sitting in Paris. Condemned for the failure of intrigues, which would have been sanctioned if successful, Genet was too wise a man to trust himself to the tender mercies of his beloved republic. He had no ambition to finish his career on the scaffold, and preferred the safety of a private life in America, to the honours of an ex-minister, and the chances of the guillotine at home. He became a citizen of the United States, and so passed away into obscurity, leaving the reputation of perhaps the *most impudent diplomatist* that was ever employed by one nation to force its designs upon another.

CHAPTER XIV.

PARTY VIOLENCE.

THE great man who held the highest post in America, and the great minister who so ably seconded his views, had thus far maintained their position against every attack. But those who could neither confute them in argument, nor circumvent them in policy, had yet a weapon which they could use with impunity against them, because it was one with which brave and honest men scorned to soil their hands—and that weapon was calumny.

In the years which followed the retirement of Jefferson from office, nothing is more remarkable than the persevering, unscrupulous, and almost savage spirit, in which the most eminent characters in the Union were assailed by anonymous writers. It was not only their public measures which were properly and fairly made the subjects for criticism, but their secret motives, and the purity of their personal honour, their domestic relations, and all the sanctities of private life, were rudely and indecently called in question. The democratic press of America seemed to have cast aside all the restraints of civilized society, and to be acting the part of common assassins, ready to stab in the dark without either hesitation or remorse. There is no blacker stain on the history of free states than the base, cowardly, and infamous conduct of these literary bravoes, unless it be the occult influence which prompted their efforts, and the condition of public opinion which could for a moment endure them.

It is impossible to determine what share Jefferson and the Republican leaders had in these outrages, but there is too much reason to suspect that they approved and encouraged them. From his retirement at Monticello (his favourite retreat) the philosopher, who had expressed his intention of detaching his mind from politics, and devoting himself wholly to rural pursuits, wrote letters filled with the wildest fanaticism, and took the warmest interest in every movement of faction. " I cannot but hope," says the gentle sage, in one of his epistles, " that the triumph of the French, and the consequent disgrace of the invading tyrants, is destined in the order of events to kindle the wrath of the people of Europe against those who have dared to embroil them in such wickedness, and to bring at length kings, nobles, and priests to the scaffolds which they have been so long deluging with human blood."—At the same time, he was constantly giving his opinion on American affairs, and repeating his old charges against the Federalists. He was in the habit of familiar intercourse with Madison, and wrote and talked freely to other leading politicians; but it seems likely that he was also in communication with some of a lower grade, and it is certain that men of scandalous repute (such as Callender, a libeller by profession) afterwards claimed rewards on the ground of services rendered. Such evidence must be received with suspicion, for it is tainted by the character of the witnesses; but there was a singular agreement between the known views of Jefferson and those advocated by the incendiary portion of the press; while *his* enemies were the persons denounced with the most violence, and held up most systematically to the contempt and execration of the people.

It is not pretended that Jefferson, or men in the

z

position of Jefferson, could ever have sanctioned
the coarse ribaldry of these attacks. Their taste,
if not their morals, must have revolted from such
brutality. In after years, when he and his friends
had come in for their share of abuse, Jefferson
complained bitterly of the licentiousness of public
writers. But those who had set the example of
personal aggression, could not possibly limit the
extent to which such aggression might be carried;
and, if they employed ruffians to do dirty work, they
ought not to have been surprised at the manner in
which the task was performed. From that time
dates the rapid degeneracy of the press, and on it
closely followed the degradation of public life. The
tone, which was first adopted by venal journalists
and pamphleteers, was transferred to official intercourse, and the daily business of the legislature.
Men, who had ceased to respect each other, soon
forgot to respect themselves; gross insults were ex-
changed between equals, and bludgeons and pistols
usurped the place of arguments; and this evil grew
and spread, till no person of eminence could take
part in the government of the country, without some
damage to his character, or at least some sacrifice
of his dignity.

What must have been the fate of others, when even the august name of Washington did not screen him from cruel affronts ? At one time, they had reached to such a pitch, that Jefferson, who had always professed the highest reverence for the President, thought it necessary to write to him, deprecating the suspicion of having had anything to do with these attacks. " I have formerly mentioned to you," he says, " that, from a very early period of my life, I had laid it down as a rule of conduct never to write a word for the public papers. From this I have never departed in a single instance." He does not say, that he never employed others to write for him ; but he goes on to insinuate, that a third party (evidently Hamilton) is endeavouring to sow tares between him and Washington, by representing him (the recluse of Monticello) as still engaged in the bustle of politics, and in turbulence and intrigue against the government. " I never believed for a moment," he adds, " that this could make any impression on you."

Washington's reply is at once a noble justification of himself, and a severe rebuke to his slanderers. " As you have mentioned the subject yourself," he says, " it would not be frank, candid, or friendly

to conceal, that your conduct has been represented
as derogating from that opinion I had conceived
you entertained of me; that to your particular friends
and connexions you have described, and they have
denounced me, as a person under a dangerous influence; and that if I would listen more to some
other opinions, all would be well. My answer in-
variably has been, that I had never discovered anything in the conduct of Mr. Jefferson to raise suspicions in my mind of his insincerity; that, if he
would retrace my public conduct while he was in
the administration, abundant proofs would occur to
him, that truth and right decisions were the sole
object of my pursuit; that there were as many
instances, within his own knowledge, of my having
decided *against* as *in favour of* the opinions of the
person evidently alluded to; and, moreover, that I
was no believer in the infallibility of the politics
or measures of any man living. In short, that
I was no party man myself, and the first wish
of my heart was, if parties did exist, to reconcile
them.

"To this I may add, and very truly, that until
within the last year or two I had no conception,
that parties would or even could go the length I

have been witness to; nor did I believe, until lately, that it was within the bounds of probability, hardly within those of possibility, that while I was using my utmost exertions to establish a national character of our own, independent, as far as our obligations and justice would permit, of every nation of the earth, and wished, by steering a steady course, to preserve this country from the horrors of a desolating war—I should be accused of being the enemy of one nation, and subject to the influence of another; and, to prove it, that every act of my administration would be tortured, and the grossest and most insidious misrepresentations of them be made, by giving one side only of a subject—*and that, too, in such exaggerated and indecent terms, as could scarcely be applied to a Nero, to a notorious defaulter, or even to a common pickpocket.* But enough of this . . . I have already gone further in the expression of my feelings than I intended."

While Washington was thus accepting the explanations of Jefferson, and comforting him with the assurance that he had never *discovered* anything to raise a doubt of his sincerity, the latter must have well known that such a discovery was likely one day to take place. Only a short time before, he had written the following letter to M. Mazzei, one of his correspondents in Europe: "The aspect of our politics has wonderfully changed since you left us. In place of that noble love of liberty and republican government, which carried us triumphantly through the war, an Anglican, monarchical, aristocratical party has sprung up, whose avowed object is to draw over us the substance, as they have already done the forms, of the British Government. The main body of our citizens, however, remain true to their political principles; the whole landed interest is republican, and so is a great mass of talent. Against us are the executive, the judiciary, two out of three branches of the legislature, all the officers of the government, all who want to be officers, all timid men who prefer the calm of despotism to the boisterous sea of liberty, British merchants, and Americans trading on British capital, speculators and holders in the banks and public funds—a contrivance invented for the purposes of corruption, and for assimilating us in all things to the rotten as well as the sound parts of the British model. It would give you a fever were I to name to you the apostates who have gone over to these heresies—*men who were Samsons in the field, and Solomons in the council, but who have had their heads shorn by the harlot England."*

Unfortunately for Jefferson, his correspondent appears to have been wanting in discretion, for the letter fell into the hands of the French Government, and by them was published in the *Moniteur.* Long afterwards, the writer laboured to prove that the offensive expressions contained in it could not apply to Washington. But it was well understood at the time, that the allusion to Samson and Solomon was meant for the President, and for none other. He and the ex-minister seem never to have met after the publication of that letter, and it is said that Jefferson studiously avoided an interview, often passing the gates of Mount Vernon without calling. Be that as it may, it is highly probable that he repented of what he had written; for, in later years, he did justice to Washington by declaring "that he was, indeed, in every sense of the word, a good and a great man."

The charges of undue partiality to England were all founded on the President's anxiety to maintain peace. Like the great Duke of Wellington, whom in many respects he resembled, he had seen too much of war to think lightly of its evils, and he

would, above all, have deplored the renewal of the
contest between the two branches of the same old
Saxon stem.   When, therefore, questions arose as
to British infractions of the rights of neutrals by
the seizure of cargoes bound for France on the high
seas, the search for English seamen on board
American vessels, and other vexatious acts of maritime power, Washington resisted the cry for an
immediate recourse to arms, and preferred to make
an appeal, in the first instance, to the justice and
good feeling of England.   It was Hamilton's suggestion that a special mission should be despatched
to Great Britain, both to arrange the matters in
dispute, and to negotiate a commercial treaty; and
this plan at once met with the President's approval.
When the time came to select the person to be
appointed, Washington's choice would have fallen
upon Hamilton himself, had it not been for the
strong opposition of personal and political enemies.
"You know," said he, "whom I wish—but for the
clamour they have raised against him."   Still he
hesitated; till Hamilton relieved him from his
embarrassment by begging to be left altogether out
of the question, and by recommending another
person as well fitted for the appointment.

"Knowing as I do, sir," he writes, "that I am among the persons who have been in your contemplation to be employed in the capacity I have mentioned, I should not have taken the present step, had I not been resolved, at the same time, to advise you with decision to drop me from your consideration, and to fix upon another character. I am not unapprized of what has been the bias of your opinion on the subject. I am well aware of all the collateral obstacles which exist.; and I assure you, in the utmost sincerity, that I shall be completely and entirely satisfied with the election of another.

"I beg leave to add, that, of the persons whom you would deem free from any constitutional objections, MR. JAY is the only man in whose qualifications for success there would be a thorough confidence, and him alone it would be advisable to send. I think the business would have the best chance possible in his hands; and I flatter myself that his mission would issue in a manner that would produce the most important good to the nation.

"Let me add, sir, that those whom I call the sober-minded men of the country look up to you with solicitude upon the present occasion. If happily you should be the instrument of still rescuing the country from the dangers and calamities of war, there is no part of your life, sir, which will produce to you more real satisfaction or true glory, than that which shall be distinguished by this very important service.

"In any event, I cannot doubt, sir, that you will do justice to the motives which impel me, and that you will see in this proceeding another proof of my sincere wishes for your honour and happiness, and anxiety for the public weal."

Chief Justice Jay, an excellent man, was accordingly chosen for this important mission; and Hamilton—freely renouncing an appointment which would have exactly suited his taste and genius, and have brought him to a country that he had long wished to see, and where his high qualities would have been recognized and appreciated—remained at his post, only to be slandered and reviled more furiously than ever. Again and again, the Secretary of the Treasury was accused of irregularities, corruption, and malversation; again and again, a searching inquiry in Congress resulted in his triumphant acquittal, and in the confusion of his enemies. But those, who could find no flaw in his political armour, could yet have recourse to calumnies, which even at this distance of time must arouse a feeling of shame and indignation. In all his dealings with men, Hamilton could challenge and defy the nicest scrutiny; but in his relations to that gentler sex, which has so often tempted the wise to folly, he was not exempt from the frailties of human nature. Thrown, a mere boy, into the wild life of camps, and since exposed to the perils of a society which had lately imported from France a somewhat lax tone of gallantry, it is enough to say that he had not always been immaculate on this head. But errors, which good men would have buried in charitable silence, and which men with the slightest spark of honour would have scorned to use against an opponent, were turned to the basest purposes in assailing Hamilton's character; and the means employed were worthy of the end in view. Vile perversions of fact, garbled extracts from stolen letters, were so arranged as to cast imputations of official fraud, which could only be answered by the exposure of private indiscretions. How affecting are the words with which he accompanied an explanation wrung from him by infamous charges! "This confession," he says, "is not made without a blush. I cannot be the apologist of any vice, because the ardour of passion may have made it mine. I can never cease to condemn myself for the pang which it may inflict on a bosom eminently entitled to all my gratitude, fidelity, and love; but that bosom will approve that, even at so great an expense, I should effectually wipe away a more serious stain from a name which it cherishes with no less devotion than tenderness. The public, too, I trust, will excuse the confession. The necessity of it to my defence against a more heinous charge could alone have extorted from me so painful an indecorum."

It is gratifying to know that the conspirators failed in their object. All that was left of gentlemanlike and chivalrous feeling rallied to the side of Hamilton; and she who had most right to complain of these revelations—true wife and noble woman—not only forgave the erring husband, but remained fondly attached to him to the last, and mourned his untimely fate with a love and a sorrow that were indeed "stronger than death."

The few preceding pages have rather anticipated events, for some of the circumstances narrated did not occur till after Hamilton's retirement from office.

They have been brought together here, as illustrative of that excess of party violence, which became so disgracefully apparent between the years 1793 and 1800. In those years were laid the foundations of that democratic despotism, which ultimately prevailed over all independence of thought and action, drove the wisest and the best from the conduct of public affairs, and gave the highest places in the commonwealth to mere flatterers of the passions of the hour. Alas! the great intellects and generous hearts which were then sacrificed have been but too fatally avenged; and America has had to pay, in rivers of blood and tears, for the fallacy that the government of a nation requires neither wisdom nor virtue.

It was in April, 1794, that Jay was appointed to the English mission, and in the following month it became necessary to send a new minister to the French Republic. On this occasion Madison and Monroe, both members of the opposition, called upon Washington as representatives of a meeting of their party, and urged him to nominate an envoy in whom they could have confidence. He asked them to name some person, and they at once recommended Colonel Burr. Washington seems to have been taken by surprise; but he answered that he had no faith in that gentleman, and must therefore decline to appoint him. A second application to the same effect met with a similar result. "But," said the President, "I will nominate you, Mr. Madison, or you, Mr. Monroe." The rejection of Burr was evidently quite spontaneous; yet it was again ascribed to Hamilton's influence, and must have added to the irritation of his old rival. To do Burr justice, however, he does not appear to have had any part in the base and cowardly libels on the Secretary of the Treasury. With all his faults, he was above such revenge. He was the man to kill his enemy, but not to stab him under the cloak of night. He left that to the tender conscience of some of his political associates.

Soon after, an insurrection broke out in Pennsylvania, on account of the excise laws. Once more Hamilton exerted all his powers to re-establish order, and maintain the authority of the government. It was a crisis in which his energetic support was of the utmost importance to Washington, for the President's right to suppress the rebellion was called in question, and he needed all the aid of

the constitutional party. That aid was given, and
the insurrection was happily put down without
bloodshed. When peace was restored, Hamilton
resolved to retire from office. Doubtless, he was
sick and weary of that constant struggle, and the
necessity of ceaseless watchfulness against ambushed
foes; but there were other reasons which made
him wish to retire, and which, if anything could
have done so, might have called up a blush to
the cheeks of his persecutors. This man, who had
held the revenues of an empire at his disposal,
and whom his adversaries had not scrupled to charge
with enriching himself at the public expense, was
in reality very poor. His official salary did not
suffice for the wants of his family, and his ministerial
duties had obliged him to abandon his practice at
the bar. He was anxious, before it was too late,
to repair his fortunes, and provide for his wife and
children. On the 1st of December, 1794, he thus
wrote to the Speaker of the House of Representatives :—"I beg leave, through you, to make known
to the House, that I have signified to the President
of the United States my intention to resign my
office of Secretary of the Treasury, on the last day
of January next. I make this communication in

order that an opportunity may be given, previous
to that event, to institute any further proceedings
which may be contemplated, if any there be, in
consequence of the inquiry during the last session
into the state of this department."

It was a challenge to repeat the charges against
him, but this time it was not accepted. The former
investigations had proved too disastrous for the
accusers, and henceforth they preferred the safer
tactics of private calumny. After waiting some
weeks, Hamilton presented to Congress a final
report on the national revenues, and a plan for
the further maintenance of the public credit. He
gave a complete account of the existing sources
of income, and considered in detail the provisions
for funding the debt, paying the interest on it,
and gradually extinguishing it. He proposed amendments in the modes of levying taxes, and securities
to render the Sinking Fund inviolable, until the
faith of the country had been fully redeemed. It
was his parting legacy to the Union; and on the
31st of January, 1795, he retired from the administration, having just completed the thirty-eighth
year of his age.

Two days after, the President addressed him in

a letter, which must ever remain as a striking testimony to his merits.

"DEAR SIR,—After so long an experience of your public services, I am naturally led, at this moment of your departure from office (which it has always been my wish to prevent), to review them. In every relation which you have borne to me, I have found that my confidence in your talents, exertions, and integrity has been well placed. I the more freely render this testimony of my approbation, because I speak from opportunities of information which cannot deceive me, and which furnish satisfactory proof of your title to public regard.

"My most earnest wishes for your happiness will attend you in your retirement, and you may assure yourself of the sincere esteem, regard, and friendship of,

"Dear Sir,

"Your affectionate

"GEORGE WASHINGTON."

To this emphatic eulogy, which would of itself outweigh all the slanders of his adversaries, Hamilton replied as follows :—"As often as I may recall

A A

the vexations I have endured, your approbation will be a great and precious consolation. It was not without a struggle that I yielded to the very urgent motives, which impelled me to relinquish a station in which I could hope to be in any degree instrumental in promoting the success of an administration under your direction—a struggle which would have been far greater, had I supposed that the prospect of future usefulness was proportioned to the sacrifices to be made. Whatever may be my destination hereafter, I entreat you to be persuaded (not the less for my having been sparing in my professions) that I shall never cease to render a just tribute to those eminent and excellent qualities, which have been already productive of so many blessings to your country—that you will always have my fervent wishes for your public and personal felicity, and that it will be my pride to cultivate a continuance of that esteem, regard, and friendship, of which you do me the honour to assure me."

In a private letter written about this time to a relation in Scotland, Hamilton thus alludes to his motives for withdrawing from the Treasury:—"In that office I met with many intrinsic difficulties, and many artificial ones, proceeding from passions not very worthy, common to human nature, and which act with peculiar force in republics. The object, however, was effected of establishing public credit, and introducing order into the finances.

"Public office in this country has few attractions. The pecuniary emolument is so inconsiderable, as to amount to a sacrifice to any man who can employ his time with advantage in any liberal profession. The opportunity of doing good, from the jealousy of power and the spirit of faction, is too small in any station to warrant a long continuance of private sacrifices. The enterprise of party has so far succeeded, as materially to weaken the necessary influence and energy of the executive authority, and so far diminished the power of doing good in that department, as greatly to take away the motives which a virtuous man might have for making sacrifices. The prospect was even bad for gratifying in future the love of fame, if that passion was to be the spring of action.

"The union of these motives with the reflections of prudence in relation to a growing family, determined me, as soon as my plans attained a certain maturity, to withdraw from office.

"It is a pleasing reflection to me, that, since the commencement of my connexion with General Washington to the present time, I have possessed a flattering share of his confidence and friendship."·

On his return to New York, Hamilton was presented with the freedom of that city, and was offered to be put in nomination as Governor of the State. This he refused, having determined to devote himself to the practice of his profession. But he could not keep clear of politics, for he was often consulted by Washington, and he was still the acknowledged head of the Federalist party. In March, 1795, the "Treaty of Amity, Commerce, and Navigation" with great Britain, which Jay had concluded in London, was received in the United States. It was a fair and reasonable arrangement of the difficulties pending between the two countries, in which both parties conceded something for the sake of peace, and, if not quite satisfactory to the expectations of the Americans, it demanded at least their candid consideration. But the Republicans had resolved beforehand, that it should meet with the most violent opposition. All the democratic machinery was set to work, and a cry was raised from one end of the Union to the

other, that America was *sold* to England, and that
the *monocrats* had betrayed the republic. After
long and stormy debates, the legal majority of two-
thirds of the Senate voted for the acceptance of
the treaty, but only with certain modifications. It
then became a question whether the President could
ratify conditionally. The cabinet was divided, and
Mr. Randolph in particular strongly opposed the
ratification. All was doubt and confusion, peace
and war trembled in the balance, and many anxious
eyes were turned once more upon Hamilton.

A public meeting was held at New York. Hamilton came down to it, and attempted to address the
multitude. But the agitators were too conscious
of his eloquence to allow him to be heard. They
raised a clamour which drowned his voice. " Fellow-
citizens," he said, " respect yourselves ! " The
answer was a volley of stones, one of which struck
him on the forehead. " Oh," said he, bowing to
the populace, " if you use such *knock-down* arguments, I shall have to retire." He then proposed
a resolution, declaring the confidence of the meeting
in the President, and affirming his constitutional
right to deal with the treaty. The motion was lost
in uproar, and the friends of the government with-

drew from the assembly. "What a head-lopping set of fellows," remarked Hamilton, "you have brought to *consider* the treaty !"

But, if he could not obtain a hearing from the mob, his influence was soon apparent in other quarters. At his suggestion, the merchants of the different seaports expressed their confidence in the President, and the better sense of the country began to speak out, in deprecation of a war with England. His ready pen, under various signatures, supplied arguments to the friends of peace ; and in a correspondence with Wolcott, his successor at the Treasury, with Bradford, the Attorney-General, and with Washington himself, he urged the immediate ratification of the treaty. An accident came to aid his endeavours. A despatch of the French minister, captured at sea, and sent by the British Government to America, implicated Mr. Randolph in discreditable intrigues with France. This decided the President to act on his own opinion, and on the advice of Hamilton. He ratified the treaty, and then handed the intercepted despatch to Randolph. The latter resigned his office, and, although he afterwards published a laboured vindication of his conduct, interspersed with virulent attacks on Washington and Hamilton, he never succeeded in removing the impression left by this discovery, both as to his own designs and those of the Republican party.

Hamilton now set to work at his profession, and was once more the leading spirit of the bar. Talley-rand, who knew him at this time, has borne testimony to his unwearied industry. "I have beheld," said he, "one of the wonders of the world. I have seen a man, who has made the fortune of a nation, labouring all night to support his family." And yet, while thus working at his ordinary calling, Hamilton never withdrew his attention from public affairs. He was still the leader of his party, and the unsalaried adviser of the President; and, as a necessary consequence, he was still the mark for the poisoned arrows of his enemies.

From 1795 to 1797, Washington found it difficult to maintain the just authority of the executive against the constant assaults of the democracy, and often had recourse to Hamilton for counsel. He had resolved to retire from office at the expiration of his second term; and, as the time approached, he determined to issue a *Farewell Address* to the American people. On this subject also he consulted Hamilton. There has been much controversy as to the exact authorship of this celebrated paper, but the fact seems to be that, while the original groundwork was Washington's own, the superstructure was in a great part Hamilton's. Already at the close of his first term, the President had consulted Madison (who then possessed his confidence) on a similar scheme, and that gentleman had prepared the draft of an address. Washington now sent this draft to Hamilton, with an explanatory introduction, a series of hints or heads of topics for further development, and a conclusion. It was upon this basis that Hamilton founded *his* draft, and, while he retained wherever he could the thoughts and language of Washington, he added much valuable matter, and brought the whole into its present form. Calm, wise, and noble, it is a monument worthy of the great man whose name it bears, and, had the American people always remembered its lessons, it would have been well for their own peace, and conducive to the happiness of the world.

As the election for President drew nigh, the sage of Monticello reappeared on the scene. When it was positively known that Washington would not again accept the Presidency, pamphlets were circulated, canvassing the claims of every possible candidate.

"Ambition, servility, pride, meanness, hypocrisy," were laid to the charge of the modest and high-minded Jay — Hamilton was a man " formed by nature to shine in a subordinate sphere "—and the intellects of Adams were " in a state of rapid decay." But there was one man who, " even in his philosophic seclusion, blushed as he received the crowning honours of his countrymen"—and the choice of the nation was plainly directed to the touching simplicity and retiring virtues of Jefferson.   At the same time, every effort was used to divide and discredit the Federalist party.   That party looked to Hamilton for advice, and he at once counselled them to unite their votes in favour of John Adams and Thomas Pinckney—the one as likely to command pretty general support from moderate men, and the other as distinguished for many estimable qualities, and sure to be sustained by South Carolina, of which he was a citizen.   The main object was, of course, to exclude Jefferson ; but some of the New England friends of Mr. Adams, fearful lest he should be elected as Vice-President only, did not give their second suffrage to Mr. Pinckney.   The result was, that Adams received seventy-one votes, Jefferson sixty-eight, and Pinckney fifty-nine.   The two former thus became President and Vice-President. Colonel Burr was among the candidates, and, although unsuccessful, could boast of thirty votes. It was clear that he was becoming an important personage in the commonwealth.

On the 4th of March, 1797, Mr. Adams took the oath of office, and Washington laid down the burden of his cares and labours. As he withdrew from the hall, there was a general rush from the galleries to catch a last glimpse of that noble and venerable countenance, and as he passed into the street the multitude thronged around him with every mark of respect and affection. He stood for a moment with his white head uncovered, and his eyes filled with tears ; but, unable to express his emotions in words, he could only wave a mute blessing to the people whom he had served so faithfully and loved so truly. "There was more weeping," writes John Adams, "than there ever has been at the representation of a tragedy"—and, doubtless, it was one of those rare occasions, when the popular heart is deeply and irresistibly moved, and gives way without restraint to the indulgence of strong, natural feeling.

But on the very day when this scene was passing in the streets of Philadelphia the following article

appeared in Bache's *Aurora*, one of the organs of
the Republican party :—" *Now lettest thou thy servant
depart in peace, for mine eyes have seen thy salvation,*
was the pious ejaculation of a man who beheld a
flood of happiness rushing in upon mankind ; if ever
there was a time, that would license the reiteration of
this exclamation, the time is now arrived ; for *the
man who is the source of the misfortunes of our country*
is this day reduced to a level with his fellow-citizens,
and is no longer possessed of power to multiply evils
on the United States. If ever there was a period for
rejoicing, this is the moment. Every heart in unison
with the freedom and the happiness of the people
ought to beat· high with exultation, that the name of
Washington from this day ceases to give currency to
political iniquity and to *legalize corruption*. A new
era is opening upon us, an era that promises much
to the people, for public measures must now stand
on their own merit, and *nefarious projects* can no
longer be supported by a name. When a retrospect
is taken of the Washington Administration for eight
years, it is a subject of the greatest astonishment
that a single individual could have cankered the
principles of Republicanism in an enlightened people,
and should have carried his *designs against the public*

liberty so far as to have put in jeopardy its very existence. Such, however, are the facts; and, with these staring us in the face, this day ought to be a day of jubilee in the United States."

And this farrago of blasphemy, absurdity, and ingratitude was the farewell of the democratic press to the Father of American Independence!

CHAPTER XV.

IT is refreshing to turn from the violence and malignity described in the last chapter, to the tranquil and beautiful home on the banks of the Potomac, where the tired hero was at length to find repose. There, in the midst of the well-known woodlands, by the side of the familiar stream, his fancy could stray back to the happy days of youth, and recall the images of old friends long departed. He has left on record that he often cast his eyes towards Belvoir, the ancient home of the Fairfaxes, now in ruins, and thought with regret of the pleasant times, before war and revolution had severed so many ties of neighbourhood and affection. But he had the consolation which springs from the consciousness of duty unflinchingly performed, and many delights and blessings seemed reserved for his honourable old age. He was venerated by all the best of his countrymen, beloved by his friends, almost adored by his family and dependents—and the envious whispers of faction could hardly reach him in those peaceful retreats. The wife of his bosom was worthy of all his tenderness, and, although heaven had denied him children, he was not without the sunshine of young faces in his house, and the glad sound of youthful voices. Mrs. Washington's son by her first marriage had left a boy and girl to the care of their grandmother, nephews and nieces were frequent visitors at Mount Vernon, and young Lafayette had there sought shelter and protection from his father's old comrade in arms. The general had, moreover, the congenial occupation of repairing his long-neglected home, putting his estate into order, and following those agricultural pursuits in which he delighted. In spite of the hardships he had gone through, his health seemed yet unimpaired, and his frame still vigorous; and it was no presumption to hope that he might continue for many years in the enjoyment of his well-earned rest.

Meanwhile, Mr. Adams had retained the late cabinet in office. They were members of the Federalist party, trusted by Washington, and likely to continue his policy. They were, moreover, in habits of confidential communication with Hamilton, whose influence would therefore still be felt in the government. Colonel Pickering, the Secretary of State, and Mr. Wolcott, the Secretary of the Treasury, were notoriously friends of Hamilton. On the other hand, the views of Mr. Jefferson, the Vice-President, were known to be with the opposition, especially on the subject of the relations of America with France. Those relations were becoming daily more and more unsatisfactory. The Directory, which had succeeded to power after the fall of Robespierre, if less bloodthirsty, was quite as arrogant as its predecessors. It had adopted a tone towards America, which appeared to be one of command rather than remonstrance. The treaty with England was held to be an offence to France, complaints of breaches of neutrality were laid against the American Government, and, when Mr. Monroe was recalled from Paris to make way for another minister, the Directory declared that no other envoy would be received from the United States, until all grievances had been redressed. This declaration was accompanied by words of insult and menace. "The French Republic hopes," said Barras, "that the successors of Columbus, of Raleigh, and of Penn, ever proud of their liberty, will never forget that they owe it to France! . . . In their wisdom, they will weigh the magnanimous benevolence of the French people, against the artful caresses of perfidious plotters,. who meditate to draw them back to their ancient slavery. . . . They will find in the French people the republican generosity, which knows how to grant peace, but which knows also how to make its sovereignty respected." Along with this bombast came measures of a stringent character, directed against the commerce of the United States. The doctrine, that free ships make free goods, which had formed part of the old treaties with France, was declared to be abolished; the French cruisers were ordered to seize all British property found on board of American vessels, and all provisions bound for England; and it was announced, that Americans serving on English ships would be treated as pirates. The policy of the French Government was evidently one of intimidation, by which America was to be coerced into compliance with the designs of her sister-republic.

But the Directory had miscalculated the character of the American people. Singularly open to the influences of cajolery, that people had yet retained the high spirit of their fathers, and were not easily moved by threats. The language of France was answered by a shout of defiance, and the French party in the United States found themselves suddenly in a hopeless minority. The President summoned the Congress to a special session, and, when he declared his determination to preserve the national honour, and recommended immediate measures for the defence of the country, he met with almost universal support and approval. He had resolved, however, to make one more attempt to adjust the differences amicably; and, with that view, Charles Cotesworth Pinckney, John Marshall, and Elbridge Gerry (two Federalists, and one Republican) were despatched on a joint mission to France. The Directory declined to receive the three envoys, but opened with them a private negotiation, the details of which would be thought incredible, if they did not rest on positive evidence. The secret agent of the French Government informed the envoys that there might be a way to arrange matters, but that a necessary preliminary would be a *douceur* of two hundred and fifty thousand dollars to the Directory, and a loan of thirty-two millions of francs to France. When the envoys proposed to enter on a discussion of the grounds of difference between the countries, the same agent said to them : "Gentlemen, you mistake the point. You say nothing of the money you are to give; you make no offer of money; on that point you are not explicit." "We are explicit enough," replied the indignant Americans. "We will not give you one farthing ; and, before coming here, we should have thought such an offer as you now propose would have been regarded as a mortal insult."

Unable to effect anything in Paris, the commissioners returned, though at separate times, to America ; but the news of their failure had preceded them, and the spring of 1798 witnessed a scene of intense excitement throughout the United States. "France pretends to levy tribute!" was the cry. "Millions for defence, not a cent to purchase peace!" Jefferson heard it with dismay, for it sounded like the death-knell of the Republican party. All the popular enthusiasm, which had formerly gathered round France and her adherents, was now turned in the opposite direction. It was the hour of triumph for the Federalists, and it seemed possible that, if they used well the occasion, they might secure for themselves a long period of supremacy.

The last decree of the French Government had subjected to capture all neutral vessels and their cargoes, if *any portion* of the latter was of British *fabric or produce*, although the entire property might belong to neutrals. This was the finishing stroke at the carrying-trade of the United States, and, combined with the treatment of the French envoys, produced a general desire for war. It was necessary to raise an army, and to prepare for all contingencies. Adams was greatly perplexed, and doubtful where to look for a commander-in-chief. But Hamilton saw from the first, that no name but that of Washington would command the entire confidence of the country, and his views were soon backed by the unanimous voice of the people. The President and the Senate confirmed the popular judgment, and Mr. McHenry, the Secretary for War, was despatched to Mount Vernon with the offer of new cares and responsibilities.

No message could be less welcome to those pleasant shades, where the veteran soldier and statesman had hoped to spend his last years in peace. But already he had written, in answer to a letter on the subject:—"As my whole life has been dedicated to my country in one shape or another—for the poor

remains of it, it is not an object to contend for ease
and quiet, when all that is valuable is at stake."
And when McHenry presented himself with the
President's commission, and at the same time handed
in a letter from Hamilton, urging the acceptance of
the appointment, Washington did not hesitate a
moment. He only stipulated, that he should not be
called into active service until his presence was
absolutely required, and that he should have the
nomination of his principal officers. He had been
too much fettered in his great campaigns, by having
men thrust upon him against his better judgment,
and he now held, that no officer of the old army
should claim precedence on the mere ground of his
former rank, but that the country should have the
advantage of the best talents, energy, and experience
within its reach. Acting upon this opinion, he
recommended, that his three Major-Generals should
be Hamilton, Pinckney, and Knox, and that the
first place should be Hamilton's.

Mr. Charles Francis Adams, in writing the life of
his grandfather, endeavours to show, that all this
was planned by Hamilton, and that he made use of
Washington as a mere instrument to force his views
on the unwilling mind of the President. It is true,

that Mr. Adams always entertained an unfortunate jealousy and suspicion of Hamilton, and that he would not of his own accord have advanced him to so high a post. It is equally true, that Washington often consulted Hamilton; but the mind of the great chieftain was as clear as ever, his intellect as unclouded, his will as firm; and when he chose Hamilton for his second in command, he was influenced by no consideration but the fitness of the appointment, founded on his intimate knowledge of the high qualities of his friend.

"Although Colonel Hamilton," he says, in addressing the President, "has never acted in the character of a general-officer, yet his opportunities, as the principal and most confidential aid of the commander-in-chief, afforded him the means of viewing everything on a larger scale than those whose attention was confined to divisions or brigades, who knew nothing of the correspondence of the commander-in-chief, or of the various orders to, or transactions with, the general staff of the army. These advantages, and his having served with usefulness in the old Congress and in the general Convention, and having filled one of the most important departments of government with acknowledged abilities and integrity, have placed him on high ground, and made him a conspicuous character in the United States and in Europe. . . . By some he is considered an ambitious man, and therefore a dangerous one. That he is ambitious I shall readily grant; but it is of that laudable kind which prompts a man to excel in whatever he takes in hand. He is enterprising, quick in his perceptions, and his judgment is intuitively great—qualities essential to a military character; and therefore, I repeat, his loss will be irreparable."

General Knox, with a pardonable sense of his own claims to distinction, declined to serve under Hamilton, who was so much his junior; but Pinckney at once accepted the appointment, and applauded the advancement of his inferior officer to the foremost place. Indeed, the acquiescence of the majority of his former comrades was a striking homage to the merits of this extraordinary man, and proved, that no personal influence or intrigue, but only a thorough knowledge of his deserts, had induced the commander-in-chief to exalt him over so many older heads.

In November, 1798, Washington came to Philadelphia, to confer with Hamilton and Pinckney on the organization of the new army. Adams proposed to nominate Burr for a brigadier-general, but Washington at once replied :—"By all that I have known and heard, Colonel Burr is a brave and able officer; but the question is, whether he has not equal talents at intrigue?" He refused, therefore, to second the nomination, and Adams was very indignant at the refusal. For five weeks, the *triumvirate* (as Adams called them) were engaged in drawing up plans for the regulation and management of the forces, while the President watched their proceedings with a restless and impatient jealousy. At the end of that time, Washington returned to Mount Vernon, where he determined to remain till actually summoned to the field. He knew that he could depend on Hamilton in all things, and that his presence would not again be required in the preliminary arrangements.

One of the charges brought against Hamilton is, that, from motives of personal ambition, he was now most desirous and anxious for war. It is said that he hoped by war to consolidate the Federalist party, to obtain for himself distinction as a military leader, and to establish his preponderance in the country. Now it is most certain that no man had done more to preserve peace than Hamilton. It was the condition on which depended the success of his financial schemes, and, soldier as he was, his humane and gentle nature abhorred the prospect of rapine and slaughter. But if war *must* come (and he saw only too plainly that, sooner or later, America was likely to be involved in the world-wide struggles of the French Revolution), he preferred that it should be with France rather than with England. He knew that the first shot fired would destroy for ever the worship of Gallic ideas and Jacobin politics; and his imagination had already conjured up the picture of a more congenial alliance, in which the two great branches of the English race, mingling their navies on the ocean, and their blood on the same fields of battle, should forget every old cause of quarrel, and become united by closest ties of confidence and friendship, for their mutual advantage, and for the common interest of mankind. It is no disparagement to the wisdom or patriotism of his views, if they included also the triumph of his party, and his own honourable fame. He would have been more or less than man, had he been indifferent to these incidental gains; but it is contrary to the whole history of his life to believe, that he ever allowed such considerations to interfere with his larger plans for the glory and the happiness of his country.

The war-cry of 1798 was not raised by any particular section of the community, but was a natural and universal outburst of indignation, provoked by the overweening arrogance of the French Government. No one joined in it more heartily than President Adams. He had said in an official message to Congress: "I will never send another minister to France, without assurances that he will be received, respected, and honoured as the representative of a great, free, powerful, and independent nation." And in his answers to the addresses, which poured in from all parts of the Union, he used language so warm and energetic that even Federalists were alarmed at its tendency. "It is not for us," wrote Hamilton to the Secretary of the Treasury, "*particularly for the government*, to breathe an irregular or violent spirit." But Adams, once roused to anger, was not easily restrained. Downright, irascible, and uncompromising, he spoke out all that he thought, without much regard to consequences. He, if any one, was responsible for stimulating the warlike ardour of the time; and, although he may have left to Congress the task of originating the principal measures taken, there can be no question that he gave his sanction to those measures, and that he did not separate himself in any way from the general policy of the Federalist party.

That policy was marked by a vigour which was sometimes carried to excess. The treaties with France were declared null and void, an army was raised, a fleet equipped, and the country put into a state of defence. But not content with these necessary precautions, the Congress passed two bills of an exceptional kind, which have since been known as the *Alien and Sedition Acts*. They were intended to strengthen the hands of the government, by giving it extraordinary powers to deal with that mass of foreigners (often the scum and off-scouring of Europe) which infested the large towns, and also with those natives of America whose attachment to France was stronger than their allegiance to their own country. In passing these bills, the Federalists imitated a political error which the Tories had not long before committed in England. They availed themselves of a moment of popular excitement in their favour, to obtain restrictions on the liberty of speech and writing, which were utterly opposed to the customs and genius of the people. The inevitable

result was a reaction, which contributed in the end
to the overthrow and ruin of their party. Nothing
can be more unjust, however, than to lay the chief
blame of these acts to Hamilton. It is quite certain
that he made use of his influence, to moderate, and
not to inflame the ardour of his friends. "Let us
not establish a tyranny," he wrote to Wolcott;
"energy is a very different thing from violence. If
we make no false step, we shall be essentially
united; but if we push things to an extreme, we
shall then give to faction body and solidity."

It is equally certain that Mr. Adams had joined,
approved, and sanctioned the Federalist policy, and
that he was more deeply committed than any one
else to the maintenance of a bold and dignified
attitude towards France. What was it, then, which
wrought a sudden change in his views? The question
seems to admit but of one answer, and that is—
jealousy of Hamilton. His grandson and biographer
virtually confirms the fact in the following passage :
"Although not by any means acquainted with the
whole truth, he saw enough to understand the
nature of the expedients resorted to for the purpose
of *controlling his will.* He had had more than one
occasion to feel that his cabinet officers were effective

instruments to this end, and that he could place little reliance upon them for the *execution of his own wishes*. Yet he was to be exposed to the world and to posterity as the responsible instrument to execute a policy, in framing which no discretion was to be allowed him. Already the outline, so far as it had been developed, alarmed him. It involved demands on the public purse, which he saw no means of supplying without risk of convulsions, and the establishment of a permanent military organization, the necessity for which he could not understand. Above all, his instincts warned him, in no dubious tones, that the extraordinary management resorted to for placing Mr. Hamilton at the head of this great power, was designed certainly to give to *him*, and in certain contingencies, perhaps, to the country itself, A MASTER."

Is not this the picture of a man—honest, well-meaning, able enough in the discharge of ordinary functions—but placed by circumstances in a position above his strength, irritably conscious of his inferiority to one powerful mind, and chafing against an influence which he yet was obliged to acknowledge? That Hamilton would ever usurp authority which did not of right belong to him, was an utterly groundless fear; but, in one sense, Adams would have done well to own him as a master— or, in other words, to have followed his advice and guidance. Had he frankly adhered to the policy of the great Federalist, and given it to the end the support of his name, character, and official station, he would have pursued a consistent course, earned the respect of friends and enemies, kept his party together, and probably have triumphed at last over all opponents. But unfortunately for himself, still more unfortunately for America, he could not conquer the personal feeling of dislike and suspicion which prompted him, at all hazards, to break through the delicate network of Hamilton's influence. It was easy to assert his independence by an act of self-will, but it was not so easy to measure the full consequences of such an act.

The President, the cabinet, and the people seemed all agreed that, if any reconciliation with France were possible, the first advances must come from her side. After what had taken place, it was clearly for the honour and dignity of America, to wait till France should distinctly propose the renewal of diplomatic relations. What then was the astonishment of the world to learn, that, on the faith of a private communication from Mr. Murray, the minister at the Hague, the President had nominated that gentleman as envoy to France! and that he had done so without the consent or privity of his own cabinet!

"He acted," says Hamilton, "like a man out of his mind. Congress being on the point of opening, his cabinet recommended a paragraph in his speech to the effect, that if France, disposed to conciliation, would *send a representative,* he would be received with the respect due to his position. To which Adams abruptly and indignantly replied, *that if France should send a minister to-morrow, he would send him back again;* and this, he declared, was his decision after mature reflection. Within forty-eight hours he intimated in his speech, that if France would *receive* with respect a minister from America, he would send one; and immediately, without waiting for the reply to his communication, or even consulting his ministers, actually appointed an envoy to that country!"

When the news of this event reached Mount Vernon, Washington expressed his extreme surprise. "But far, very far indeed," writes he, "was that surprise short of what I experienced the next day, when, by a very intelligent gentleman immediately from Philadelphia, I was informed that there had been no *direct* overture from the government of France to that of the United States for a negotiation." And this was literally the case; for, although Mr. Murray had obtained *indirect* assurances of the more amicable disposition of the French government, this was surely not the way in which the insult of dismissing the former envoys could be redressed, or the relations of the two countries be placed on a satisfactory footing.

In spite of what had occurred, Washington did not relax his efforts to bring the army into an efficient state. From his rural solitude he kept up a constant correspondence on the subject, and his letters show that the general aspect of affairs filled him with apprehension. "I have for some time past," he says, "viewed the political concerns of the United States with an anxious and painful eye. They appear to me to be moving by hasty strides to a crisis; but in what it will result, that Being, who sees, foresees, and directs all things, alone can tell. The vessel is afloat, or very nearly so, and considering myself as a passenger only, I shall trust to the mariners (whose duty it is to watch) to steer it into a safe port."

In the trouble and confusion, however, which the President's late proceedings had occasioned, many Federalists cast longing looks towards Mount Vernon, and it seemed likely that, when an opportunity offered, Washington would again be called to the helm. It would have been much against his wishes, and it is doubtful whether anything short of the imminent danger of the country could have induced him to consent to a third term of office. But he was spared the necessity of choice, and the pain of refusal. The month of December, 1799, set in with cold and wet, but found him still vigorous and active. He was frequently on horseback, going the rounds of his estate, and putting everything into order, so that no reproach might attach to him, as he said, "when he took his departure for the land of spirits." He was occupied with arrangements for hutting the troops during winter, and with writing to Hamilton on the plan of a military academy. On the morning of the 12th he addressed a letter to his faithful lieutenant, which he closed with the assurance of his "very great esteem and regard." He then mounted his horse, and rode for some hours through a storm of snow, hail, and rain. He returned apparently well, but found the next day that he had taken a severe cold. He treated it lightly, but grew worse towards evening, and in the night became alarmingly ill. With his usual consideration for others, he would not have any one disturbed before morning. Medical aid was then sent for, bleeding and other remedies were tried, but without avail. His breathing had become difficult, and he was unable to swallow. "I find I am going," he said; "my breath cannot last long." He then gave directions about his will and papers, spoke affectionately to his wife, his secretary, his servants, apologized for the trouble he gave them, and added: "Well, it is a debt we must all pay to each other; and I hope, when you want aid of this kind, you will find it."—And with such kind speeches, as long as he could speak, and the same noble simplicity that had distinguished his whole life, the hero, statesman, and patriot passed away from a sorrowing world.

For, at the rumour of that death, every sound of faction was hushed, and even calumny was awed to silence. Through the length and breadth of America ran the thrill of a great emotion, and a common sympathy once more united her people. A solemn and religious gloom overspread the Union, accompanied by every outward sign of respect, and even foreign countries joined in the national mourning. Far away over the ocean, the mighty fleets of England lowered their unconquered flag at the news ; and the young soldier of France, then in the first flush of his glory, ordered his victorious standards to be veiled with crape. But, like all men of genuine worth, Washington was mourned the most by those who had known him best. "I shall soon follow him," said the wife, who for forty years had partaken of all his cares and honours; "I have no more trials to pass through." "There can be few who equally with me participate in the loss you deplore," wrote Hamilton to Mrs. Washington. His family, his friends, his servants, these were the true witnesses to his virtues; and the grief which darkened the face of a whole continent fell with a still deeper shadow on the quiet happiness of his home.

His will had been prepared not many months before, and, along with ample provisions to satisfy the claims of kindred and affection, it contained one remarkable clause, giving freedom to all his slaves

after the demise of Mrs. Washington, and charging
his estate with the maintenance of the sick, the old,
and the infirm, and with the nurture and apprentice-
ship of the children. Born and bred a slave-owner,
he had always treated his negroes with the kindness
of a father; but he felt that slavery was in itself
an evil, and he wished to see it gradually abolished—
while the term he fixed for the manumission of his
own slaves, and the wise and humane precautions
with which he accompanied it, are sufficient to prove
(if any proof were needed), that he would never have
dealt with this subject rashly or intemperately, or
without due regard to the rights, the interests, and
the welfare of all parties concerned.

They laid him in the family vault at Mount Vernon, where he had himself desired to rest. The
silence and the beauty of nature encompassed the
spot, and for many years the pilgrim, who came to
visit it, was undisturbed by any ruder association.
Since then, the hostile forces of a divided empire
have encamped on the banks of Washington's beloved river, and fought for possession of the soil
which holds his remains, like Greeks and Trojans
contending over the body of Patroclus. But no
change of circumstance, or madness of men, can

desecrate the sylvan scenes, which his life and death
have hallowed ; and his memory is enshrined for
ever in that proud temple of history, where few
have left a greater, and none a more unsullied
name.

CHAPTER XVI.

THE TIE.

WHILE the death of Washington, following near on the imprudence of Adams, was felt to be a heavy blow to the Federalist party, two men were anxiously watching to improve the occasion for their several purposes. These men were Thomas Jefferson and Aaron Burr.

In the temporary triumph which French insolence had given to the Federalists, and when most of the Republican leaders were inclined to despair of their faction, Jefferson had retained his coolness and presence of mind. His policy was to wait for events, and to take advantage of the least indiscretion on the part of his opponents. The Alien and Sedition Acts first gave him an opportunity to stem the torrent of Federalist success, and there can be no doubt that he was the instigator of that resistance in Virginia and Kentucky, which led to the earliest attempt to *nullify* the acts of Congress by a vote of the State legislatures. But his efforts would probably have failed, if Adams had not thrown the game into his hands by dividing the Federalist party. From that moment he saw that he had only to bide his time, and the intestine feuds of his adversaries would leave them at his mercy.

But while Jefferson was thus scheming and waiting, Burr was animating his partisans with the fire of his own restless disposition, and gathering round him all the daring and ambitious spirits amongst the younger members of the democracy. He was at this time in pecuniary difficulties, embarrassed by the result of various speculations, and exposed to some private slanders, which appear to have been without foundation; but he never relaxed his energy in the pursuit of his political objects, and the more desperate his fortunes, the more determined he was to force his way to power.

A new election for President was approaching, and no Washington was there to throw the weight of his influence into the scale. Meanwhile, the schism in the Federalist camp was complete. Not only had Mr. Adams resolved, that General Hamilton should not be left in command of the army, but he had denounced that gentleman in conversation with an extraordinary display of acrimony, had accused him of being the leader of a British faction, and had got rid of Colonel Pickering and Mr. McHenry from the administration. On his side, Hamilton saw that it was hopeless again to co-operate with Adams. Already in January, 1800, he writes: "The leading friends of the government are in a sad dilemma. Shall they risk a serious schism by an attempt to change; or shall they annihilate themselves, and hazard their cause, by continuing to uphold those who suspect or hate them, and who are likely to pursue a course for no better reason than because it is contrary to that which they approve?"—But, by the May following, his mind was made up. "I will never more," he says, "be responsible for him (Adams) by my direct support, even though the consequence should be the election of Jefferson."

The plan for the electoral campaign, as proposed by Hamilton, was as follows. General Charles Cotesworth Pinckney was to be started as the *second* Federalist candidate, and it was hoped, that, while many would still vote for Adams, parties would be so divided as to secure Pinckney's election for President. The friends of Mr. Adams have ex-

hausted their vocabulary, in denouncing what they
call the *treachery* of this scheme; but there does not
appear to be any good ground for such a charge. If
the Federalists were in a majority, they were of
course free to choose the candidate they preferred.
If they voted unanimously for Adams, he would be
President; if only a portion of them voted for him,
it would show that the second candidate was the
man of their choice. There was no conceivable
reason why Mr. Adams should enjoy a prescriptive
right to their suffrages. It may be true, that the
splitting of votes favoured the success of the opposite
party; but this was a contingency, which Hamilton
and his friends were surely entitled to risk, to prevent the supremacy of a man who had described
them as a British faction.

The truth seems to be, that the Federalists could
not in any case have carried the election. Their
divisions had already paralysed their strength, and
revived the courage of their opponents, whilst the
ebb and flow of public opinion (inconstant in democracies as the moon) had once more given the
majority to the Republicans. "The question is not,
I fear," said Fisher Ames, "how we shall fight, but
how we and all Federalists shall fall"—and the

result proved the correctness of his judgment. Still Hamilton struggled to gain votes for General Pinckney. He undertook a journey through the New England States, was in communication with most of the leaders there, and tried to induce the Federalists generally to act independently of Mr. Adams. It was during the heat of this contest that a singular incident occurred. Provoked by the bitter attacks of the President on himself and his friends, Hamilton had prepared a letter on the *Public Conduct and Character of John Adams, Esquire,* and had proceeded so far as to have it printed. It is supposed, that he intended it for private circulation, and perhaps to hold in reserve for some future opportunity; but it seems clear, that it was not meant for present publication, when, by mere chance, it fell into the hands of Colonel Burr. That unscrupulous personage, it is said, met the printer's boy with a basket full of pamphlets for General Hamilton, and managed to obtain a copy. Extracts were instantly inserted in the Republican journals, and Hamilton had no alternative but to publish the entire pamphlet. It contained a severe criticism of the President's public career, and some exposure of his personal foibles; but the faults charged against him were chiefly those of vanity and temper, and there was nothing after all in the sketch inconsistent with a belief in his honesty and good intentions. It was, however, attended with mischievous effects, for it widened the breach between the rival sections of the Federalist party, inflamed the angry feelings already existing amongst them, and hastened the inevitable catastrophe, which involved them all in a common ruin.

When the final result of the election was made known, it was found, that neither of the Federalist candidates had been returned, and that two of the Republicans had exactly the same number of votes. While Adams counted sixty-five suffrages, and Pinckney sixty-four, both Jefferson and Burr could boast of seventy-three. It was, therefore, A TIE, and, by the provisions of the Constitution, the choice between the two devolved on the House of Representatives.

The Congress met for the first time at the new city of Washington, and the most pressing question for settlement was the succession to the Presidency. The proper and dignified course for the Federalist party was obvious enough, and was never doubtful for a moment to the clear intellect of Hamilton.

It was to acknowledge themselves defeated, to retire from the contest, and to leave to the Republicans the responsibility of selection between their own two candidates. Whatever had then occurred, the Federalists were in no way answerable for the consequences, they were not brought into connexion with either of their opponents, and they remained an unbroken phalanx as far as their adversaries were concerned. The time would come, when they might once more assert their influence, and, in the meanwhile, they would retain all the advantages of a perfectly independent position.

But, unfortunately, the Federalists were in no temper to follow this prudent advice. Maddened by the reverses they had sustained, they were determined to seize every opportunity of revenge, and to inflict an injury, if they could not secure a triumph. They were still powerful in the House of Representatives, where, of the sixteen States that now composed the Union, they commanded the votes of six, and neutralized those of two. But the voices of nine States were required to elect a President, and, although there could be no doubt that the Republican majority intended Jefferson for that office, it would be possible to defeat their object

by giving the Federalist support to Burr. There
may have mingled with this calculation some hope
of gaining over Burr to the Federalist cause; but
the main design was to exclude Jefferson, and so
practically to reverse the decision of the national
vote.

It was an unwise and unworthy policy, which did
more harm to the party that adopted it than all the
plots of their enemies. That honest and able man,
Gouverneur Morris, at once protested against it, on
the plain ground of right. "Since it was evidently
the intention of our fellow-citizens," he said, "to
make Mr. Jefferson their President, it seems proper
to fulfil that intention." And a little later he wrote
to Hamilton, complaining that the excitement amongst
their political friends rendered them deaf to the voice
of reason, and that it was dangerous to quote an
opinion in opposition to their plans. "You who are
temperate in drinking," he adds, "have never, perhaps,
noticed the awkward situation of a man who continues
sober after the company are drunk."

But Hamilton, whom no danger from friend or foe
ever held back from his duty to his country, had
strongly urged his opposition to the intended scheme.
He wrote private letters to many of the leaders of

the party, and laboured incessantly to convince them
of the perils of an alliance with Burr. The most
remarkable of these letters is addressed to Mr.
Bayard, and may be taken as a complete exposition
of Hamilton's views on the subject. "I was glad to
find, my dear sir, by your letter," he says, "that you
had not yet determined to go, with the consent of
the Federal party, in support of Mr. Burr; and that
you were resolved to hold yourself disengaged till
the moment of final decision. Your resolution to
separate yourself in this instance from the Federal
party, if your conviction shall be strong of the
unfitness of Mr. Burr, is certainly laudable. So
much does it coincide with my ideas, that if the
party shall, by supporting Mr. Burr as President,
adopt him for their official chief, I shall be obliged
to consider myself as an *isolated* man. It will be
impossible for me to reconcile with my notions of
honour or policy, the continuing to be of a party
which, according to my apprehension, will have degraded itself and the country.

"I am sure, nevertheless, that the motives of many
will be good, and I shall never cease to esteem the
individuals, though I shall deplore a step which I
fear experience will show to be a very fatal one.

Among the letters which I receive, assigning the reasons (*pro* and *con*) for preferring Burr to Jefferson, I observe no small exaggeration to the prejudice of the latter, and some things taken for granted as to the former which are at least questionable. Perhaps myself the first, at some expense of popularity, to unfold the true character of Jefferson, it is too late for me to become his apologist; nor have I any disposition to do it.

"I admit that his politics are tinctured with fanaticism; that he is too much in earnest in his democracy; that he has been a mischievous enemy to the principal measures of our past administration; that he is crafty and persevering in his objects; that he is not scrupulous about the means of success, nor very mindful of truth, and that he is a contemptible hypocrite. But it is not true, as is alleged, that he is an enemy to the power of the Executive, or that he is for confounding all the powers in the House of Representatives. It is a fact which I have frequently mentioned, that, while we were in the administration together, he was generally for a large construction of the executive authority, and not backward to act upon it in cases which coincided with his views. Let it be added, that in his theoretic ideas he has considered as improper the participation of the Senate in the executive authority. I have more than once made the reflection, that, *viewing himself as the reversioner*, he was solicitous to come into the possession of a good estate. Nor is it true that Jefferson is zealous enough to do anything in pursuance of his principles, which will contravene his popularity or his interest. He is as likely as any man I know to temporize; to calculate what will be likely to promote his own reputation and advantage; and the probable result of such a temper is the preservation of systems, though originally opposed, which, being once established, could not be overturned without danger to the person who did it. To my mind, a true estimate of Mr. Jefferson's character warrants the expectation of a temporizing rather than a violent system. That Jefferson has manifested a culpable predilection for France is certainly true; but I think it a question whether it did not proceed quite as much from her popularity among us as from sentiment; and in proportion as that popularity is diminished his zeal will cool. Add to this, that there is no fair reason to suppose him capable of being corrupted, which is a security that he will not go beyond certain limits. It is not at all improbable that, under the change

of circumstances, Jefferson's Gallicism has consider-
ably abated."

Hamilton then proceeds to consider how far the
Federalists would gain by substituting for Jefferson
a man of extreme and irregular ambition like Burr.
He combats the notion, that the very selfishness of
that artful and dexterous intriguer will lead him to
adopt sound views of policy. He shows that, however Burr may break with the Republicans, it will
certainly not be to join the Federalists. He will
take care not to disoblige his present supporters,
"and he will always court those among them who
are best fitted for tools. He will never choose to
lean on good men, because he knows that they will
never support his bad projects; but, instead of this,
he will endeavour to disorganize both parties, and to
form out of them a third, composed of men fitted by
their characters to be conspirators and instruments of
such projects."

He goes on to say, that Burr had blamed him
(Hamilton) for not having improved the situation
he once was in, to change the government; that,
when told it could not have been done without guilt,
he had answered: " Great souls care little for small
morals;" and that, when it was observed the thing

was never practicable, from the genius and situation of the country, he had only remarked : "That depends upon the estimate we form of the human passions, and of the means of influencing them."

"The truth is," continues Hamilton, "that, with great apparent coldness, he is the most sanguine man in the world. He thinks everything possible to adventure and perseverance ; and, though I believe he will fail, I think it almost certain he will attempt usurpation, and the attempt will involve great mischief.

"But there is one point of view which seems to me decisive. If the Anti-Federalists, who prevailed in the election, are left to take their own man, they remain responsible, and the Federalists remain free, united, and without stain, in a situation to resist with effect pernicious measures. If the Federalists substitute Burr, they adopt him, and become answerable for him. Whatever may be the theory of the case, abroad and at home (for so from the beginning it will be taught) Mr. Burr must become, in fact, the man of our party ; and if he acts ill, we must share in the blame and disgrace. By adopting him, we do all we can to reconcile the minds of Federalists to him, and we prepare them for the effectual operation of his acts. He will, doubtless, gain many of them, and the Federalists will become a disorganized and contemptible party. Can there be any serious question between the policy of leaving the Anti-Federalists to be answerable for the elevation of an objectionable man; and that of adopting ourselves, and becoming answerable for, a man, who on all hands is acknowledged to be a complete Catiline? 'Tis enough to state the question to indicate the answer, if reason, not passion, presides in the decision.

" You may communicate this and my former letter to discreet and confidential friends."

But the counsels of moderation and wisdom were thrown away on the excited passions of the hour. The Federalists persisted in voting for Burr, the House was equally divided, and thirty-five ballotings took place without a result. For seven days the contest was continued with dogged obstinacy, amid the threats of the Republicans and the indignant murmurs of the people. Burr claimed the credit of taking no part in this intrigue; but Jefferson evidently suspected him of acting indirectly through agents. As it turned out, the only effect of the struggle was to complete the ruin of the Federalist party. The unseemly strife was at length terminated by Mr. Bayard, Hamilton's correspondent. Finding the case hopeless, he declared his intention of voting for Jefferson ; others stayed away, and, on the thirty-sixth ballot, the necessary majority was obtained. But this late and forced concession could not repair the mischief already done, and the party, which had been most distinguished for devotion to the Constitution, paid dearly for neglecting the advice of the great constitutional leader.

On the 4th of March, 1801, Mr. Jefferson was inaugurated President of the United States, and Mr. Adams, wrathful and implacable, refused even to be present at the installation of his successor. "The last day of his political power," says Jefferson, "the last hour, and even beyond midnight, were employed in filling all offices, and especially permanent ones, with the bitterest Federalists, and providing for me the alternative either to execute the government by my enemies—whose study it would be to thwart and defeat all my measures—or to incur the odium of such numerous removals from office as might bear me down." It may be added, that Jefferson preferred to encounter the latter danger, and that his example has since been generally followed in America. It

has been one of the great evils of the system, that
the accession of every new President has been
accompanied by innumerable changes in the inferior
posts, and by the disturbance of official relations
from one end of the country to the other.

Wearied and desponding, Hamilton saw the
supreme power passing into the hands of his enemies, and the pile he had reared with so much
toil shaken to its foundations. The unchecked flood
of democracy was breaking in upon all sides, and he
felt that henceforth nothing would be able to resist
its course. "Mine is an odd destiny," he wrote to
Gouverneur Morris. "Perhaps, no man in the United
States has sacrificed or done more for the present
Constitution than myself; and, contrary to all my
anticipations of its fate, as you know from the very
beginning, I am still labouring to prop the frail and
worthless fabric. Yet I have the murmurs of its
friends, no less than the curses of its foes, for my
reward. What can I do better than withdraw from
the scene ! Every day proves to me more and more,
that this American world was not made for me."

CHAPTER XVII.

THE DUEL.

IN the neighbourhood of New York, but still in the midst of rural scenery, and not far from the ancient village of Manhattan, Hamilton had purchased a small estate. The ground was undulating, and adorned with fine old trees, a pleasant lawn spread in front of the house, and the balcony of the drawing-room commanded a magnificent prospect. Harlem River, and Long Island Sound, and many a scene endeared by its own beauty, or made interesting by old recollections, were visible from this lovely spot. Hamilton called it *The Grange*, after the name of his grandfather's house in Scotland, in the bonny shire of Ayr; and thither he often retired from the labours of his profession, to enjoy the society of his family, and the refreshment of a country life.

He had laid aside the truncheon of command, and

was once more a busy man at the bar, and, although he could never keep quite clear of politics, they no longer occupied all his thoughts. He could occupy himself with his garden—"a very usual refuge," he says, "for a disappointed politician"—send to Carolina for melon-seeds and paroquets for his daughter, play at soldiers with his boys, and spend summer evenings with his friends on the green slopes of his domain. A great sorrow came to darken this cheerful picture. His eldest son, a promising youth of twenty, was killed in a duel arising from a dispute at the theatre. It was a bitter grief to the father and all the family; but it only foreshadowed the worse calamity that was to follow.

While Jefferson, during the first years of his administration, was filling every place with his partisans, reducing the army and navy to satisfy the tax-payers, and doing all in his power to increase the influence of the democracy, Colonel Burr was by no means content with his share of the spoils of victory. He was indeed Vice-President; but he found that he had scarcely any direct weight with the government, that his immediate friends were not appointed to office, and that the leaders of the

Republican party were inclined to keep him in the background. It was a dangerous game to play with such a man, and he once more cast about him to obtain a lever for his ambition. He not only endeavoured to strengthen his own faction, but he carried on a kind of political flirtation with the Federalists, and some of them cherished a hope of a return to power, by the help of what Hamilton called "Burr's flying squadrons." It was after an interview with Jefferson, in which he vainly tried to extort from the President some definite pledge, that Burr resolved to act quite independently, and to start as a candidate for the Governorship of New York. Could he succeed in this election, the highest post in the Union might yet be within his grasp. But to succeed he must have the support of the Federalists, and that support was yet in some measure dependent on Hamilton. The latter declared against him, and, although he polled 28,000 votes, he was defeated by a majority of 7,000. It was the last drop in the cup. Burr looked on Hamilton as the evil genius of his life, and it is only too probable that, from that moment, he determined to destroy him.

The election took place in the spring of 1804.

Monstrous stories are told, that Burr devoted three months to pistol-practice before calling out his intended victim, and that he set up a mark in his own grounds to shoot at. It is not necessary to believe these tales. They rest on no good evidence, and have all the character of vague popular rumours. Burr was a brave man—a man of iron resolution—with steady nerves, and no doubt a fair mastery of his weapon. It is very unlikely, that he would have thus waited to train himself for combat. It is far more conceivable, that the delay was caused by the want of a decent pretext for a quarrel.

That pretext was at length found in the columns of a newspaper. A letter from a Dr. Cooper to a friend, with reference to the late election, had appeared in one of the journals. It contained this passage: "General Hamilton and Judge Kent have declared in substance, that they looked upon Mr. Burr to be a dangerous man, and one who ought not to be trusted with the reins of Government. *I could detail to you a still more despicable opinion, which General Hamilton has expressed of Mr. Burr.*" And this wretched gossip, such as was going about with regard to all the public men of the day, was made the ground to fasten an offence on Hamilton, and to force him to risk his life in a personal encounter.

On the 17th of June, Burr sent for Mr. Van Ness, one of his most intimate friends, and requested him to deliver a note to General Hamilton. It called attention to the passage in the published letter, and added: "You must perceive, sir, the necessity of a prompt and unqualified acknowledgment or denial of the use of any expressions, which could warrant the assertions of Dr. Cooper."

Hamilton might well be surprised at this demand. It was clear, that whatever opinions he had expressed to his friends, with regard to the fitness or unfitness of a particular man for office, were privileged communications, which could not with propriety be called in question. At the same time he did not wish to evade the subject, and asked time for consideration. On the 20th he sent a reply to Burr's note, in which he declined to make the acknowledgment or denial demanded. He could attach no meaning to the words *more despicable* as used in the letter, and he could not consent to be interrogated as to *the inferences* drawn by *third parties*, from what he had said of an opponent during fifteen years' competition. He was ready to avow or disavow any *definite* opinion, which he might be charged with having expressed of any gentleman. He trusted that, on reflection, Colonel Burr would see the matter in the same light. If not, he must abide the consequences.

To this Burr returned an answer, which seems intended to prevent the possibility of compromise. "Your letter of the 20th instant," he says, "has been this day received. Having considered it attentively, I regret to find in it nothing of that sincerity and delicacy, which you profess to value. Political opposition can never absolve gentlemen from the necessity of a rigid adherence to the laws of honour and the rules of decorum. I neither claim such privilege, nor indulge it in others. The common sense of mankind affixes to the epithet adopted by Dr. Cooper the idea of dishonour. It has been publicly applied to me under the sanction of your name. The question is not whether he has understood the meaning of the word, or used it according to syntax, and with grammatical accuracy; but whether you have authorized this application, either directly, or by uttering expressions or opinions derogatory to my honour. The time *when* is in your own knowledge, but no way material to me;

as the calumny has now first been disclosed, so as to become the subject of my notice, and as the effect is present and palpable. Your letter has furnished me with new reasons for requiring a definite reply."

When Mr. Van Ness delivered this uncourteous epistle, Hamilton said that it was not such as he had hoped to receive; it contained several offensive expressions, and closed the door to a reply; but he was even yet willing to enter more fully into explanations, and, if Colonel Burr chose to give another turn to the discussion, he was at liberty to withdraw that letter.

Other communications followed, through the intervention of Hamilton's friend, Mr. Pendleton, and, for ten days, the correspondence and interviews continued. Hamilton showed throughout a conciliatory temper, and a wish to do everything consistent with honour to bring about an amicable arrangement. He gave Van Ness a paper in his own handwriting, in which he stated, that, if Colonel Burr chose to inquire the purport of any conversation between General Hamilton and Dr. Cooper, General Hamilton would be able to reply with truth, that it turned wholly on political topics, and had no relation to Colonel Burr's private character. And he added, that he was ready to make an equally frank answer, with regard to any other conversation, which Colonel Burr would *specify*. But Burr was not so to be turned from his prey, which he pursued with the savage eagerness and obstinacy of the bloodhound. He persisted, "that the partial negative General Hamilton was disposed to give, with the reservations he wished to make, were proofs that he had done the injury specified ; " and refused to accept anything short of a *general* disavowal of *all* imputations on his character. This he was not entitled to ask, and, as he well knew, Hamilton could not grant. But the reasons, which Burr advanced, were in fact of secondary importance. His motives were only too apparent. He had said in his heart : " This man has crossed me for years in all my schemes of ambition. I admired his talents, but he refused my homage. I offered him my friendship, but he repelled the offer. I would have shared with him the three idols of my soul's worship—pleasure, and glory, and power. But he chose to go his own way, with his fine phrases of public virtue, to thwart me at every step, and to foil my best-laid plans. He did it at his peril ;

and now the alternative shall be *his life* or *mine.*"

But why did Hamilton accept the challenge? Before answering this question, it should not be forgotten, that a complete and most beneficent change in public opinion with regard to duelling has taken place within the memory of one generation. The absurd and barbarous custom, which staked the most valuable life against that of any scoundrel who could pull a trigger, and which, though it flourished in every Christian country, must be condemned by every possible code of Christian ethics, has now been happily consigned (in England at least) to the same limbo as the witchcraft and astrology of the middle ages. But, when Burr challenged Hamilton, and for many years after, it prevailed almost universally, and exercised a tyrannical influence over men of all ranks and conditions. Many of the leading statesmen of that day were engaged in duels, and, a quarter of a century later, the greatest soldier and subject of the British Crown, then holding the highest official station, thought it necessary to go out and fight in defence of his political consistency. Habit, example, prejudice, all were in favour of accepting a challenge, especially when offered by one military man to another; and no one could refuse it under those circumstances, without incurring a certain amount of popular contempt and obloquy.

And yet it must be acknowledged, that, in consenting to fight with Burr, Hamilton committed a grave and fatal error. Often enough, in the course of his splendid career, he had dared to stand alone, and to brave alike the malice of enemies, and the senseless clamour of mobs. In this instance also, he would have done well to prefer his duty to God, his family, and his country, to any mere pressure of public opinion. He should have refused to expose a life, on which so much depended, to the chances of a marksman's fire; and the studied and deliberate malignity of his adversary would have justified him in the eyes of all honourable men. It may be said, that a soldier's courage, like a woman's chastity, is not able to endure even the suspicion of a stain. But the man who had earned in his youth the name of the *Little Lion*—who had turned the tide of battle at Monmouth Court House, and been the first over the ramparts at the siege of Yorktown— had surely no need to prove his valour by engaging in private combat. The truth is, that, with all his magnanimity, Hamilton was not exempt from mortal imperfections; and among them none was more prominent than the extreme sensitiveness of his pride. He could not bear the whisper of a doubt affecting his military honour; and he, who had defied the multitude on questions of public principle, sacrificed his convictions to their breath in a matter of personal reputation. He seems to have feared also, that his refusal to fight would diminish his influence, and so impair his future usefulness. But, whatever the grounds of his resolution, he determined to accept the challenge, and to risk his own life in the combat, while he abstained from taking that of his deadly foe.

He informed Colonel Burr, through Mr. Pendleton, that he had yet some business to transact, and private affairs to arrange, but that he would meet him with as little delay as possible. The seconds conferred together to settle the preliminaries, and at length fixed on the 11th of July, at seven o'clock in the morning, for the time of the encounter. The place was to be Weehawken, on the Jersey shore of the Hudson, the weapons pistols, and the distance ten paces.

The fact, that a fortnight elapsed between the

acceptance of the challenge and the meeting, and
that during the interval the secret was known to
several persons, adds a peculiar character to the
lamentable circumstances of this duel. One would
have thought that some friend, warned in time,
would have interposed between these two men—
both distinguished, both followed by faithful adherents—to save them from a cruel fate. One would
have hoped that even the heart of the aggressor
would have relented, at the cool contemplation of
what he was about to do. But no warning came,
no friend interposed, and the heart of Colonel Burr
remained hard as the nether millstone. Both the
principals went about their business as usual; and it
was long remembered how well Hamilton had pleaded
his causes, how kind and courteous he had been to
his friends and clients, how gentle and amiable to
all men, during that dread period of suspense. Daily
he returned to *The Grange*, and saw his wife and
seven children gathered about his table, and listened
to the gay talk and innocent prattle, which he knew
might so soon be changed to wailings of anguish and
despair. The 4th of July came round, and both
Hamilton and Burr were present at the banquet of
the *Cincinnati*. Late in the festival, some of his old

comrades urged Hamilton to sing the ballad of *The Drum*. He was at first reluctant, but at length yielded to their wish, and sang it in his best manner. Burr leaned on the table, and looked steadfastly at him during the performance. But no word passed between them, and their next meeting was the last.

On the 9th of the month Hamilton executed his will. He left everything he possessed, after payment of his debts, to his *dear and excellent wife*. "Should it happen," he says, "that there is not enough for the payment of my debts, I entreat my dear children, if they or any of them should ever be able, to make up the deficiency. I, without hesitation, commit to their delicacy a wish which is dictated by my own. Though conscious that I have too far sacrificed the interests of my family to public avocations, and on this account have the less claim to burden my children, yet I trust in their magnanimity to appreciate as they ought this my request. In so unfavourable an event of things, the support of their dear mother, with the most respectful and tender attention, is a duty, all the sacredness of which they will feel. Probably, her own patrimonial resources will preserve her from indigence. But in all situations they are charged to bear in mind, that she has been to them the most devoted and best of mothers."

And now the eve of the fatal day had come. Hamilton sat writing late into the night, and left a paper, containing an explanation of his motives. In this interesting and affecting document, he avowed that he had shrunk from the coming interview—that his religious principles, his regard for his family, and his duty to his creditors, were alike opposed to it—that he should hazard much, and could gain nothing by it—that he was conscious of no ill-will to Colonel Burr, apart from political opposition, which he hoped had proceeded from pure and upright motives. But there were insuperable difficulties, intrinsic and artificial, in the way of an accommodation; *intrinsic*, because he had really, at various times, made severe remarks on Colonel Burr—*artificial*, because the explanation had been demanded in such a manner as to preclude a peaceful discussion. Then follows a passage which, in its candour and generosity, is quite characteristic of Hamilton. " As well because it is possible," he says, " that I may have injured Colonel Burr, however convinced myself that my opinions and declarations have been well founded, as from my general principles and temper in relation to similar affairs, I have resolved, if our interview is conducted in the usual manner, and it pleases God to give me the opportunity, *to reserve and throw away my first fire`;* and I have thought even of *reserving my second fire,* and thus giving a double opportunity to Colonel Burr to pause and to reflect. It is not, however, my intention to enter into any explanations on the ground. Apology—from principle, I hope, rather than pride—is out of the question. To those who, with me abhorring the practice of duelling, may think that I ought on no account to have added to the number of bad examples, I answer that my relative situation, as well in public as in private, enforcing all the considerations which constitute what men of the world denominate honour, imposed on me, as I thought, a peculiar necessity not to decline the call. The ability to be in the future useful, whether in resisting mischief or effecting good, in those crises of our public affairs which seem likely to happen, would probably be insepa-rable from a conformity with public prejudice in this particular."

There is, at all events, something very consolatory in the above mournful sentences. They show that

Hamilton went to the ground with no hostile or murderous intention—that he went to risk his life in deference to a prejudice he despised—but that he had fully resolved to spare the enemy who was hunting him so remorselessly to the death, and only to use his weapon in the last extremity of self-defence. Is it presumption to hope that those last thoughts and words, preserved and registered by angels of love and pity, have pleaded eloquently for him at the bar of heaven? And may we not safely leave him in the hands of that supreme tribunal, in humble but perfect reliance on the mercy of *his* Judge and *ours* ?

The morning of the 11th of July rose warm and bright over the waters of the Hudson, when a boat was seen to glide from the New York to the Jersey shore, and Burr and his second, landing beneath the heights of Weehawken, ascended to a grassy ledge about twenty feet above the river, and there stood waiting for the arrival of the adverse party. They were not kept long in suspense. A few minutes before seven Hamilton's boat touched the rocks below, and he and his friend, Mr. Pendleton, mounted to the same spot. A surgeon was left with the boats, to be called if his services were required.

Gravely and courteously the principals saluted each other, and the seconds proceeded to measure the ground, and to cast lots for the choice of position. When the principals were placed, Pendleton said to Hamilton: "Will you have the hair-spring set?" "Not this time," answered the other, quietly; and in those words was the confirmation of the resolve he had taken, to spare the life of his enemy.

The pistols were handed to the principals, and the seconds inquired if they were ready. Both replied in the affirmative, and a moment's pause ensued. Then the fatal word was given, but Hamilton remained motionless. Burr raised his pistol, took deliberate aim, and fired. Hamilton sprang forward, involuntarily discharging his pistol, and fell headlong upon his face. As he saw him fall, an expression of something like regret passed over the countenance of Burr; but Van Ness hurried him from the ground, for the surgeon and the boatmen were approaching. They found Hamilton half lying, half sitting on the grass, supported in the arms of his second. The ball had entered his right side, and the pallor of death was on his features. "Doctor," he said, "this is a mortal wound,"—and he swooned away with the effort.

They carried him down the rocks, and placed him tenderly in the boat. The surgeon applied the usual restoratives, and he began slowly to revive. His eyes wandered—he murmured: " My vision is indistinct "—but soon after he caught sight of a pistol lying near him, and his first thought was for the safety of others. " Take care of that pistol," he said; " it is undischarged and still cocked; it may go off and do harm. Pendleton knows that I did not intend to fire at him."

Then he remained silent till they approached the city. " Let Mrs. Hamilton be sent for," he said, as they drew near the wharf; " let the event be gradually broken to her, but give her hopes." His friend, Mr. Bayard, was waiting at the landing-place. He had heard from his servant, that General Hamilton and Mr. Pendleton had crossed the river, and he guessed the nature of their errand. When he saw his poor friend lying at the bottom of the boat, he burst into tears and lamentations. Hamilton alone was calm, and gave the necessary directions. They conveyed him to Mr. Bayard's house, and despatched messengers for his family.

It is best to draw a veil over that closing scene. Suffice it to say that he lingered for thirty hours

in great agony, but retained his composure and
self-command to the last. He tried, with failing
voice, to comfort his broken-hearted wife—he fixed
his dying looks with unutterable tenderness on his
children—and he resigned his soul to his Maker
with the unaffected penitence and submission of an
erring, but noble nature.

When the result of the duel was first known, it
spread consternation through the city. In a moment
all was forgotten, except the services and the fame
of the victim. That very populace, which at one
time had received him with acclamations, and at
another had stoned and hooted him in the streets,
now thronged, with pale faces and tearful eyes, to
glean the slightest intelligence of the state of the
illustrious sufferer. Bulletins were issued hourly,
and the people waited for them with intense and
breathless anxiety. When his death was at length
announced, a cry of sorrow for his fate, and of
execration on his murderer, burst from the lips and
hearts of the multitude. On the day of his funeral
the whole city was in mourning. The procession,
which followed him to the grave, comprised men
of every degree, without distinction of parties. The
minute-guns from the batteries were answered by

the French and British ships-of-war in the harbour. On the steps of Trinity Church, Gouverneur Morris, with the four sons of the deceased by his side, pronounced a solemn oration in memory of his slaughtered friend; and when they had laid him in the earth, and the parting volley had been fired over his remains, the vast crowd dispersed in silence, and each man carried to his home the impression of a profound grief. Nor was this feeling confined to New York. It spread rapidly through the Union, and found utterance in every variety of form. Speeches, and sermons, and poems innumerable were composed in honour of Hamilton, towns and villages in all parts of America were called after his name, and never, since the death of Washington, has any event produced so universal an expression of sympathy on that continent, as the untimely and lamentable end of the great Federalist.

Well might they grieve for *him*, who had left none like himself in all the wide area between the Atlantic and Pacific, and to whom the subsequent history of America has furnished no equal. Into the forty-seven years of his mortal career, he had compressed such an amount of difficult and laborious service, as few men have ever rendered to any country in the longest term of human existence; and, when he fell, his great powers were in their meridian fulness, and their exercise was never more needed than at the moment of their loss. Every generous and every selfish consideration combined to make his death a subject for national mourning. And so, in the first days of remorseful sorrow, America wept for Hamilton as for her favourite son —and then, with the strange inconsistency of democracies, forgot at once his precepts and his example, and yielded to the downward current that was bearing her far away from all the principles of his life.

CHAPTER XVIII.

THE DEMOCRACY.

WITH Hamilton fell the last hopes of the Federalist party. Burr's fatal shot had destroyed more than his great rival. It had cut the ground from under his own feet, and left Jefferson in undisputed possession of the field. From the day of the duel, Burr ceased to be a political leader, and his name was held in horror by the great majority of his countrymen. A coroner's jury returned a verdict of *Murder*, and the Vice-President had to fly and conceal himself until the first fury of the people had blown over. After a time, his friends seem to have obtained a promise that no criminal proceedings would be taken against him; but his position was gone, and he was in most respects a ruined man. Driven from his profession, overwhelmed with debts, abandoned by one faction, and denounced by the other, he appeared to have no choice but to sink into obscurity and be forgotten. It was under these circumstances, that his wonderful energy contrived a scheme of matchless daring, which only proved how true had been the instinct of Hamilton, when he warned his country against placing power in the hands of this reckless adventurer.

The United States had just acquired Louisiana by purchase from France, but the Spaniards still held extensive possessions to the West of the Mississippi, and the border-land was inhabited by a wild, unsettled population, not very strict in their allegiance to any power. After the death of Hamilton, Burr went to travel in the South-Western regions, descending the Ohio in a boat, and afterwards proceeding in the same manner to New Orleans—a voyage which, with stoppages by the way, took him sixty-seven days. He returned on horseback through the wilderness, halted at Natchez, Nashville, and other places, made himself well acquainted with the habits and feelings of the people of those parts, and, if he is not much belied, conceived the most magnificent project that ever dazzled the eyes or mingled with the dreams of ambition. He hoped that a war with Spain was at hand; but, whether

it broke out or not, his design was to assemble a
host of restless and adventurous spirits on the
frontier, and to take the first opportunity that might
offer to invade the Spanish dominions. The conquest
of Texas, the ultimate subjugation of Mexico—all
those plans of lawless aggrandizement, which have
since bewildered and misled so many of his countrymen—were present to the mind of Burr. It is
said that the throne of Montezuma was his object,
and that he saw himself already at the head of a
new empire, which was to absorb the valley of the
Mississippi, and the Western States of the Union.
It is certain that he laboured incessantly to collect
money, stores, and adherents, and that he was
making every preparation for a warlike expedition,
when he was betrayed by one of his confederates,
and arrested by order of the President. He was
brought a prisoner to Richmond, and there tried
on a charge of treason. He was attacked and
defended with equal violence and passion, but the
evidence failed to prove the charge, and the jury
returned a verdict of *Not Guilty*. Burr's own
account of the matter was, that the object of his
proposed expedition was to settle lands on the
frontier, and *not* to levy private war, or to separate

the Western from the Atlantic States. He was accordingly acquitted; but the outcry raised against him made it prudent for him to leave America for some time, and he embarked under a feigned name for Europe.

For several years, he led the life of a wandering exile—in England, in Sweden, in Germany, in France. Suspicion seems to have followed him wherever he went, and he was frequently reduced to extremities for want both of cash and credit. He retained his taste for intrigue, his talents, energy, and courage; but the ghost of Hamilton must often have crossed his path, and barred his way to the recovery of fame and fortune. It is related, that, when in Paris, he wrote to Talleyrand requesting an interview, and that the latter replied: "The Minister for Foreign Affairs will be happy to see the late Vice-President of the United States; but M. Talleyrand thinks it due to Colonel Burr to state, that he always has the miniature of General Hamilton hanging over his mantel-piece."

At length, the exile returned home, and was allowed to spend the rest of his days unmolested; but his society was generally shunned, and he lived in poverty and seclusion. He was indebted for the few comforts of his last years, when old and stricken with paralysis, to the ministry of that charitable sex, which had never ceased to regard him with a romantic interest. He lingered on to the age of eighty, and then died in obscurity—his end forming a singular contrast to the brilliancy of his youth, and the stormy ambition of his manhood. Let us hope, that this prolonged period of existence was not granted him in vain; and that, in sickness and solitude, he learned to repent of the great crime, which robbed America of her foremost statesman, and stained his own soul with blood.

Meanwhile, Jefferson had endeavoured to maintain his power by the same arts that had acquired it. His object was " to sink Federalism into an abyss, from which there shall be no resurrection," and to complete the revolution he had begun, by giving entire sovereignty to the populace. He chose indeed to govern—but to govern by submission to the democracy. From his Presidency dates that utter prostration of the intellect of America to vulgar ignorance and clamour, which has made the tenure of office in that country a reproach and degradation to the holders. Every dyke and barrier, which still remained to check the advancing flood, was gradually swept away. The States followed each other in the course of change, and, through the succeeding years, broke down the last remnants of strength and stability in their institutions. Universal suffrage (or something nearly approaching it) everywhere took the place of the old qualifications for voters. The rights of citizenship, once jealously guarded, were lightly bestowed on all comers, without limitation or precaution. In some States, the independence of the tribunals was attacked, by making the judges removable, or only electing them for terms ; in others, the abolition of existing grants and endowments left the ministers of religion more and more at the mercy of their flocks. The whole tendency of the time was to submit the governors to the governed, and to treat authority and obedience as the old-world fancies of a worn-out superstition. Hence the rude familiarity in manners, the arrogant self-assertion, the untenable claims to social equality, and the general want of reverence, which make so strong an impression on visitors to the United States. Of course, all this did not grow up in the Presidency, or even in the life of Jefferson. But it is from the triumph of him and his partisans, and the fall of their gifted opponents, that we trace the unchecked progress of the democratic stream. And henceforth it was not *one* party only, but *all*, that shared in the abject worship of the popular idolatry. Many factions have since arisen in the United States, with various professions of opinion, and under many different titles—but all have alike acknowledged the practical supremacy of the mob, and striven to gain its support by flattering its passions and prejudices. No politician has since addressed the American people, as Hamilton used to address them ; and they, in their turn, have substituted the mere agents of their will, for leaders that could guide their judgment, or statesmen that could rule the republic.

Therefore it is, that the history of the United States presents from this time such singular contrasts to the world. On the one hand, favoured by the circumstances of their climate and geographical position, their immense and fertile territory, their chain of lakes and rivers, and a thousand other natural advantages, and by the constant tide of immigration for ever setting in from the shores of Europe—they have enjoyed a material prosperity, such as was never before bestowed on man by a beneficent Providence. Nowhere, probably, have the labouring classes been blessed with so many com-

forts, or with such fair prospects for themselves and
their children. Nowhere has commerce flourishe⟨
more abundantly, or such wide-spread wellbeing
rewarded the industry of a nation. The number
of the States has been nearly trebled, the people
have multiplied tenfold, the desert has bloomed
into a garden, towns and cities have sprung up
like Aladdin's palaces, and all the discoveries of
science have been as genii of the lamp to this
energetic race. And yet, on the other hand, in
the midst of wealth and apparent progress, there
have not been wanting signs of social, moral, and
political deterioration. Not only has this been
visible in the decay of ancient manners, and the
decline of honourable feeling, but also in the loss
of all independence of thought, and in the blind
submission of the understanding to the freaks and
fancies of the multitude. One by one, the higher
class of minds have retired from public life, and
left the stage to the dulness of mediocrity, and to
the intrigues of adventurers. Nothing can be more
dreary than the records of that half-century of
ever-deepening gloom—relieved here and there by
a flash of light from the intellectual activity of a
Clay, a Calhoun, or a Webster, but, in the main,

rolling darkly along on its obscure and blundering course, till all difference of principle is absorbed in a selfish contest for pelf and power. Then, while the mantle of Washington passes from one lay-figure to another, all great questions are suppressed, all inquiries stifled, all difficulties evaded or shuffled out of the way; and the American people, soothed by the voice of flattery, and plunged in an atmosphere of self-delusion, are content to admire their own perfections, and look down with contemptuous pity on the rest of the world—till the inevitable END comes, and history affords one more example, that no nation can safely dispense with the services of its ablest citizens, or confide its government with impunity to the management of inferior men.

It would be idle to ascribe the catastrophe to any one party, or to any particular series of measures. Sooner or later, it must have come in the natural sequence of events. It was not because this or that question pressed for settlement, and that the interests of the States were divided on many important subjects; but because the vessel of the Union was drifting helplessly on the waters, without helm, or pilot, or chart, or compass, and the democracy looked on with careless indifference, foreseeing, anticipating, and preventing nothing. It suited them better to indulge in visions of boundless prosperity and glory and to use the language of ostentation at home, and of unprovoked defiance abroad, than to give a thought to the dangers that were gathering around them ; and the first notes of civil war aroused them from the dream of a fool's paradise, to find their empire rent asunder, and the most terrible of calamities about to fall upon them.

It would, perhaps, be still vainer to inquire what would have been the result if Hamilton's life had been spared. Both Adams and Jefferson lived to a great age—dying in 1826, by one of the strangest coincidences in history, on the same day, and on the anniversary of the Declaration of Independence—yet the troubles were still far distant, and they knew not of the evil to come. Though Hamilton was younger than either, he could hardly have survived them many years. He had already foretold the perils that menaced the republic, and his provident wisdom might have guarded against some of them ; but it is more than doubtful whether he could have succeeded in stemming the tide of democracy, or in reviving that Conservative party which alone could have saved the Union.

Yet, if it be permitted to dwell for a few moments on a picture of fancy, and to conceive Hamilton still alive, and taking a prominent part in the government of his country, it may not be uninstructive to consider what would have been his policy.

In the first place, he would have prepared for the crisis long before it came. As far as his influence extended, he would have trained his countrymen to meet adversity with patience and dignity, by accustoming them to the accents of reason and moderation. But, more than this, he would have grappled boldly with the questions at issue between the States, and have laboured to arrange them amicably, while it was yet time. He would have taken care not to step one hair's breadth beyond the limits of the Constitution, but within those limits he would have applied his whole soul to the task of reconciliation. With what scorn would he have looked down upon those personal and party feuds, which were withdrawing the attention of politicians from the great interests of the country! How indignantly would he have denounced the petty jealousies of trade, which were sacrificing the industry of one section of the Union to the protective tariffs of the other! And how anxiously would he have sought for the solution of that awful problem of slavery, which was fast escaping from the hands of the statesman, to fall into those of incendiaries and fanatics on both sides !

With regard to slavery, Hamilton had from his youth upward been opposed to it. Embracing all men, black and white, in his comprehensive and genuine humanity, he desired to see them all happy and free. He well knew the evils inseparable from a state of serfdom, and he would not willingly have trusted any mortal with irresponsible power over his fellow-creatures. But he also knew, that the right to possess negroes was interwoven with the laws, the customs, and the interests of large numbers of his countrymen, and that it had been recognized and confirmed by the whole course of American legislation. North and South had origi- nally shared in the practice, and both still profited by a commerce which was based on the growth and extension of slave-labour. The present race of planters had inherited their slaves from their fathers, held them by the same title as any other property, and, in spite of some glaring and horrible exceptions, treated them in general with more kindness than was often bestowed on the negro by the inhabitants of the free States. Hamilton was too just to impute the existence of the institution, still less its flagrant abuses and scandals, to any peculiar wickedness in the slave-owners. He was too wise to expect them to make sacrifices for principle, in which the rest of the Union was not disposed to join, and so to become scapegoats for the sins of the whole republic. He would have seen that, if the question was ever to be satisfactorily adjusted, it could only be by approaching it with large and liberal views—by dealing with it equitably and generously—and by calling on every citizen, in every portion of the empire, to take his full share in the cost and the burden of curing this national disease. He would have seen that, under the most favourable circumstances, the result could only be brought about slowly, gradually, cautiously —for the sake of every person and interest concerned, and especially for the sake of the negroes themselves. He would have seen that to continue, and even to extend the institution, was the undoubted legal right of the several States—that to circumscribe, and ultimately to abolish it, was a matter of high policy for the Union—and that these two things could only be reconciled by mutual forbearance, wisdom, patriotism, and a common desire to promote the public good at the expense of some private advantage. He would have seen that to stimulate sectional differences, by making them the ground for party contests, and ignoble struggles for place, was to render all agreement impossible, and to prepare the way for a violent disruption. He would have spoken the whole truth, appealed to the judgment of North and South alike, deprecated every breach of the law, and every attempt at coercion, and have trusted to time and reason to effect a peaceable settlement of this great controversy.

He would probably have failed. His voice would have been drowned in the senseless roar of the democracy, the antipathy between the Northern and Southern States would have gone on increasing, and the day of separation would have arrived. What then would have been Hamilton's course? If any one had laboured indefatigably to cement the Union, *he* was the man. He cherished it with the jealous love of a parent, and would have grieved to miss a single star from the bright American constellation. But Hamilton was essentially a practical statesman, and would have understood at once the full meaning of the fact before him. Had it been some local rebellion for a temporary purpose

—such as the old resistance to the excise laws—
he would undoubtedly have supported the central
government, in strong and bold measures to suppress
it. But when ONE THIRD of the States had deliberately resolved to separate from the remainder, when
the only alternative was acquiescence or war to
the knife, he would have perceived that one of
those "mortal feuds" had come, which, in the words
of the *Federalist,* "do not fall within any ordinary
rules of calculation," but really "amount to revolutions, and dismemberments of empire." He would
have felt that the *old* Union, as conceived by its
founders, had virtually ceased to exist—that the
"government by consent," which was its essence,
had become a thing of the past—and that a republic
maintained by force was no republic at all. Then,
although he loved union much, he loved freedom
more, and would never have consented to sacrifice
the reality to an empty name. The mere extent
of territory would have had little value in his eyes,
if no longer to be inhabited by willing members
of the commonwealth. He would have bowed to
the force of circumstances, and have preferred *two*
confederacies to *one* despotism. Nor could he have
failed to see, that the North would find many

compensations for the loss of its Southern allies—
that it would get rid at once of the whole difficulty
of slavery, and be able to establish within its
borders a more manageable and homogeneous government. And, with regard to the negroes, he would
rather have left them to the gradual influence of
time and opinion on their old masters, than have
committed them to the cruel and terrible chances
of insurrection and servile war, in which defeat or
victory would be alike fatal to them. In a word,
he would have counselled his countrymen to antici-
pate the issue of the contest, and apply themselves
at once to negotiate such terms of pacification, as
might best conduce to the honour and happiness
of all.

This, or something like this, if I have not quite
mistaken the character and opinions of Hamilton,
would have been the tenour of his advice, had he
lived in the present day. Of course he might have
failed to convince his fellow-citizens, or even to
obtain a hearing from the excited and maddened
democracy. But, at all events, there would have
been *one* voice raised in favour of humanity and
reason—a voice too bold to be silenced, too weighty
to be altogether neglected—the voice of one who

had given his whole life to the people, and would have cheerfully laid it down in their service, but who loved them too well to flatter them, and had never shrunk from telling them the unvarnished truth. Even now that voice speaks to them in solemn accents from the tomb, and warns them not to destroy the work of the founders of the republic. "Do not sacrifice," it says, "the end to the means. The Union is worthless without liberty, and liberty can only be saved by ending this unnatural war. If our empire must be maintained by the sword, it is not for this that we threw off the yoke of England, or devised the Constitution of the United States. That Constitution must perish in the attempt to force our dominion upon unwilling subjects, and its wreck and ruin will alone remain as the monument of all our baffled efforts and blighted hopes."

And let Americans be assured, that the country, which next to his own Hamilton most loved and prized, views their present calamities (whatever foolish people may affirm to the contrary) with feelings of deep sympathy and regret. No provocations on their part—no rash or unfriendly words, whether spoken in the pride of success, or the bitterness of disappointment—can ever make us forget that they are men of our own race, brothers of the same blood, heirs of the language and literature, the history and traditions of England. Nor can all the excesses of democratic violence, nor the infusion of foreign elements into the nation, nor those mysterious influences of climate which have wrought so marked a change in their outward appearance, have wholly obliterated from their minds the remembrance of our common origin. We believe and trust, that the English virtues yet flourish in thousands of American homes, and that English memories are still warm in millions of American hearts. We could not persuade ourselves, if we would, that all ranks and classes of a kindred people are united in bitter hostility to the land of their fathers. When we turn, indeed, to their public speakers and writers, we see but few signs of moderation or candour; and, were we to judge by the utterances of the platform and the press, we should really despair of the future relations between the countries. But our hope is, that, roused by the peril of the times, the cultivated intellect of America may start from its long sleep, and resume its natural supremacy over all the multitude of her citizens; and we can frame no better wish for her and for the whole world, than that she may find other Washingtons to rule her empire, other Hamiltons to guide her councils—to wean her from mad dreams of ambition, conquest, and aggrandizement, and bring her back to the happier domain of law and liberty, civilization and peace.

Meanwhile, the curse of civil war which has fallen upon the great republic—traceable in its causes to that uncontrolled licence of the democracy, which has substituted mere self-will and caprice for knowledge, experience, and wisdom—may serve as a warning and a lesson to other nations and people. It may teach the remaining colonies of Great Britain to be slow in breaking the "golden link of the crown" which binds them to the mother-country, until they have secured for themselves institutions firm enough and strong enough to resist the strain of popular violence. It may teach those nations of Europe, which are struggling manfully to obtain the old English privileges of free thought, free speech, and just and equal government, to base the rights thus acquired on the broad ground of practical and constitutional liberty, not on any fanciful application of democratic theories. Above all, it may and must teach the people of England, to be content with the

manifold blessings they enjoy, and not to risk them
by rash experiments. More devotedly than ever
shall we guard that time-honoured Throne,

> " ————Whose deep foundations lie
> In veneration and the people's love ;
> Whose steps are equity, whose seat is law."

And because we know, that it can never be maintained by cold calculations of utility, we shall
cherish those sentiments of loyalty and personal
attachment which unite the highest with the lowest
in joy and sorrow—as when, of late, the death of an
illustrious prince cast a shadow over every English
home, and the arrival of a royal bride made a holiday
round every English hearth. In the same temper,
we shall grudge no mark of reasonable deference
and respect to that ancient Nobility, which, mingling
in all the pursuits of daily life, and constantly
recruited from the ranks below it, exists amongst us,
not as an effete and obsolete order, but as a real
power in the state, balancing the two extremes. Nor
shall we fail to support that National Church, which,
by its wise moderation, has saved us alike from the
gloom of infidelity on the one side, and the wild
extravagance of religious fanaticism on the other—
confiding the care of our parishes, not to bigoted

priests or ignorant zealots, but to kindly and educated gentlemen, good fathers of families, for the most part models of a Christian life, and centres of civilization in their several neighbourhoods. And, along with these venerable institutions, we shall study to uphold the dignity of the Commons' House of Parliament, and resist every attempt to establish the brute force of numbers, in place of the virtual representation of the spirit and intelligence of the country. In a word, we shall cling faster than before to the old laws, the old franchises, the old customs of England ; and, by so doing, we shall best preserve that glorious inheritance of freedom, which we have derived from a long line of patriots and statesmen, and which I trust in God we shall transmit unimpaired to distant generations.

INDEX.

R. CLAY, SON, AND TAYLOR, PRINTERS, BREAD STREET HILL.

BY THE SAME AUTHOR, CROWN 8VO. PRICE 7s. 6d.

TEUTON: A POEM.

A DREAM, with meanings haply understood
  By those, for whom these runic lines were strung—
The men, who boast the old Teutonic blood,
  And speak in divers tones the Gothic tongue.

O brave descendants of the mighty race,
  That spurned the axes and the rods of Rome !
Sons of the North ! whate'er the special place,
  Which time and fortune may have made your home !

We hail you—from this isle of ancient fame,
  Where Saxon laws have kept a people free,
And still the Viking's children proudly claim
  The chief dominion o'er the conquered sea—

We hail you brothers ! not by blood alone,
  But word and deed ; for, let what will befall,
We Northmen have a story of our own,
  And thoughts, and feelings, common to us all !

That story have I sketched in colours faint,
  Pale emblems of our struggles, hopes, and fears,
And in a single life essayed to paint
  The moral changes of a thousand years.

Weak is the hand, which dared a task so high,
  And oft, perchance, the effort has been vain ;
But let your sympathies each want supply,
  And bind the broken links in memory's chain !

Then may you trace, through legend, tale, and song,
  The Northern mind from its poetic youth,
Awakening early to the sense of wrong,
  The love of freedom, and the quest for truth—

May see it bravely battling for the right
  With ignorance, superstition, bigot rage,
Till crowned a victor in the glorious fight,
  And monarch of the new and wondrous age !

But, with the gain, you there will find the loss,
  Presumptuous errors, wanderings far astray,
Clouds of despondency and doubt, that cross
  The brightness of the full meridian day—

The restless search, the cold and barren lore,
  Which science, culture, intellect impart,
Till suffering cleanse the soul, and faith restore
  The simpler, holier wisdom of the heart !

" TEUTON is a poem, and written by a poet."—*Athenæum*.

" A riddle like this needs no interpreter. Its propounder does not lose himself in any imaginative depths, but displays, even while allegorizing, the practical aspect of the Teutonic mind. His language is simple, pure, and forcible."—*Guardian*.

" One short extract from the conclusion of the poem will give the reader a fair idea of the simple, manly, and in general harmonious language, in which Mr. Riethmüller has clothed his allegory."—*Economist*.

LONDON : BELL AND DALDY, 186, FLEET STREET.